# The Door on Half-Bald Hill

Books by
Helena Sorensen

The Shiloh Series

*Shiloh*

*Seeker*

*Songbird*

# THE DOOR ON HALF-BALD HILL

Helena Sorensen

RABBIT ROOM
PRESS

Published by
Rabbit Room Press
3321 Stephens Hill Lane
Nashville, Tennessee 37013
info@rabbitroom.com



ISBN 9781951872038

Printed in the United States of America

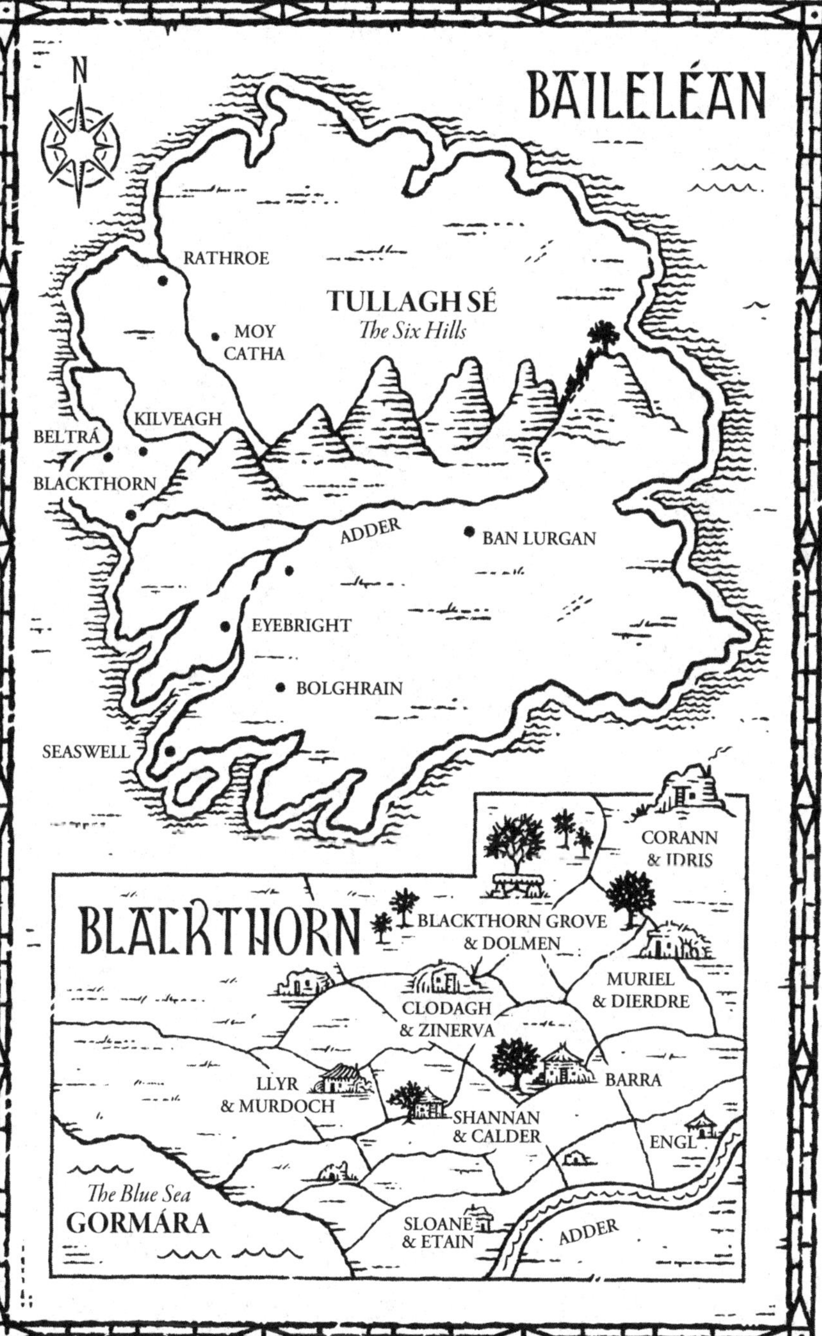
N
BAILELÉAN
RATHROE
TULLAGH SÉ
The Six Hills
MOY
CATHA
KILVEAGH
BELTRÁ
BLACKTHORN
ADDER
BAN LURGAN
EYEBRIGHT
BOLGHRAIN
SEASWELL
CORANN
& IDRIS
BLACKTHORN
BLACKTHORN GROVE
& DOLMEN
MURIEL
& DIERDRE
CLODAGH
& ZINERVA
BARRA
LLYR
& MURDOCH
SHANNAN
& CALDER
ENGL
The Blue Sea
GORMÁRA
SLOANE
& ETAIN
ADDER

# PERTH

ᛈ

THOSE WHO HAVE GATHERED in the inner grove await my words. Their forms are immaterial, and many cannot speak on this plane of existence. Yet they listen. They strain to hear the voice of the mighty sorcerer, the great druid.

But how can I tell of the Tír Ársa that was? Of the days before the coming of the Fir Bolg? Once, the telling was sweet. Now I taste nothing but the bitterness of the path ahead.

I close my eyes, open them. Sighing, I begin.

"Our people lived long, and the land yielded increase; the drinking horns overflowed. The forests bristled with wolves and bears and stags. A man could plunge his hands into the river and draw them out full of salmon. The celebrations of the eight-fold wheel were so lively and high-spirited that one might roll on into the next—the solstice into harvest or the equinox into Newmoon—without pause in the feast or the dance.

"And the druids—" My words falter. How deep the memory cuts. We were kings among men!

"In those days we drank from wells of knowing as deep as the Blue Sea, Gormára. For us, the moon and stars came close. The speech of animals unraveled mysteries, and the trees divulged their secrets."

Again, I hesitate. Silent fog moves through the grove and the forms around me shift.

"My days are spent. Soon I must leave the sunlit lands to follow the path of our ancestors." I look on the gray faces gathered around me. I have made war. I have made peace. I have raised the groves of Baileléan. And soon I will be on every plane as they are on this one—gray, immaterial, emptied of the potency of my magic.

"Much I have taught you of the wisdom of Tír Ársa, of the ogham signs, and the eight-fold wheel. But the wheel turns. It presses me down into the soil and raises you up before your time. Your knowledge is not yet full."

I step back, opening a space in the center of the grove.

"None of you alone can carry the mantle of Druid. Yet a druid is many things to his people. His roles may be sundered thus—"

Using the butt of my iron staff, I make the sign for birch in the gray soil of thought. A tree springs up, its trunk white and straight, its leaves small and rounded.

"The birch is the tree of beginnings, of purification, of fire. Let the birch stand in honor of the Bard, who summons the inner flame. The Bard will be poet, musician, and prophet. He will learn the history of our people, all our laws and our lore. The Bard will be Keeper of the Word."

I brush out the marking with the sole of my foot, and the birch tree vanishes. I make the sign for yew, and what springs from the ground is twisted, tortured, old as time. Hidden among its needles are clusters of berries.

"The yew is the tree of long life. It sees the passing ages of the world. Yet to eat of its fruit is death. Let the yew stand in honor of the Ovate, who summons the inner priestess to stand in the balance between life and death, between mortality and immortality. The Ovate will be healer, diviner, seer, master of augury and divination."

Once again, I erase the marking with the sole of my foot. Once again, I make a sign in the gray soil. An oak tree sprouts, growing high overhead. Mistletoe hangs from its branches.

"The oak is the storehouse of wisdom. Its seeds germinate in sunlight, and its branches pull lightning from the heavens. Let the oak stand in honor of the Druid, who summons the inner sage. The Druid will be teacher, philosopher, and sorcerer. His is the study of the stars and the great luminaries. His is the ordering of the forces of nature. Let him maintain the balance of the world."

I move to blot out the mark in the soil, but my strength falters, vanishes. The trees of the inner grove ripple like water. The forms around me waver, and some of them call out. "Master!" "Druid!" I stumble, planting my iron staff over the sign in the soil. It trembles and sets down roots, sends trunk and branches high, high. I cannot hold it. I fall back, peering up into the canopy.

In a moment, the movement stops. My vision clears. But I do not know what to make of the tree. Its height is so great that its crown is lost in the gloom overhead. Yet an archway cuts through its trunk. I can see the shadowy grove on the other side.

What brings this portent now, unbidden?

The living iron confounds me.

It is not a tree.

It is a door.

# IDRIS

# 1

IN MY DREAMS I HEAR THE KEENING of the banshee. It is a strange lullaby, wild and haunting, born of an inconsolable sorrow. Once it would have silenced me. Before the Bloodmoon, the banshee's cry would have quickened my heart to a frenzy of fear. Before the Bloodmoon, that herald of coming death sounded over an eight-fold wheel of celebration, a single dark note in the joyous music of the turning years. But which of us anymore weeps to hear the banshee's cry? It has become the anthem of our people. For death comes to us all.

The song fades, and I rise to the dim plane of half-sleep. Here I linger, eyes closed, waiting for inspiration. Corann says the waiting is key. And the darkness and the silence. But it's more than external quiet, more than stillness of lip and limb. It's the inner grove I seek. That is the place where the light of inspiration comes, where the sacred Word is revealed to me. That is where I meet the ollamh within, the bard whose stories shape worlds. So Corann says. But I hear nothing. My feet are cold, and my empty stomach protests. What is the worth of an ollamh who sees all the history of his people, all their laws, their words and their ways, yet cannot see their future?

I open my eyes. A heavy sigh escapes my lips and forms a cloud over my face. I should stop, await the coming of the creative flame, but I would rather seek a fire that comes at my call. The peat is stacked outside. If I hurry, I can toss a lump or two into my tunic and get back into the hut before I feel the chill. That is my thought. But I open the door as the last of the starlight breathes over the quiet of the grove, and I stop. The blackthorn trees are coated with frost. Fine white crystals cover sulfurous leaves and blue-black sloeberries. Long black thorns jut from ten thousand slender branches. The ground is frosted white. I stand a moment watching as the sun's approach silvers the sky. A thrush breaks the stillness with its high, trilling song. Farther on, inside the grove, a raven utters a throaty complaint.

The prick of the cold air inside my nose and the ache of the frost on my bare feet recall me to the present. There is peat to gather, a fire to light, porridge to boil. Another, larger, task awaits me then. The year has waned to its end. Tomorrow another year is born. Tonight is the celebration of Newmoon, and it falls to me to make the crowns.

The peat is covered with straw and cloth. I take two chunks and return the covering to its place. The frost burns my feet. Three steps back to the doorway and I'm wrapped in the close dark of our little cave hut.

Corann's bedroll lies against the opposite wall. As always, the old man is gone, up with the morning stars and roaming.

I wonder at times if Corann is a man and I am not. But I think it more likely that I am a man and Corann is nearer a god. He is tireless, though he hardly sleeps. He seems to feel neither heat nor cold. He disappears for days, taking no provisions. Are all druids so vital, so mysterious?

I roll my mat into a bundle and scoop oats from the bag on the floor. One handful in a wooden bowl. I'd like to eat a dozen handfuls. But there isn't enough water. I add a little water from the bucket at the back wall. This is our hoarded store. I set the oats to boil, raise the bucket to my lips, sip the water. It is cold and only a little bitter. I'll drink from the grove later, when the frost melts.

The water bubbles, and I stir the oats with a stick. I toss a few brambleberries into the bowl and mash them and eat. When I finish, the bowl is so clean it needs no washing. I set the bowl on a shelf and prepare for the morning's work. Using narrow strips of cloth, I wrap each of my fingers. I wrap the palms of my hands and secure the cloths. I would wrap them again, but I mustn't be hindered. That would only increase the danger. Thick, clumsy hands are no better than bare hands.

I slip a leather satchel over my head and rest it on one shoulder before banking the fire and leaving the cottage. Outside, the frost catches the light of the rising sun and hurls it back from leaf and branch and stone. My eyes are dazzled. I think of Perth, standing on the eastern shore of Baileléan, watching the flash and flicker of moonlight on the golden swords and shields of the Fir Bolg. Probably Perth was not afraid.

I am.

~

There are fifty-seven blackthorn trees in the grove that gives our village its name. Three times nineteen trees of strife and ill omen. Three times nineteen slender gray trunks whose branches wear thorns as long as my thumb, one thorn at least for every sloeberry. We'll need a hundred crowns for the ceremony. I spread my cocooned fingers and say a few words over them, a little spell of protection. Then there is nothing to do but reach in. Moving my hands gingerly, pinching between the thorns, I cut the narrow ends of the branches from the trees and twist them into crowns, securing them with little knots. Some of the berries I pop into my mouth. Others I drop into my satchel. The crowns I rest on the floor of the grove, beneath the branches of the blackthorns.

It is many hours' labor. I would work faster, but I dread the thorns. During my second autumn in Blackthorn, I lost my footing in the grove and caught hold of a branch to steady myself. The rocky ground would have been far kinder. Four blackthorns pierced my right hand, two coming clean through and protruding from the soft flesh between my knuckles. The wounds bled so freely that before I reached Corann's hut, I fainted. He found me, carried me inside. For days I was fevered, plagued by dark visions. My hand swelled and burned, and the skin around the punctures turned greenish, putrid. Corann cut it away. He made poultices of precious honeysuckle, applied primrose oil, and still it took two cycles of the moon before I regained the use of my hand.

The wrapping helps, and I am careful, but the day is long, the work tedious. Once I bend a branch too far. It whips back, and some of the thorns snag the cloth on my left thumb. My breath freezes in my throat, and I clench my teeth against the coming pain, but the thorns only graze the skin. The air in my lungs escapes in a frosty puff. I pull away from the tree and pause.

Nothing has changed. The song of the thrush is the same, and the cawing of crows. The cows low in the pastures. In silence, the sun passes overhead, and the frost drops from the trees. But I feel a presence, an impending pressure. Her eyes are on me. I know it.

Slowly I turn. She is sitting at the base of a blackthorn on the other side of the clearing where the portal tomb stands. Over her head are the sulfurous leaves, the blue-black berries, the deadly thorns. Behind her is the smooth gray bark. Her hair is wild, matted, a haze of pale yellow like winter sun. Some strands are bound with threads of blue and brown and black. Over a tattered cream-brown peplos she wears an orange shawl dyed from bramble roots. It is wrapped backwards, over her thin shoulders, under her arms, around her waist, and knotted in front. The top makes a harsh, straight line across her collarbones. Her hands rest in her lap. And her eyes—deep-set, heavy-lidded, the blue of winter ice—are partly open. I cannot see where she is looking. She could be in a meditative state, wandering the far-off groves of her consciousness. Such preparation is critical, for this is Zinerva. Tonight, at the celebration of Newmoon, she is initiated. Tonight she goes down into death. Tomorrow, with the birth of the new year, she replaces

Clodagh as Ovate of Blackthorn. No doubt she waits beneath the blackthorn tree in hope of communicating with the ancestors. She will need a guide for her journey if she is to return to the soil of Baileléan.

"Hello, Bard," she says.

She never refers to me as "Ollamh," though I am the Master Poet. I carry the gold branch. To be called "Bard" is no insult; it is high honor. But issued from her lips, the word pricks like a thorn.

"The banshee," I ask, "did she cry for you?"

"Perhaps," she says.

There is no sadness in her voice.

"Do you fear the journey?"

Her lips spread. A small smile. She turns aside and cuts her eyes toward me. "The spirit is reborn in the place of greatest darkness, Bard. I go tonight to be born anew. What have I to fear?"

"But your guide..."

"She has come." Zinerva flicks a glance toward the branches of the tree over her head. An owl is perched there, its talons threaded through the thorns. Its feathers are mottled, gray-brown and white. Its face is a blossoming mushroom of white. Its eyes are yellow.

I feel a sinking inside me. Had I thought Zinerva would enter the Underworld and not return? Had I hoped as much? Until this moment, I did not know it. Now her success seems assured. She has asked help of the ancestors, and they have sent her the surest of guides, one with keen sight in darkness. After this night, she will grow more powerful.

"Finish your task, Bard," she says, and rises. I make no reply. My traitorous mind is wordless and still. The owl pushes off from its branch and flies after her. A knot of crows hops along behind, following her measured footfalls as she winds her way through the blackthorns.

I am alone in the grove.

# 2

CORANN RETURNS FROM HIS WANDERING long after the midday meal. I have finished the crowns. Sloane and Barra have helped me gather wood and peat; we have piled them in the clearing where the portal tomb stands. I have sipped a little water and washed my face with oil. Now I watch Corann set his hazel wand at his feet and slide his wiry arms into his black robes. He anoints himself with a few drops of primrose oil. There is no sound in the hut but the little roar of the peat fire, and I wish, not for the first time, that Corann would tell me something of his travels. He smells of frost and starlight, and a yellow birch leaf is stuck in his hair. It's likely he's been to Kilveagh, but unless I ask, he'll never offer the tale. He would be glad, I think, to speak no word outside the ceremonies of the eight-fold wheel. But I covet his wisdom and knowledge, and I long for the comfort of speech.

"It's too late in the year for primrose or honeysuckle. Did you seek the white bull?"

Corann adjusts his cloak and raises his face to mine. The firelight catches on the white hairs of his beard and on the long white strands that frame his face. The gray hairs recede into the dark and flashing gray eyes look through me, his head canting to the side.

"I seek the wisdom of the ancients," he says. "I seek a sign."

I know this. What more has he ever sought? I grit my teeth against the flood of questions I haven't time to ask. "Anything?"

"The ravens gather. I saw flocks wheeling over the Tullagh Sé, coming from the east."

Not a heartening omen. "Zinerva has her guide. An owl."

Three little mounds of flesh appear between Corann's brows. His eyes narrow, straining at the wall behind me. Or perhaps he seeks wisdom beneath my cloak, within my flesh. He'll find none.

He turns and takes his walking stick in hand. The hazel wand stays here tonight, for Clodagh, not Corann, presides over the celebration of Newmoon. He is gone in a flash of black robes and a whiff of primrose.

I was ten when I came to Blackthorn to apprentice to Dermot, the bard. I had come to the village with my parents and my two sisters every year at Newmoon, and Dermot read the signs and declared that I was to be the next Bard of Blackthorn. It was a great honor, and a mighty undertaking for a boy of ten, for twelve years of training stretch before a first-year apprentice. I hoped to bring honor to my family and to the village of Kilveagh, but I was frightened as I slung a bedroll over my shoulder and fell into step with the other travelers who journeyed to Blackthorn. I remember how my father smiled, how my mother blushed.

That night they wore the blackthorn crowns, and Clodagh spoke of the parting of the veils between the worlds, and the fires burned. It looked to me as though all Baileléan had been set ablaze. I searched the crowd for Dermot's friendly face. I left the grove and peered into the villagers' cottages, one by one, and when dawn came stealing over the horizon I fell asleep under an ash tree.

My father found me and roused me with the news of Dermot's death.

"Dead?" I asked, uncomprehending. Dermot was Bard of Blackthorn. He had read the signs.

My father's answer was pained. "The villagers spoke of it last night," he said. "The bard went into the hills."

The Tullagh Sé. The Six Hills. There was not a child in Baileléan who did not learn at his mother's breast to fear the name. *The hills are haunted. The hills are hers.*

But I would not return home to Kilveagh. My father trusted the signs. He placed a steadying hand on my shoulder and walked me to the eastern end of the village, to a stone hut built right against the first of the Six Hills. Its outer walls were curved, built of stacked stones rising to a rough peak. Its roof and its back wall were the rock and soil of the Tullagh Sé. I clung to my father's side, panicked. *The hills are haunted. I cannot live here.*

He knocked at a door of weathered gray wood. Between the boards were curls of leaf-green lichen. I fixed my eyes on them until they swung back into a dim, musty cave and Corann appeared. He nodded to my father, turned to me. I can still feel the weight of his gaze, see the stillness and wildness that mingled in his eyes. The snap of sorcery hung around him like a fog. He spoke my name. "Idris." He motioned for me to follow and retreated into the hut. My father gripped my hands and kissed me on both cheeks, and his smile was like sunlight on my face. Then he was gone, and I was to learn history and poetry and lore and magic from Corann, Druid of Blackthorn.

Those first months were bitter, for though the Bloodmoon had already brought suffering and death to the Antae, I had seen its horrors from the safety and warmth of my mother's hearth. I had heard the news of plague and blight from my father's kindly voice. Then one morning I found myself in a dim hut at the western edge of the Six Hills with a short-tempered old man who terrified me. When I woke in the night, troubled by dark dreams, there was nowhere to turn for comfort. And often, when I rose, I found myself alone.

During the first year Corann taught me the ogham signs, slowly and singly. I would follow as he walked the groves, and he would stop, touch his walking stick to a tree, press the tip of the stick to the ground, and make the symbol in the dirt. Oak: one line running from earth to sky, two pointing westward, toward the sea. Birch: one line from earth to sky, one pointing east, toward the Tullagh Sé. Ash: one line from earth to sky, five pointing east. Blackthorn: one line from earth to sky and four intersecting at an angle, like claw marks. I thought at first that Corann despised me. He scarcely spoke to me. I had been apprenticed for some time before I understood that Corann scarcely spoke to anyone. He presided over ceremonies. Occasionally he spoke with Barra. That was all. The rest of his waking hours (when does he sleep?) were spent in wandering, in the search for wisdom.

I know he longs to speak with Perth. Perth would know what plagues the land. Perth would divine the source of the blight, the bitter water. Perth would restore the balance. But Perth is many years gone, and Corann has yet to divine anything of use, or even to answer the question of why. His agitation increases with every turn of the wheel. Even in his silence he is restless, searching the inner groves for the wisdom of the ancients.

Now he hurries out to the celebration of Newmoon. Tomorrow brings a new year, a new ovate. The mighty Corann grows desperate.

I carry no torch tonight. The village swarms with them, and the bonfire is lit in the blackthorn grove. People have come from Beltrá and Seaswell and Eyebright, from Bolghrain in the south and Moy Catha in the north. None will come from Rathroe, for there is strife between them and us. They will keep to their ring-fort.

I should go down into the grove at once and take up my crown, greet my father and those who have journeyed from Kilveagh. I should keep a watch on Zinerva, and Clodagh as well. But I feel a terrible dread of the coming ceremony. So I skirt the steep rise of the hill, heading south. I climb the worn steps of a stile, passing over one of the many drystone walls that make a patchwork of our pastureland. I stop beneath the red leaves of a rowan. It grows from a rocky crag, with its roots embedded in stone, and it has become a cherished resting place. Here I seek a moment's solace while the stars shine down on the village that has become my home. The noise of the celebrants drowns the distant roar of the sea, but the rushing of the Adder is close, clear. Corann says a poet receives inspiration beside the brink of running water, and I have spent countless hours testing the truth of his words. On this night, as never before, I long for the light of inspiration. I long for a word of hope.

A candle is blown out, and the windows in Deirdre and Muriel's cottage go dark. The door swings open, and I find I cannot breathe. My mouth is dry, wooly. Deirdre comes first, a basket braced against her hip. Behind her is Muriel, her hair like sunlight on frost. Even in the dark, it shimmers. She has pinned it back, away from her face, and it cascades over her green shawl. She walks with Deirdre toward the grove, through patches of firelight and pockets of shadow. My pulse hammers in my throat. Arlan called his beloved Meréd "the delight of the ages, the gem of time." Yet he knew nothing of beauty.

Silence falls over the grove, and I stir from my thoughts. The ceremony is beginning. I hurry down into the trees, catching up a blackthorn crown as I go. I shiver as I set it lightly on my brow. Hundreds are here, crowned as I am, waiting. They circle the clearing, and I slip through the crowd, pressing in, hoping to catch Clodagh's words. Those who know my face pull aside to let me pass. This is the ovate's night, but still I am the ollamh, and that is high honor.

Clodagh stands in the clearing. Her robes are black, and a black hood obscures her face. I catch glimpses of her chin, her nose. But her eyes are hollow sockets, sunk deep behind her cheekbones. She stands with the fire at her back. In front of her is the portal tomb, the dolmen—two upright stones supporting a broad, flat capstone. Zinerva lies still, spread out on the capstone, while Clodagh raises her hands to the waning moon and speaks.

"Tonight we celebrate Newmoon. Tonight the doors of all worlds stand open. Artek's veil is drawn aside and the gates of the Underworld are flung wide. This is the timeless time, when the dead and the living dance together!"

The celebrants raise a shout, though they are careful in their movements, and while their voices ring over the grove, their heads are still and turned toward the clearing. When the noise dies down, Clodagh continues.

"Here among the blackthorns we are reminded." Her hood swivels slowly left and right, invisible eyes scanning the attendants. "Here among the blackthorns we are called to face the necessity of death. Each of us must go down into the place of greatest darkness, for that is where the spirit is reborn."

The owl drops from the sky, alighting on the edge of the portal tomb. Zinerva does not move.

"For death is the fountain of life!"

Another cheer from the crowd. It seems a long time until they are quiet. This part of the ceremony I do not understand. So many have died since the Bloodmoon, and no life has come surging back from the darkness. Where is the victory in that?

"On this night, one of our own completes her training. She descends to the Realm of the Ancestors to seek the wisdom of the ancients."

Zinerva sits up and tilts her head to the sky. Clodagh raises a bony hand, palm up, fingers spread. The wrinkled, bluish skin holds a small collection of seeds. Yew. It is deadly. I've seen cows and sheep dead as stone with bits of yew still in their mouths, the pieces hardly damaged. Clodagh drops the seeds into Zinerva's mouth.

"Tomorrow, at the dawn of the new year, Zinerva will return to us."

Clodagh has not finished speaking before Zinerva twitches on her stone bed. Her muscles jerk, convulse. She gasps for air, just once. Her back arches high over the stone. There is not a sound from the crowd. Then she slumps against the capstone. Clodagh extends two bony fingers, sliding Zinerva's lids over her eyes. The owl utters a harsh cry, spreads its wings. Underneath, they are white as cream. It bats the air and rises over the grove, soaring eastward into the haunted hills. The celebrants erupt again, and Devlin pounds out a driving rhythm on the bodhrán. It carries the people toward the bonfire, where they remove their crowns and toss them into the flames. They've brought their hoards of honey mead. Tonight the dancing will be wild, the merrymaking fevered. Tomorrow begins another year of blight.

I do not join in the feast or the dance. My eyes are fixed on the portal tomb in horror and fascination. I cannot help myself. I approach the dolmen. Zinerva's head is rolled to the side, her neck twisted at an awkward angle. There is no flutter of movement at her eyelids, no measured rise and fall of breath to stir her orange shawl. She is absolutely still. I look up, searching for Clodagh. The old ovate has moved to the edge of the clearing, but she sees me, fixes black hooded hollows on my hand as I lift it to Zinerva's wrist. The skin is already cool. I press my fingers against it. Nothing. The bodhrán hurries its rhythm, and the claves join in. The dancers leap and spin, and still I wait. But there is no breath, no rush of blood in Zinerva's body. Whatever the morning brings, for tonight, Zinerva is dead.

# 3 )

THE HISTORIES OF OUR PEOPLE tell of others initiated in this way, at Newmoon. The ceremonies of the eight-fold wheel began in the time before times, long before the Antae fled to Baileléan, in the dim dawn of Tír Ársa. I learned the stories at Corann's hand, and as the ollamh it is my duty to preserve them. Yet Zinerva's journey troubles me. I am afraid of her going, afraid of her returning. Perhaps because she is the first to be initiated since the Bloodmoon.

I was a small boy when it happened. They say the moon was full, bright, the red of a new wound. The Bloodmoon comes only once in every nineteen years, when the paths of sun and moon collide. So it has been since the beginning. But this was a Bloodmoon like no other. They say there was thunder in the east, that the banshee cried all night long and for many nights thereafter. They say the puka came to every door, peered through every window. They say he called the names of every man of us, every woman, every child. Some followed him.

Hundreds had died—laughing warriors with the strength of bulls, red-cheeked maidens, chieftains of wealth and renown, mothers of ten—before they found the source of the plague. The river Adder. The water drank their vigor, laying waste to their bodies in days. The living took to boiling the water. It made no difference. Many more were lost. They went to the springs, and for a time the plague was halted. A spring near Kilveagh quenched the thirst of four villages, but in a few years its water was as bitter as the river's. The great ring-fort at Rathroe was supplied by a spring just beyond the outer wall. When word spread that their water was sweet, people journeyed far to get a taste of it, to bring full water skins and full buckets home to their families. But the men of Rathroe abandoned the age-old custom of hospitality and demanded an extravagant price for the water. They extended the boundaries of their ring-fort. There was bloodshed.

What, then, remained to be done? Long years past, my people left Tír Ársa, fleeing the Fir Bolg to make our home in the Crone's domain. Farther west and farther west the enemy pursued. Past the haunted hills to the curve of land where the Adder spreads its tongues. The river's source is behind us, in the Tullagh Sé, and the hills are hers. Those who have gone in seeking answers have not returned. There is no more land to the west. There is nothing but the sea.

Eighteen times the wheel has turned since the Bloodmoon. But the bitter water from the Adder seeps ever farther, filling the old cooking pits, souring the soil, poisoning the flowers, wilting the crops. We raise new drystone walls to keep it out. They branch from our little cottages like so many arms, elbowing our neighbors, clinging to the little unspoiled land we call ours. Calder says the Tullagh Sé and all the land between here and the sea wore a cloak of flowers once. His back is not as strong as it was, so I help him feed and pasture the cattle, and often he talks of pink foxglove and spotted orchids, of spring gentian and bluebells and eyebright, of green hedge parsley and white wood sorrel. Once, Calder says, you could scarce put your foot down without bruising a clump of primrose.

I made him draw the shapes of the flowers. He took a fragment of rock, his eyes shining, and scratched it against an upright in the drystone wall. What he drew was nothing like the ogham signs. Those are straight, harsh, unbending. Calder drew delicate arching stems, clusters of blossoms as light and airy as sheep's wool, curving buds as lovely as the hollows in a woman's throat.

Lines on stone, that is all they were. Yet they filled me with sorrow. I closed my eyes, seeking some image to enflesh Calder's scratchings. I found nothing. I cannot remember fields in flower.

We have the gorse. There is that. The shrubs are green nearly all the year, and their hearty yellow blossoms line the drystone walls, brightening the dying land. Without the gorse we would starve. The beaten branches feed the cattle; the ashes fertilize our two remaining fields; the blossoms provide honey and mead.

But too many things have been lost. Beneath the capstone where Zinerva lies, inside the portal tomb, there are too many bones. It's as if, during the Bloodmoon, some ancient thunder broke open the door to the Underworld. Death came rushing out, not one night in the year, but every night in the year, every day, for eighteen years. If the great luminaries keep to their courses, the Bloodmoon will come again next year. What will become of us then?

The atmosphere in the grove is oppressive. Hours pass while the dancers spin and the rhythm of the drum batters my mind. I am restless, uneasy. I feel a sudden kinship with the boy of ten who searched the village of Blackthorn for a man already dead. Something is about to shift, but what I do not know. I leave the revelry and turn toward the village.

The first cottage south of the blackthorn grove belongs to Clodagh and Zinerva. The shutters stand open, and as I pass I catch the usual scents of gorse and birch gum, ashes and ale, animal fat and flesh, barley and oats and berries, feathers and wool and filth. There is a stale smell of dusty bones and old feathers. And something more, something sour, like spoiled milk, like corrupted magic. I cover my face with my cloak.

I turn westward, toward the sea, and pass the cottage where Llyr and Murdoch live. I have only ever seen the two mending their coracles and nets and lines or carrying them down to the shore. Llyr is teaching Murdoch the secrets of the Blue Sea, Gormára, and since, with every breath, the Adder dumps more bitter water into the ocean, they must sail far from shore to find fish. A fleeting hope causes me to glance in the window, wondering if they've caught a salmon. It is a sacred creature. In all our tales, the salmon bestows knowledge. Corann covets it, but there have been no salmon since the Bloodmoon.

My steps are aimless, agitated. I clamber over the drystones, passing an empty cottage on the western edge of the village, one of three such places in Blackthorn. There is not a village in Baileléan without an empty cottage or two. The wheel turns. A once-mighty people dwindles. Bitterness and blight, and too many bones in the portal tomb.

I see Zinerva's small body spread out on the capstone. I wonder what she is seeing now. Has she passed the gates of the Underworld? Has the darkness enfolded her? I wonder with whom she speaks. And will she truly return? And how? Even on this night, when the doors between the worlds are flung wide, how can death give up its dead?

Almost due east of the empty cottage are three more cottages, each nearer the Tullagh Sé than the last. Calder and Shannan's cottage sits in the shade of a tall ash tree. Beyond is the home of Barra, Chief of Blackthorn, the fourth to assume that role since the Bloodmoon. We are running out of men to lead us. Further still, in the shadow of the easternmost hill, lies Deirdre and Muriel's cottage. But they are with the others in the grove.

I go to the river. In the darkness, by the sound of running water, perhaps I can quiet my mind. Perhaps I will receive a prophetic word at last. I pass the cottage where Sloane and his sister, Etain, live. The peat is piled high, covering two of the walls from ground to roof, sod rising to sod. The steady splash and babble of the river makes itself heard above the thumping music in the grove. Is there consolation in the sound? Inspiration? Time is fluid, Corann says. Like water. Will it lift me in its currents and carry me away? I sit on the drystone and wait while the moonlight glances off the wrinkling waters of the Adder. I slow my breathing, focus my thoughts. The sound of running water carries me . . . where?

A muffled sob disturbs my descent into the inner grove. A light burns in Engl's cottage. It is the southernmost cottage in Blackthorn, perched on the bank of the Adder. Engl's candle often burns through the night. I know why she weeps. I know I am helpless to relieve her suffering, but I rise and hurry along the riverbank, glad of the tallow that seals my boots against the sodden ground.

One shutter hangs open. Engl sits on the floor, her candlepot beside her, her baby in her arms. She has wrapped him tight with cloths. His face is feverish, his eyes glassy. She tries to coax a rag into his mouth. She wants him to suck some of the tea from it. I've seen her do it many times, seen Zinerva pound the blackthorn bark and boil it for her. The baby will not take it, and Engl weeps and rocks him.

I do not know how long I stand at the window, watching while Engl tires, while she curls on her side, the baby under her arm, while she strokes his face and dozes, while the candle gutters and goes out. I know nothing but the scene of Engl's suffering until a salt-whipped wind touches my face and I hear a cry from the grove. It spreads, and I turn, anxious footfalls hurrying me back toward the blackthorns. The moon has sunk, and far down in the west, the stars are going out. The noise in the grove rises to a roar and falls away in an instant. Silence.

I enter. The faces I meet are awed, the lips parted, the cheeks flushed. Every back is rigid, every eye directed toward the dolmen. The owl is perched on the capstone. Zinerva sits beside him. She faces Clodagh, but her heavy-lidded eyes search the crowd. She finds me, stops. She smiles.

In this wide-spun moment, while Zinerva holds me fast with her eyes, I feel the burden of time, the great rush of years mounting before me like a storm wave. They will bury me, press me down into the Underworld. On a high plain, in the pale dawn light, in the open air, I gasp for breath. Zinerva's eyes release me, and we wait, every one of us, to hear what she will say. What word has she brought from the ancients?

She allows the spell of silence to linger a moment longer. Two moments. I can see how she devours our wonder, our worship. Another moment, and another. At last she speaks, making no effort to raise her voice. Our ears strain through the grove, hanging on each word.

"My spirit is reborn," she says.

A small rushing sound, as scores of onlookers suck the frosty air through their teeth.

"The Veiled One offered me passage through her realm. I have spoken with Madigan."

Now the air rushes out of every mouth. Madigan. Hero of a Hundred Battles. Madigan who took up the trunk of a mighty yew and made it his cudgel, who broke the foundations of Tír Ársa so the Antae could escape the pursuit of the Fir Bolg.

"He told me of his fall at Moy Catha, how the battle plain was scattered with heads as numerous as the grains of sand in the sea, as the hailstones in spring, as all the leaves on all the trees of all the sacred groves of Tír Ársa."

She pauses again, and now it seems that no one breathes. She has ensorcelled us, every one.

"It was by the sword of Arlan, son of Artek, King of the Fir Bolg, that Madigan fell. But the Hero of a Hundred Battles bears no ill will against Arlan. And he sends a message to the Antae."

Even the birds are silent. Not a breath of wind disturbs the blackthorns. I cannot feel my heart beat.

"'In death,' says Madigan, 'I have found at last the life I sought. And though the spray of the salt sea on my face and the softness of a woman's skin are pleasures indeed, here I have found the comfort of darkness and the quiet of eternity. Do not fear death. Embrace it as a friend, as a lover. It waits to return your embrace.'"

Zinerva pauses while the words settle over us, while our backs bow beneath the weight of this ancient wisdom. If Madigan says it, it must be so. Mustn't it? The faces around me are baffled, disconsolate. What wisdom had we hoped the ancients would send? Did we imagine that those long dead would give us the key to life?

Zinerva steps down from the capstone and the owl alights on her shoulder. She retreats to the side of the smoldering bonfire, and after a moment of awed silence, the celebrants file past the portal tomb and brush their fingers over the stone. They pass out of the grove, some singly, others in tight, nervous clusters. The sun emerges from its resting place and fans its full glory over the Tullagh Sé. Dew sparkles on the blackthorns' yellow leaves, on the blue-black berries and cruel thorns.

After a time, only a small assembly remains, tarrying in the shadows of the trees on the edge of the clearing. My father has lagged behind the company from Kilveagh. He wraps me in a fierce embrace before he leaves the grove. Corann's face is raised to the sky. He watches the passing clouds, seeking a sign. Does he hope to divine some word that contradicts the wisdom of the ancients? Eighteen years he has roamed the groves of Baileléan, the inner groves of the mind. Eighteen years he has sought an answer for the blight, the bitter water. Eighteen years he has read the earth, the sacred animals, the sun and moon and stars and clouds, seeking for a way to restore the balance, to right whatever it is that has wronged us. But if Zinerva's word, if Madigan's word, is to be believed, he has wasted his years. His search is futile. He turns, leaning heavily on his walking stick, and disappears.

Clodagh stands like a queen in the clearing, meeting no one's eyes. A queen does not have to. She flicks a glance at Zinerva, and in the lift of her chin I see pride, triumph. When Corann, defeated, leaves the grove, she glides across the clearing. Her steps are smooth, limber, graceful. She says nothing to Zinerva as she passes. Her green-black cloak brushes Zinerva's feet and she, too, is gone.

Now I stand alone among the blackthorns while Zinerva fills the clearing. She is small and slight, yet the place throbs with her presence. I cannot turn away. The owl fixes round gold eyes on me. The pupils are narrow, thin black needles in a sea of gold. Zinerva runs a finger over the creamy feathers on its breast. She turns to face the gaping mouth of the dolmen. Its joints frame her and she peers into infinite darkness, unafraid. She turns and strides out of the grove, the new Ovate of Blackthorn, and master of death.

# 4

CORANN IS NOT IN THE HUT. Little wonder. The hazel wand is gone. Has he set out to divine for water? To work some sorcery? He heard Zinerva's message. What does he mean to do? My body is weary, my mind addled, my spirit heavy. I sink to the floor beside a cold fire, forgetting to unroll my sheepskin mat. I am asleep before my head falls against my outstretched arm.

In sleep I seem to pass through Artek's veil and enter the glorious gates of the Many-Colored Land. I walk through woods that are not unlike the woods of Baileléan. The trees spread the same branches, the water sparkles in the same light, and the air rings with birdsong. Yet here there is more green in the leaves, more purple in the heather, more gold in the bands of sun that pierce the forest canopy. On the edges of my vision, there is movement. It is a rush like the rush of water, neither fast nor slow, and I know that I glimpse the graceful passing of the Shí. I long to speak with them and fear the sight of them in equal measure. We breathe the same air, they and I. But I no longer tread the soil of Baileléan. They are leading me, I know not where. I turn my steps toward the light of their garments and follow.

We seem to travel for many days, but I feel neither hunger nor thirst, for the brightness of the wood and the light of the Shí are sustenance enough. We pass through groves of ash and hawthorn, birch and hazel. Sometimes I see things new and unfamiliar. Chasms yawn to the south and east. Mountains rise in the north. And each step carries me farther, hurling me through the splendor of that place, holding me fast to the path of the Shí. At last we come to a great, black tree, wide across as three strong men. It fills my vision, and my eyes travel up from roots like well-muscled arms to bark that is uniformly black to branches holding firm against a stiff wind. The leaves are like oak leaves, but I stretch my hand to touch them and flinch. They are hard as iron.

I wake sweating and rise. The smoky dark of the hut pushes the light of the Many-Colored Land from my vision. The fire has been banked, and the hut is warm. Out the window, the sun goes down to its grave in the west. I have slept through the day. The first day of the new year spent in dreaming. And what a dream! The tips of my fingers tingle, remembering the cool, unyielding leaf of the oak.

Oak.

The oak is the cosmic storehouse of wisdom, the sacred tree of the druid. Is the tree a sign of the wisdom from the ancients, the wisdom Zinerva has already revealed? Or does this tree signify some new wisdom, some new insight? And why iron? Apart from its power over the Fir Bolg, it holds no sacred meaning, no significance. None, at least, that Corann has taught me.

There are too many questions. They are stacked like the peat outside Sloane and Etain's cottage. They are heaped like the hills of the Tullagh Sé. The years pass, and the answers do not come. I could ask dozens, hundreds. And Corann is nowhere to be found.

A little salted beef, a mouthful of sloeberries, two sips of water, and I abandon the hut. I am too restless for meditation. My hands itch for some task to busy them, and there is always work to be done.

A few of the villagers are at work in the clearing, gathered around the remnants of the bonfire. They shovel the ashes of the blackthorn crowns into two wheeled carts. Barra is there, and Calder, Sloane and Etain, and Deirdre. No sign of Muriel. I suppose it's just as well. I am tired, filthy, burdened in heart and mind. I would rather she see my face shine. I would rather she see my strength.

The others are tired and thoughtful as well. There is little talk around the heap of ash. I touch Deirdre on the shoulder and take her shovel in hand, filling the cart in a moment or two. She walks at my side as I steer the cart out of the grove, heading west of the blackthorns to the fallow fields north of the village. Here the ground is not so wet, and we harvest small crops of oats and barley in early autumn. The ashes will fertilize the ground, lying beneath the winter snow and strengthening the soil for spring planting. Deirdre hands me the shovel she brought from the grove and I scoop the ruins of the bonfire and spread them over the earth. I am careful to keep the shovel low, to limit its rise and fall lest the wind carry our labors away. Deirdre goes behind me, tamping the ashes into the ground with her mallet.

She's a lovely girl, Deirdre, with a broad white forehead over sad green eyes. Her nose and cheeks are spattered with freckles, and her lips are full and pink. No more than fourteen or fifteen, I believe, but as good a friend as any I've known. I am more at ease with her than ever I was with my sisters, and she is easy with me. Like Muriel, she was to be apprenticed to Clodagh. She came to Blackthorn with that esteemed intention. Then she met the Ovate of Blackthorn at the ceremony of Newmoon and refused the apprenticeship. Among the Antae, there are no words to describe such a slight, such an offense to the ovate's power and position. To fell a tree or to refuse hospitality to a traveler are crimes scarcely more terrible than this. Deirdre's father and mother were shamed. They shut their doors against her. I don't know what would have become of her if not for Muriel. Muriel was first to refuse the apprenticeship, first to settle in an unfamiliar village in an abandoned cottage, under the rancorous gaze of Clodagh. Muriel forged the path, and well Deirdre knows it. The two have hammered out a life for themselves in the cottage by the hill, and their labors on behalf of the people of Blackthorn have all but banished the villagers' memory of their slight against the Ovate.

Yet Corann still frowns on our friendship. Clodagh and Zinerva are no small adversaries.

Deirdre is studying me. I lean on the shovel and meet her eyes. She knows which question stands at the forefront of my mind. *Where is Muriel?*

"Engl," she says.

Helping with the baby. Of course.

The rest of my thoughts will be just as clear to her. Zinerva's words, Madigan's message. We had hoped for other wisdom from the ancients. We had hoped for answers, for relief. We needed no more invitations to death. Are not all our waking hours filled with the struggle against it? And in spite of all our warring, all our seeking, does it not prevail? I read the same despair in Deirdre's eyes.

"If I had apprenticed," she begins.

I try to stop her. "Don't."

"I might have found another way, another word."

"From the dead? What word of hope did we think to find in the Underworld?" I take the shovel in one hand and drive it into the ground before a heavy sigh empties me of my fury, and I am drawn back to the desolation of my failure as ollamh. "It is mine to speak the Word, Deirdre. I am filled with words. I choke on words. But they are dead—they are the history of our people, our past. When I look to the future, when I seek a word of hope, I find nothing."

She takes my hand. Her forehead falls against my shoulder. I twine my fingers through hers, and we stand on the ancient soil of Baileléan while the sun sinks through a bank of gray clouds into the Blue Sea, Gormára.

Calder and Barra pass with a load of ash. They say nothing.

It is some days before I understand that Zinerva is ill. I finish the spreading of the ashes with Deirdre and the others. When the fields are covered, we take what's left to scatter around the houses, a reminder of the necessity of our own death, and a boon to the soil. I catch glimpses of Muriel. She carries a pot of soup to Shannan, one to Engl. She beats the gorse with Deirdre's mallet, collects peat from the stack outside her cottage. Her hair is fine, like spun gold. The wind whips it away from its pins and golden strands blow over her face. I yearn to brush them back from her eyes, her mouth.

The fosterlings join us in the work. As we move from cottage to cottage, scattering the ashes, Pixie and Vaughn stand in the path of the wind and try to catch the black snow in their hands. They skip over the ash-carpeted earth, driving the fine powder into the ground. Brennan follows, pushing a cart.

Sloane spreads the ash with a concentrated vengeance. His sister, Etain, works beside him. Barra and Calder move the cattle from pasture to pasture, guiding them over the stiles or through little gates in the drystones. The cattle would hinder us. Once, Pixie clambers over a stile and pats the nose of the cow Calder is leading. I am struck by the sight of them: the old man so near to death and the little child so shadowed by its presence.

Calder's wife, Shannan, keeps to her cottage under the ash tree. Llyr and Murdoch return to the sea. Engl nurses her child.

And Corann wanders the groves of Baileléan. Only Clodagh and Zinerva fail to show their faces. It is not unusual. The two have never joined us in the common labors of spreading ash or beating gorse or gathering sloe.

But on the third night of the new year, when starlight rains down on the Tullagh Sé and I have eaten my supper and spread my bedroll by the fire, there is a tap at the door. Engl is here, with a bundle pressed to her shoulder.

"Could I trouble you to make some more of the tea?" she asks.

My confusion keeps me standing at the door a moment, looking out at her over the threshold. "Zinerva—"

"Ill," she says. "Since Newmoon."

Again I hesitate. Zinerva looked so vital after her return from the Underworld. She appeared before us like one out of legend. She looked as though she could have challenged all the hosts of the Fir Bolg and brought them to their knees with one pointing finger.

Engl clears her throat, pats the bundle in her arms.

"Come in." I step back and she enters the hut. She seems uncertain, uneasy. The dwelling of the druid and the ollamh, she thinks, is no place for her. She stands at the edge of the fire, retreating from the walls, the ceremonial robes, the wands and walking sticks, as though her touch would taint them.

I snatch a piece of blackthorn bark from a hollow in the back wall. It will take some minutes for me to pound the bark, to boil the precious water and make a tea. The silence is strained, awkward. I never know what to say to this poor woman. If he chooses, the ollamh can exercise the *glam dicin*, the words that harm, that curse. I have never done so. I don't believe I could. But is there no counterpart to the *glam dicin*? Are there no words that bless, that heal? Did Perth know them? Or were they lost in the flight from Tír Ársa? With a smooth stone I pound the bark in a shallow bowl. The peat fire snaps; the baby whimpers, and Engl scarcely breathes.

I set the cauldron on the embers, pour a little water into the bottom, watch as bubbles form and rise. Engl kneels, leans back on her heels, and sets the baby in her lap. The boy's face is bright, damp. His mother unwinds his wrappings and spreads a hand over his chest. The water boils. Wisps of steam rise, and I drop the beaten bark into the water and slide the cauldron from the embers. A few moments more while the tea steeps. I strain the mixture, catching the tea in another pot. Engl reaches out, drops the corner of her shawl into it, and soaks up some of the tea. She runs her finger over the baby's nose, and he makes a feeble effort to open his mouth. Quick as thought, she tucks the tea-soaked shawl between his lips and pulls him close.

She rises with care, balancing the pot in one arm and the baby in the other, and turns her face to the ground. "Thank you, Ollamh." The eyes she raises to mine are red and weary. And though I am the Keeper of the Word, master of the laws and lore of our people, I cannot think what to say. I have done so little for her. I do not know how to receive her thanks. She turns, waits a moment for me to open the door, and goes.

I take my cloak from its hook and trace her footsteps along the eastern edge of the grove. When she climbs over the stile, following one of the longer drystones toward her cottage, I turn west. The cottage where Clodagh and Zinerva live is close, twenty paces or so from the grove. In the trees nearest the cottage, ravens are gathered. They make no harsh cries. They are silent, watchful. On the corner of the sod roof, Zinerva's owl rests, its head swiveling left and right over the village. It stops as I approach and fixes a golden gaze on me, but it makes no sound. I step as softly as I can through the squelching soil, moving to the corner of the cottage. The chimney belches its sour fumes, and bands of flickering light bleed through the shutters. One stands ajar, and I peer through, searching the dark for a glimpse of Zinerva.

She is wrapped in a sheepskin, huddled in the corner. Her face is deathly pale. Her eyelids flutter over glazed eyes. Sweat trickles from her temples and forehead and beads on her upper lip. A little bowl of herbs sits on one side of her, a bowl of water on the other. I cannot see Clodagh. Has the plague come to claim the Ovate of Blackthorn? She knows the healing arts, and she is especially gifted in divination and sorcery. What is it that could master Zinerva? Could it be that her journey to the Underworld has altered her? Drained her, more like. Time will tell.

There are other owls perched in the branches of the blackthorns. Their white faces are bright against the blue-black feathers of the ravens. Their heads turn. They follow my progress out of the village, but still no sound escapes their throats. I close the door of the hut, shutting out the starlight and the unknown and the ovate who returns from death and the druid who searches the world for wisdom.

# 5

Now comes the winter, when the leaves loose their grip on the branches of the blackthorns, the rowans, the ash, and the birch. The blackthorn grove is bare and skeletal, with just a remnant of sloeberries to sustain the birds. The rest we have harvested, and hawthorns, elders, and rowans are plucked clean. Some of the berries we use for dye, but most go to make hedgerow wine. For weeks, the berries ferment in kettles and pots and cauldrons, whatever comes to hand. Then the wine is sweetened with honey and set aside for the Feast of the Fertile Earth.

The days are brief. The wind is biting. I begin to recall the constant burn of cold at my feet, my nose, my fingertips. One afternoon after the berry harvest, I sit on a stone by the barley fields and look down over the sloping western edge of Baileléan. Half a day's hard journeying would bring me to the sea where, many miles from shore, Llyr and Murdoch are tossed by the waves and buffeted by the wind. My eyelids close, and I try to imagine the sea in the time before times, when the world was new. Bits of old stories, those I've collected during my training, rise to my tongue.

. . . *where black seals barked and dived . . .*

. . . *when great whales came heaving from the green-hued void . . .*

. . . *Over the endless rhythmic billowings of the ocean wastes, Murron's coracle was carried to the Many-Colored Land . . .*

There are some who say that Llyr has crossed the sea in his coracle. He has found no new home for the Antae, but I must ask him what he has seen.

I open my eyes and search the sky. It's two years since I received the gold branch, since the swan-feather cloak was wrapped around my shoulders and I became the Bard of Blackthorn, Master Poet, Ollamh. Hundreds of stories I hold in my memory, but still I do not truly fulfill my role. An ollamh has wisdom. An ollamh has foresight. His knowledge of the past allows him to look into the coming days. Yet for all my labors, still I hear no word of truth, see no vision of our future. My meditation has been fruitless. The inner grove is barren, the creative flame cold. Perhaps Dermot read the signs awry.

I turn my energies to divination, hoping the clouds will give some sign. I lie back on the stone so that nothing impedes my view. I see clouds, nothing but clouds. They are dense, low-hanging, with a greenish cast that warns of coming snow. Something in their tight weave makes me think of a sheepskin, and I raise my hands as if to grasp a seam of cloud. I would pull it down and spread it over my feet to warm them.

But this is foolishness. This is not how inspiration comes, and I will divine nothing with such fancies. If Corann saw, he would flare his nostrils and expel a brief, sharp blast of disappointment. Then he would turn and head out into the trees. It's no use.

Before the Bloodmoon, or so they say, the great bards would spend days and weeks lying in a field of primroses before they donned the swan-feather cloak and shook the bells of the gold branch and captivated the Antae with tales of unimaginable wonder. But the creeping bog has made an end of the primroses. There's scarcely a flower to be found on the western half of Baileléan.

Apart from the yellow blossoms of the gorse. I do not know why I should begrudge the gorse. Without it, we could not feed the livestock. I should help Deirdre beat the branches. My mind is dull; I will give my hands some work.

She's in the pasture between her cottage and Corann's hut. The rowan tree rises over her, bare of leaves. Its roots plunge into the rocky hillside, and it leans into the wind like a bent old blind man reaching for a handhold. A pile of gorse branches is spread beneath her. The branches will feed the cattle, but not before they're softened with a good beating. She raises her mallet and brings it down with a fierce and practiced stroke. I think that Deirdre was born with a mallet in her hand.

I reach the drystone wall and she pauses, straightens. I climb the stile and go to her side. The branches of gorse are stacked higher than my knees. I lean to either side of the pile, looking for an extra mallet.

"Inside," she says, and watches the color rise in my face. Her eyes light, and for a moment I despise her and the ease with which she enters and leaves the cottage where Muriel dwells.

I decide to knock at the door, hoping Muriel will come and open it, hoping she'll invite me in. Instead she calls an invitation, and I gather what moisture I can summon to lick my lips and swallow. I lift the latch and step inside. She is kneeling by a large kettle, stirring a cloth in a deep red dye. Her hands and forearms are stained. Her hair is tucked behind a small pink ear. One strand is stained with red.

"Ollamh," she says, and lowers her chin to her chest.

I try to swallow again. There is nothing in my mouth but ash. I find voice enough to speak her name and return the nod of greeting. It is not customary for the ollamh to bow his head to anyone, not even the chief. Muriel smiles, and she returns to her work. I hurry to the wall where the mallet rests and grab it, closing the door behind me when I go.

It's a relief to find Deirdre hard at work. She will not tease me now she's found her rhythm, so I fall in beside her, bringing my mallet down on the gorse when hers reaches its highest point above her head. We beat out a fine counterpoint, we two. Once I catch her glancing at me, but there is no laughter in her eyes. Only understanding, and a flicker of something else. Impatience, I think.

"You've seen Zinerva?" she asks, between strokes.

"Yesterday. In the grove."

"She looks well."

She does. It took a full cycle of the moon for her to recover from her journey, but now she bears no scar, no sign. It seems clear that she has triumphed, that no plague has come to claim her. We should rejoice.

The mallet warms in my hands. The muscles in my back and arms warm to the work. I think less of the wind.

"Will you honor me with a story, Ollamh?"

"You know the stories of our people, Deirdre."

"But it is pleasant to hear you tell them." She never breaks her rhythm, though her face is splotched with color. The hair that frames her white forehead is damp with sweat.

"Not today. My heart is heavy."

"Mine as well." I catch a strange gleam in her eyes as she continues. "Tell me of the days when the cattle spread over the hills like drifts of snow. Tell how the warriors were more fierce and the women more fair. Tell of a time when the honey dropped from the comb and the otters played in the rivers . . ."

*. . . and the air smelled of apple blossoms.* She is luring me in, enticing me with the opening lines of a familiar story. It tells how Weylin of the Shield made war with Angus of the Mighty Arm, and how the two made peace in the very same day; how the feast that followed was full of brawling and boasting, and every warrior had the finest cuts of meat, and every cup overflowed with mead. I sigh. "Another day."

"Barra will ask you. Soon. What good does it do to put off the task?"

"It is one thing to remember and recite."

"But memory and foresight issue from the same fountain."

"No!"

She sighs. The mallet falls. The branches of gorse are bruised, crushed, ready to be used as fodder for the cows and sheep. In my frustration I have stopped. I stand watching her, searching for explanations, dreading the task Barra will lay at my feet.

"What future can I prophesy, when—"

"I know," she says. She sets the mallet on the ground and leans against the handle, catching her breath. She wipes the sweat from her brow with the back of her finger.

"Zinerva has already—"

"I know."

My anger cools. Deirdre means no offense. She understands something of my position.

"I fear for you," she says.

And this time I speak the words, "I know."

Who can stand against Zinerva when the mighty Madigan speaks through her, when the ancients stand behind her, when death bows before her?

Suddenly, out of the storm of questions that rages in my mind, a single question rises. "Deirdre, at Newmoon, when first you came to Blackthorn and met Clodagh, what did you see that made you refuse her?" She has told me that a dark vision drove her from the ovate, but nothing more than that.

Deirdre stares at me. She looks as though her knees might give way beneath her. A darkness passes over her face while she searches her memory, searches for words. At last, slowly, they come.

"I saw a door in a hill, and a black passage beyond."

She trembles. I take her arm, but she does not see me.

"I was carried along the passage and into a kind of tomb. My bones ached with the cold of that place, and as I stood and waited, the tomb grew darker. You would have thought there was no more room for darkness, but there was. And though I saw no face, heard no voice, I felt the presence of Death. I felt its fingers rake across my skin, felt its breath condense around me. I had not known fear until that night. I ran from the grove and hid."

Her face is pale. I press my lips to her forehead, hoping she cannot see how her words have unnerved me. I had not thought Clodagh as fearsome as that. To invoke such a vision in Deirdre without herbs or incantations? The Ovate is healer, seer, diviner, and midwife. She is the priestess of realms and times. She opens the doors to healing and new life. Yet that high honor Clodagh despises. Her power, her very presence, points to one door. Death's door. Surely Zinerva is no less to be feared, now she has taken Clodagh's place.

"Go in and rest. I'll take the gorse."

For once, she nods and retreats into the cottage. I scoop armfuls of the beaten branches and carry them over the drystones to each little irregular patch of pasture. Half a dozen cows lumber over. They munch the fresh fodder with relish. Three times ten sheep bleat their gratitude when I spread the branches for them. The sound is cheering after the horror of Deirdre's vision. I don't know why I should begrudge the gorse.

# 6

The wheel turns.

The sun reaches its weakest point, its death. We rise in the early dark, for the winter solstice is celebrated in a cluster of oaks west of Kilveagh, and we must make the journey and complete the rites before sunrise. We stow a few provisions in our satchels, wrap ourselves in our warmest cloaks, and take our flagons in hand. Corann walks at the head of the procession, wearing gray robes and carrying a tall staff. I follow him, with Zinerva at my side. Her cheeks are bright, pricked by the cold air, and she walks quickly, with great energy. The waxing moon, as it sets, shines through scudding clouds, lighting the snow and our path to the grove.

Behind Zinerva is Clodagh, and Barra behind me. I can hear the butt of his great spear as it thumps against the ground, like another leg to bear Barra's weight. The rest trail behind: Shannan (leaning on Calder's arm), Llyr and Murdoch, Muriel and Deirdre, Engl and the baby. Sloane and Etain will keep to the back, and doubtless the fosterlings are sleepy and subdued. The snow is soft, feathery. It hushes our passing.

The starlight was crisp when we left Blackthorn, but it fades as we journey, melting into the gray of the coming dawn. After three hours' walking, we reach the grove. To the east are the birch woods of Kilveagh, but here a grove of ancient oaks spread their bare limbs to shelter a sacred clearing. We wait at the outer edge of the grove, silent, while some of the Antae from nearby villages fall in with us. Only three druids remain in all of Baileléan. Since one keeps to the ring-fort at Rathroe and the other lives some days' journey south, in Bolghrain, those of the Antae nearer the Tullagh Sé join us for the rites.

The last of the villagers takes his place. There is no sound but the distant roar of the sea. Corann raises his arms, holds them up, drops them. He takes a single step forward, and his foot falls beside the roots of a broad oak. In that moment, half muffled by the small crunch of Corann's foot pressing against the snow, there is a whisper. I have never heard such a thing, not with my ears, not in any of the hundreds of tales stored in the caverns of my memory.

A whisper? Of what? Not question or dissent. Corann is the druid. Corann presides at the celebration of the winter solstice. Who would dare to speak, to utter any sound, when first he enters the sacred grove?

I cannot tell if Corann heard it or not. But others did. The air around us tightens, and I feel a strange tension that was not present a moment ago. But there is no time to explore it. Corann has gone in among the oaks, and we must follow.

The clearing is small. We press back against the trees so that Corann has room to perform the rites. Through the bare branches to the east, I watch the sky pale. From a purple as deep and liquid as hedgerow wine, it thins and softens. The change is gradual, hypnotic. I am startled when a band of luminous pink blooms over the Tullagh Sé. Corann finishes the rites and speaks.

"Cast away, O man and woman, whatever impedes the appearance of light."

I asked Corann once what the people brought to winter solstice before the Bloodmoon. What did they carry in their flagons? What horrors did they cast away then? He only looked through me as though my body were immaterial and furrowed his brow. "I can't remember," he said.

There is a space between Corann and me, a chasm I can never bridge. He lived a life before the Bloodmoon. He gained a seat of honor over a diminished but vibrant people. He feasted with them, loved them. He loves them still. But the memory of that world is fading, blotted out by the search for answers. He is losing the thing he hopes to restore.

The Antae come to the heart of the clearing and empty their flagons of bitter water. What else is there to bring? It is the bitter water that poisons the fields and drowns the flowers, that alters the soil and causes the bog to creep over the good, green land. It is the bitter water that carries away the strongest among us and leaves the children and the aged.

When the common people have done their part, they step back. My hand is cold, the muscles cramped around the flagon.

I step to the spot of bare earth where the issue of the Adder has melted the white snow. *Cast away, O man, whatever impedes the appearance of light.* Knowing no truer impediment, I tip the flagon and watch the water spill out on the ground. There is comfort in this ceremony, though every year we cast away, and every year the Adder is unchanged. For a short time, in the biting cold before dawn, it is the flagon, and not me, that is empty. I step back with the others to wait.

Zinerva is next. Last year, I followed her, but now that she is Ovate of Blackthorn, she supersedes me. She is to go last.

She takes too long stepping from her spot, too long walking to the center of the clearing. Strangely, she carries no flagon. She raises nothing, empties nothing, only stands by the spot of bare earth a moment and returns to stand beside Clodagh. But there is something changed. She has left something behind. It lies on the dark soil, at the edge of the snow, scarcely visible. What has Zinerva cast away?

Corann hesitates, narrows his eyes at Clodagh, then completes the ceremony. He lights a small lantern with his flint and raises it on the crook of his staff. We all turn to face the east, to watch the birth of the sun.

After a pause, a few moments' silent meditation, the grove begins to empty. The celebrants set off in many directions, and I take advantage of a moment when backs are turned. I crouch beside the spot of dark earth and pick up a little scrap of wood no larger than my thumb. Birch. A knot forms in my belly. It is not likely that a piece of birch would find its way to the heart of an oak grove, and birch is the tree of the bard. Zinerva is sending a message. She implies that I, the Bard of Blackthorn, impede the light.

"Ollamh."

We have left the grove. Our tracks lie before us, guiding us home to Blackthorn. This time the procession is noisy, and Pixie and Vaughn and Brennan run circles around the rest of us. Others talk as they go, and Barra has fallen into step beside me. The bronze tip of his tall spear burns in the morning sunlight. I know what he has come to ask, and I am glad he walks at my side. I do not want to meet his gaze.

"When I was a boy," he says, veering around the question I feared and into a story, "Olwen was Bard of Blackthorn. When she wished to speak, and the bells of the gold branch sounded, everything else was forgotten. I saw hungry warriors walk away from a roast boar just as it began to drip, saw wives leave their cooking pits just as the water came to a boil. Boys would leave their fiercest games unfinished. We lived in horror of arriving too late, of missing even one drop of the honey-words that dripped from Olwen's mouth. I sat in my mother's lap one evening, while Olwen told of the Cogath Tornech, and I remember nothing of the sun setting, or the moon rising and setting, or the sun rising again. I only remember how her words held us in thrall. When the story was ended, Olwen spoke of the richness of the coming harvest." He turns to me. "I've never seen another such yield," he says. "Enough barley for three winters."

Barra is a great, hulking man. I believe he could lift me into the air with one of his meaty hands. He was born to be a warrior, but not against the ills of plague and starvation. His young wife was one of the first to go after the Bloodmoon, and it took the heart out of him. He watched as night fell on three chiefs before him, and now he is left with a dying people, three fosterlings, a roaming druid, a disquieting ovate, and me. Barra would be better suited to making demands, to giving orders. He should shake me until my bones rattle, until the stories of our past and the promises of our future come pouring forth. At the least, I should offer them freely. The great ollamhs, like Olwen, merely walked from their homes with the gold branch in hand, and the people came at once, silent and expectant. But Barra is reduced to asking that the poet recite. In stories, in hints. And I am reduced to refusing.

"I cannot."

"Please, Ollamh."

My face burns with shame, but I do not reply.

"If you begin," he says, "if you begin with Tír Ársa, or with Genevieve or Perth, if only you open your lips to speak the sacred Word, perhaps foresight will come. It may come."

The sinking in his voice as he sounds those final words, the hopelessness—I cannot bear to hear it. "How can I? The Word was spoken at Newmoon. You heard it with your own ears."

"No," he says. His voice is low, but his words have sharp edges. There is much he holds back. "You are the Custodian of the Word. You are its keeper."

"Not more than the ancients."

He stops. I seem to hear his thoughts churning. He cannot speak against the wisdom of the ancients. He cannot deny it. And he can say no word against the ovate. None. He pounds the butt of his spear into the snow. "The ancients tell us that death is the path to life," he says. The words come slowly. He is careful. "Today we mark the sun's death, yet we know it will be born again. The trees of Baileléan are bare and still, yet we know that spring will waken them." He pauses while our feet carry us back over the path we trod this morning, in darkness. Now the snow sparkles and the sky is blue. "There are many deaths a man may die and still feel the sun on his face."

Barra clings to the hope that Zinerva's words might be seen in many lights. But if her account is true, Madigan spoke of ultimate darkness, of the quiet of eternity. He did not speak of pain or sleep, but of surrender. No, not surrender. Embrace.

"Zinerva said..." I stop, correct myself. "Madigan said that we must embrace death as a friend, as a lover. I do not think he spoke of seasons."

Barra is quiet for some time. The easternmost of the Six Hills looms before us and grows until it fills our vision. We catch sight of the fallow fields, the grove. I hadn't noticed how much the blackthorn trees resemble arms. Maybe the ancients stretch their arms from the Underworld and spread many-fingered hands to catch the light of the sun. Do they long to feel the sunlight on their faces?

At last we can go no further together. I must stop at the hut in the hillside, and Barra must take the children back to their cottage. I thought he had done speaking, but he stops and steps in front of me. He waits until I meet his eyes.

"Your words are not less than hers. You have partaken of the creative flame. You have drunk from the well of knowing. Speak, Ollamh."

He gives me no time to respond. He calls to Pixie and Vaughn and Brennan, and when they come to the drystone, he props his spear against the wall and lifts them each over the stile before climbing through himself. The passage is too narrow for him. He takes it on an angle. Then he reclaims his spear and sets off through the pasture.

I am not long in the hut before Corann comes through the door. It is not like him to spend the day here. I wonder if the ceremony has tired him. He removes his ceremonial robe and hangs it on a peg. Corann is the druid, the storehouse of wisdom. There is so much he has not told me. Only enough to finish my training, and nothing more. Calder says he came to Blackthorn to study under a mighty druidess called Sheridan. Yet Corann has never spoken the name. Not to me.

"Will you go out again?" I ask.

He cants his head, squints toward the wall behind me. "No," he says. In the issue of the word I hear his weariness. His shoulders stoop, and the lines on his forehead are deep. His mouth is pinched. His eyes, always so piercing, are unfocused. I do not like to see it. Three druids remain. Only three. And the vital, energetic Corann has never given me cause to fear that soon there may be two. Suddenly I am afraid. I do not want to be left alone with Clodagh and Zinerva.

"Were you pleased with the ceremony?"

He settles himself beside the fire and adds a chunk of peat. It catches on the smoldering embers, and flames leap up. He warms his hands. For a time, he studies the flames. Even by the fireside, at the end of weariness, Corann seeks wisdom, searching for signs in the tongues of fire.

"All the rites were performed," he says at last.

I want to shake him. That is not an answer.

He senses my frustration. I think it crackles at the sides of my head. I know something of sorcery, too.

"You have never learned, Idris, how to ask a proper question. You wait for me to illuminate the mysteries of earth and sky, of time and eternity. But you could have already grown wise. A well-packed question carries its answer on its back."

I see the drystone walls in spring, the slime trails left by the snails who carry their homes on their backs. Like answers. To the right questions.

I feel a sense of urgency. Corann is present with me now, in body *and* mind. That is a rare gift. But what question is the right one to ask? There are too many questions. They are heaped in my mind, mounded, piled. They've not been sorted. I grasp for one and fling it at Corann.

"Did you eat the yew at your initiation?"

He does not look up from the fire. Instead he sighs. There is no sound from his lips. His body sighs, as if some of the air, some of the strength, leaves him. "The yew is the tree of the ovate, not the druid. I ate mistletoe, and I did not come to harm."

I feel a spark of hope. Corann has done what Zinerva did! He can speak for the ancients as well as she.

Corann senses my misunderstanding and frowns. "I did not journey into the Underworld." Each word is weighted. "I ate mistletoe, and I did not come to harm."

Then Corann has not returned from death. Corann has not mastered it. In all Baileléan, has only one done that? And there is the heart of my fear—that the Antae should turn for wisdom and guidance to one who urges them to embrace death, to run into its arms; and that I should have no other word to offer them.

Barra says there are many deaths, but I read in Corann's eyes, in the slump of his body, that he has divined no other interpretation of Madigan's message. I feel the pull of despair. *The blackthorn is the tree that reminds us of the necessity of our own death.* Necessity. I understand that the body dies. We all go the way of the earth and the ancestors. But the old tales tell of the Many-Colored Land, and in my dream I walked there. Why does no one speak of that place? We speak only of the Underworld, the Crone's Realm. And there are not enough of us who still ask why.

"At Newmoon, Clodagh says . . ." I stop. Clodagh. "What of Clodagh's initiation?"

Corann brushes the question aside with a flick of his fingers. "She was not initiated in Blackthorn, and Clodagh is many years my elder. There may be no one left alive to tell of her initiation."

I am surprised when Corann offers more. "Clodagh and Zinerva make much of this message. But it was not always so.

An ovate could return with any vision of other realms, and it would serve."

Strange. "At Newmoon, then," I ask, returning to the question, "Clodagh says the veils between worlds are open. She says *worlds*, yet I hear nothing of the dead coming among us, nothing of the Antae passing into the Many-Colored Land."

There is a smile in Corann's eyes. They are clearer than they were. "That is better," he says. "Though you've asked no question."

"Are the doors between worlds truly open at Newmoon?"

Corann gazes into the fire while I search the caverns of memory for stories that tell of passage between realms. If the songs and poems are true, our people lived a life of such zeal and passion that they had no wish to leave this world, even for the delights of the Many-Colored Land. Something troubles me, though. I know hundreds of stories, but Corann taught me as he had time and patience. He did not line up tales on a string and pass them to me one by one. History and lore came tangled together in a knot.

"Are there any tales that speak of the Underworld before we came to Baileléan?"

Corann looks at me now. At me, not through me. "There was the boy, Innis."

The name jerks a memory from the dark. "He killed his brother, and went down into the Underworld to allay his guilt."

The mounds of flesh gather between Corann's brows. "He returned. In other tales, Innis travels with Boden the Archer."

"Has no one returned since we came to the Crone's Domain?"

"I think the Crone does not give up her dead."

"Even on the night of Newmoon?"

Corann's gaze is answer enough. To one question.

Foolishly, I voice my frustration. "But why the blight? Why the bitter water?"

"That question has consumed me these eighteen years."

"Then why does it carry no answer on its back? If it is the right question, how is it you have found no answer?"

Corann holds me with his eyes. I sense the great span of years that lies between us, some forty years of wandering the groves of the mind, of learning the speech of the stars, of studying the courses of sun and moon, of endless searching and broad experience. I feel very small.

"I see the coming of calamity," Corann says. "In the clouds, in the water, in the leaping of the flames. I see a change that will shake the world to its foundations. What I do not see is a path of escape or a means to bring the world into balance. Something has set it off its courses, and I do not know how to right it."

Disaster. Ruin. *Calamity*. Worse things are coming. Have I known it all along? Have I seen it in the gathering of storm clouds and the assembling of carrion birds? The village of Blackthorn is small. Of a sudden, I feel the narrow limits of the grove and the drystones, the cottages and the Adder. I want to see what Corann sees when he roams the groves. Perhaps there is a word, an answer that waits for me, dangling like a leaf from a dead branch or buried in a foxhole or bubbling up through the bog. Perhaps I can set the world back in its courses.

"When you go out again, Corann, may I go with you?"

He banks the fire and stretches out on his back, interlacing his fingers over his belly. The long white strands that frame his face fall away. He closes his eyes. "Do what you will," he says.

When I open my eyes, Corann is making ready. I have never seen him set out with anything more than a cloak, his hazel wand, and his walking stick. But the sun has not yet begun to rise behind the Tullagh Sé, and Corann is rummaging through the bundles and phials jammed into the recessed shelves on the back wall. Sometimes he lifts a bundle, sniffs it, raises it to his eyes, and drops it into a satchel. The work is studied and nearly silent. For Corann, it is unusual. He is the druid, the philosopher, the friend of the stars, the dweller in groves. The healing arts are Zinerva's province. But he is putting ash leaves into the satchel. Rowan leaves, rowan berries.

Ah. Corann is hoping for visions.

He stops at the bottle of primrose oil. It is almost empty. Not enough primroses. He stares at the bottle, turns, and squints over my head.

"Will you never get up?" he asks.

I am not fool enough to ask when we leave. I should hurry

and gather my things and hope I am not left behind. But where will Corann go? And what do I bring? Since I began my apprenticeship, I've traveled no farther than the oak grove. I stuff my feet into my boots, pin my cloak at my left shoulder, and make a survey of the hut. My ceremonial swan-feather robe hangs in a corner. It should be aired and dusted before Snowmelt. I'll see to that when we return. I own no weapon, no wand, no staff. The sacred Word is my instrument. I glance at the shelf where the gold branch rests. I am glad I do not have to carry it with me. Beside it are the bodhrán and claves, the dord and the eagle-bone flutes. No need for them either. I wonder what Corann eats in the woods. Berries? Bark? Starlight? I grab a satchel of my own and fill it with slivers of dried beef, a bag of oats, two handfuls of dried sloeberries, and a skin of clean water. I check the hedgerow wine, fermenting in a bucket in the warmest part of the hut. The smell is strong and promising. I wrap it in a sheepskin and give it a pat.

"Are you ready? I have passed many lifetimes in watching you prepare."

For Corann to wait is a kindness. I hurry out the door and close the latch.

He heads north, toward Kilveagh, keeping the hill to his right. The Six Hills are more mountains than hills. When I raise my head, following the rise of the hill at my shoulder, I can see no eastern sky. The hill blots it out.

When I was a boy, I sometimes followed Corann on brief excursions, for I was lonely, and Corann had become everything to me: teacher, mentor, provider, guide, father, friend.

It was rather like being left on the seashore with an enormous clam that held a mouthful of pearls. If I stayed beside the clam at high tide and low, I might catch it with its stony lips parted. If I was brave, I might even reach in and take something. Or I might get my fingers smashed.

In those days Corann was more often in the hut, or among the villagers. It is only the persistence of the blight that has kept him so much away, so much in search. His gait is smooth, his steps long. He does not stand as tall as I, but it is hard to keep pace with him. I sense his desperation, his determination. Zinerva's triumph, I think, has fed his frustration. Who would not feel impotent beside one who has overcome death?

I expected a long walk. Corann has packed for an extended journey. He is in earnest. But we reach the birch woods of Kilveagh in a few hours, and there Corann slows and drops his satchel.

I have always loved birch trees. In spring, their leaves are greener than the hillsides; in autumn, more golden than sunlight. I have a memory of lying beneath the birches of Kilveagh with one of my mother's bowls. I was very small, but as the yellow leaves drifted down, I imagined that I gathered a great wealth of gold. Strange to think of a time when gold was more valuable than water. Now the trees are bare, their trunks white against the snow. They stand tall and straight, with thin, graceful branches. They are so unlike the twisted blackthorns.

Corann seats himself on a tumbled stone and closes his eyes. It is not yet midday. Sunlight slants through the branches, and Corann's face is dappled gold. There is another stone, not far off.

I go and sit and rest my legs. I look back at Corann, thinking to find him resting from the morning's journey. But he is meditating. The set of his body is unmistakable: eyes closed, forehead slightly raised, back straight, hands resting palm-up on his knees. Every muscle is focused, every thought stilled.

I should do likewise. Kilveagh is the place of my birth, and this is the grove where I played as a boy. These are the trees of the bard, and I feel a kinship with them. I mimic Corann's stance. My thoughts, first rushing in torrents, gradually slow to a trickle and dry up. The sound of my breathing grows remote. I descend. Into darkness. Into silence.

I wait.

I begin to sense the presence of something, in the dark. It gives off no scent, makes no sound. But I feel its weight. Some of the air has been displaced, and the spaces around it are tightly packed. The hair on my arms stands up. I can taste my fear.

It grows. Spreads. In this inner darkness, where I had thought to find light and insight and inspiration, I find nothing but an all-consuming presence. It is larger than I am, stronger than I am. It speaks the final word. *Death.*

"Idris."

Corann's hand is on my shoulder, and the sky is blue. The wind sets the birch trees groaning; their branches crack and sway. I gasp for air, remembering Deirdre's vision. The doorway, the passage, the presence of death.

"Take this," he says, and places a skin in my hand. I raise it to my lips. A bitter wine? No. A tincture of gorse. I take another sip and return the skin to Corann.

He studies me a moment before turning his scrutiny on the grove. He rises, takes the stone knife from his satchel, and makes a mark in the bark of the nearest birch. One line running from earth to sky, and another, half as long, extending from the midpoint on the right side. The ogham sign for birch.

Corann returns the knife to the satchel and pauses. I think he is gauging my strength. I stand to show him I am ready, hoping, as ever, that he cannot see inside me. I do not want him to see my fear. He faces east, and we journey again into the shadow of the first hill.

When we stop to sleep, the sky is black, and the first of the Tullagh Sé lies to the south. I miss its shelter. The winds from the north and east are brutal, sharp as blades. And I forgot my bedroll. The night will be long.

For some days we skirt the northern edge of the hills. I walk alongside Corann, struggling to match his speed, and it comes to me that this is a well-worn path. Who but the Druid of Blackthorn can say how many such journeys he has made, how many groves he has marked? Corann is master of every meadow and waste, every tussock and solitude. We journey with the hills looming over our shoulders to the south and the plains stretching out forever to the north. Here and there we stop to eat, and Corann digs roots and forages for berries. How any berries could still brighten a branch of rowan or elder or bramble is beyond my knowing, but Corann can always find them.

We are careful with our water, only drinking from the skins when there is no time to stop and melt snow. At night we replenish what we drank during the day. This is winter's gift, and since the Bloodmoon we receive it with profound gratitude.

My sleep is poor. The hills are haunted, and we walk beneath them, hard against them, as though no horrors dwell there. I hear the screeching of bats and owls, the disconsolate cawing of the ravens, and my heart grows lean. I do not know where Corann leads.

We come at last to a stand of hazel. Fresh snow covers the ground. Little clumps of snow perch on every loop of the tiny, curling hazel branches. I stand aside while Corann goes in among the bare trees and steps lightly around each trunk. He is feeling the ground with the soles of his feet. I know what he seeks. Hazel nuts. They give visions; they give knowledge. Corann looks ahead of him as he goes, but his thought is bent on the ground beneath the snow, on what his feet can tell him of hidden things.

He makes several passes, circling each tree twice or three times before emerging from the grove.

"There are no nuts," he says. "The trees no longer flower."

He was here in the spring, then, watching to see if the hazel trees would flower.

He stoops over a branch that has broken under the weight of the snow and tucks it into his satchel. It might serve some purpose later. He removes the stone knife and marks one tree with the ogham sign for hazel. I lean to left and right, counting the trees so marked. Three times ten and eight besides. Has he sought visions under every tree in Baileléan? Corann rises and strides past. We continue the journey east.

The nights grow bitter. Even huddled by a fire I can find no warmth. My body seems to shrink away from the cold, my muscles to harden against it. I can find no rest. During the day, I can hardly keep my feet. I stumble through the deepening snow while my head nods. Corann gives me elderberry syrup and pushes on. We find small groves of rowan, oak, elder, and hawthorn. In each of them, no matter the bite of the wind or the depth of the snow, we sit and wait for visions. But I struggle to clear my mind. My teeth are gritted against the cold. I shiver, and hunger screams over the quiet of the inner grove. Now, too, I fear to descend. I fear what waits for me in the darkness. I see nothing, and if Corann sees visions he does not speak of them. At the end of each vigil, he marks a tree with his knife, and we continue our search.

The land to the north is unvarying. Snowy fields stretch to the sea, with no drystones to cut and quarter them. The Six Hills, on our right hand, are never different and never the same. Always they loom above us, blotting out great swaths of sky. There are birdcalls and wind, and the trees groan under the weight of the snow. Yet each grove has its own character, and I tremble whenever we pass a valley that lies between the hills. It is a passage, a doorway into the Tullagh Sé. The hills were here before the Antae. *The hills are haunted.*

Ten days have passed since the solstice. I woke this morning beneath a blanket of snow. It falls so thick I can scarcely see

Corann where he lies on the other side of the sleeping fire. I sit up, rub my hands against my upper arms, twist my fingers in front of my mouth and expel a bit of breath to warm them. It is nothing like enough. There's no sense in wasting a scrap of tinder, though. Not unless Corann means to stay here. I pray by all the powers of earth and sky that he does not.

A bedroll and an extra cloak. It is difficult to fix my thoughts on anything else. I imagine a roaring fire, a mound of sheepskins. I think of August, of harvest, when the sweat pours into my eyes and the sun burns my cheeks. Once or twice, I seek warmth in meditation, but I cannot focus, and the stillness only leaves me colder, aching with cold.

Corann wakes. His cloak rises in the drumming snow, and I see his face. His beard is coated with snow and ice, but his eyes are bright, alert. He stands and brushes the snow from his shoulders.

"We must find shelter," he says.

Yes, we must. But where? Corann would not look kindly on the question. Any fool can see there is no shelter to be found to the north or east. We are far, very far, from the shelter of the cottages in the west. There is nowhere to go but south. And there is nothing to the south but the Tullagh Sé.

Shivering, I gather my cloak around me. "You don't mean to go in."

Corann's face is set. He rolls his blanket and places it in his satchel, and his movements are sure. He shows no sign of cold or hunger. Does he enter the hills for my sake?

"I need no shelter, Corann."

"Twelve years I spent, pouring words into your ears while

you dogged my steps and plagued me with questions. I'll not have my labor wasted."

There is a smile in his words, but I cannot understand his resolve. "I can contend with the snow. Corann, the hills are hers! Dermot . . ."

"Dermot and I had begun a search of the hills when he disappeared."

My mouth hangs slack. "How far . . . ?"

"The third hill." He gives me a look that stops the questions in my throat. He takes his walking stick and sets it before him, placing both palms on the handle and lowering his head. I cannot see his lips flutter as he speaks the words of power. The snow falls too thick between us. But I see the light that blooms at the top of his walking stick. It is bright, with a greenish cast, nothing like true flame. This is druidic fire. Only a druid can summon it, and the fire serves none but its master. What Corann needs now is not heat but guidance, and so the fire blazes from his walking stick with such brilliance that the sheets of falling snow part like curtains.

We enter a narrow valley between the third and fifth hill. According to Corann's description, the fourth hill rises between the two, further south. For now it is veiled in the gray of morning and the falling snow. The hills on either side of us, however, are conspicuous. They watch, holding their breath as we penetrate the horror and sanctity of the Six Hills. I wonder if they will crowd together and close the valley, if they will trap us, if we will ever escape. This is forbidden domain.

# 8

On entering the Tullagh Sé, I am astonished to find that I feel something apart from fear. The fear is present, palpable. But the hills provide a shelter from the bitter north wind. Though the fall of snow is heavy, I am warmer than I have been in many days. I had not thought that fear and relief could be bedfellows.

We push southward, climbing. The valleys are choked with snow, and we hope to find a dense wood, a cave, anything to cover us and offer a respite from the weather. The boundaries of my stomach seem to have deepened since the solstice. I feel their deep-down profundities, the gnawings of hunger in places I had not known before. This morning I think that no honey mead could be sweeter than a simple bowl of porridge. I remember the warmth and pressure of a mouthful of sticky oats sliding down my throat.

There is no sign of sun, but I think it must be several hours after sunrise when Corann stops and turns to me. I raise my hand to shield my eyes from the druidic fire. He lowers the walking stick and sets it on the ground at his side.

"Ahead," he says. He turns back into the path and leaves me to wonder. Would it be foolish to ask *what* lies ahead? How can I learn to ask a well-packed question when Corann always leaves me with infinite questions? I never know where to begin.

I follow Corann. His dark robes protect me from the brightness of the druidic fire. I lift my feet high, stepping into the snow as lightly as I can, pushing forward, leaning into the next footfall. It is tiresome work. But before long, I see a darkness ahead. Slowly the darkness rises, expands. It is a tree—ancient, broad, weighted with snow. Its trunk is twisted, full of muscles and sinews and hollow cavities larger than my fist. Its roots spread wide before they pierce the soil. They make a kind of confused skirt beneath the canopy of green needles. A yew. Tree of the ovate. Tree of the ancestors, of death and rebirth. Tree of memory.

I had hoped to find shelter before we sought more visions. I had hoped for warmth and food and sleep. I had hoped my body would be rested, my mind cleared, when next we sought for answers in the inner groves. But this! This is a gift.

Corann steps beneath the branches. The lowest are more than an arm's length over his head. I step in behind him.

The moment I enter, I sense it, smell it, taste it, feel it on my skin. The air is alive. The druidic fire casts its light up into a thousand-year-old domain of needles and branches and berries. A coat of snow gives a soft, woolen cast to the lighted world beneath the tree. But there is nothing else of softness in this place. There is an energy here that is sharp as a blade, ancient as the Blue Sea, fierce as the Fir Bolg.

Corann settles himself on the skirt of roots and presses his hands against the top of his walking stick. The druidic fire is quenched. He will need all his reserves for the descent into the inner grove.

I sit on the other side of the yew, in the gloom that only follows the brilliance of druidic fire, and breathe. Fear consumes me. I must will some calm into my shaking arms and legs, for the need is too pressing. I cannot waste this precious chance.

Tree of the ancestors, of death and rebirth.

Tree of memory.

The visions come in three bright bursts, one after the other.

A ridge of white stone with a village beside.

Lovers embracing.

A monstrous tree of black, with leaves like oak leaves.

Darkness. A gentle rise to awareness. I feel the roots beneath me, hear the hiss of snowfall. My hands and feet are numb. How long have I been sitting? It could not have been more than a moment. I open my eyes. Corann stands at the edge of the branches, looking out into the snow. The druidic fire burns again on his walking stick. He senses my return, glances over his shoulder, fixes me with an appraising stare. I stand, dropping my eyes, and make an effort to stomp the blood back into my feet. As Corann leaves the sheltering canopy and the light of the druidic fire recedes, I turn to catch a glimpse of the primeval trunk. Corann has made no mark. I think he is wise.

I follow him into the falling snow.

Corann finds a cave before nightfall. I stagger in and collapse against the wall. Corann, forty years my elder, makes up the fire. It is true fire this time. We need the warmth.

When the spark from Corann's flint catches and the flames begin to rise, I pull a little bowl from my satchel and fill it partway with water. I go to set it on the edge of the fire, but my hands are shaking. I burn my fingers and spill the water, dampening the fuel and quenching the flame.

Corann begins again without a word of reproach. I sort through the remainder of my food, busying my hands, warming them, and trying in vain to turn my thoughts from my empty belly. The spark catches again, and the fire grows, and I make myself wait. A little longer. A little longer. When I trust the steadiness of my hands, I set the bowl on the edge of the fire and pour the water.

Whole ages of the world seem to pass while I watch the water heat. The bubbles form with infinite patience, as if the journey from the base of the shallow bowl to the skin of the water were as vast as the journey from ocean floor to crashing wave. The bubbles multiply, quicken. At last, the water boils. I drop a handful of oats into the bowl and stir them with a stick. They are tough and chewy when I wrap my fingers in the edge of my cloak and pull the bowl from the fire. I burn my lips on the first bite.

I glance at Corann. He sits by the fire, watching the flames. He eats nothing, drinks nothing. I feel strange offering him a portion of my oats. In all our years together, we have not often shared a meal. But I extend the bowl, raise my brows. He refuses the offer with a wave of his hand, and once again, I feel the gap between us. He is accustomed to hunger and exposure and exhaustion. He has not aged past that strength, but into it. If he knew no sorcery at all, he would still be a man to be reckoned with. He is one with the elements.

The hood of his cloak has fallen back. He studies the fire in perfect quiet while I finish my porridge. I scrape the bowl with my fingertips and stuff the last sticky remnants of the oats into my mouth. I return the bowl to the satchel, sip from my waterskin, and move to lie down.

Corann speaks.

"I have never searched beyond the third hill," he says. "Never this far."

I straighten and watch him. I cannot tell by his tone if he is ashamed.

"The hills are haunted," I say.

"The hills are *hers*," he replies. He looks hard at me. "Perth warned me against dealings with her."

"Perth? You've met with Perth?" The great sorcerer. First among druids. He taught us the magic of Tír Ársa, the ogham signs, the eight-fold wheel. He lived three hundred years.

"Long ago, in the inner grove."

"Was it then that you brought down lightning on a holly tree?"

Corann nods once. "At Snowmelt."

This man. The secrets he holds. The knowledge! He has spoken with the great sorcerer. He has called down lightning on the sacred tree of the Crone, on a tree that repels lightning. Is Corann's sorcery as powerful as the Crone's?

He dismisses the thought before I can voice it.

"The hills are *hers*. They dropped from her cloak as she flew over Baileléan in the time before times. It was not Baileléan then. Only the western shoulder of Tír Ársa. Nothing but a desperate flight from the Fir Bolg could have driven us into the Crone's domain. We are trespassers here, for all this land is hers. If she wished to claim it, she could push us into the western sea. But she has chosen the Tullagh Sé."

I know the tale well. It was Corann who taught me, and it was in the silence and darkness of a cave such as this that I wove the words into the fabric of my memory. The Crone has many names: Hag, Veiled One, Mountain Mother, Keeper of Death's Door. But apart from her betrayal of Arlan and Meréd, I know little of her doings.

"What did Perth say of her? She enters so few of our stories."

Corann's eyes narrow. "She enters all of them. All the stories of the Antae. The battles we have fought? The land we have cultivated? Our celebrations and even our search for answers—all have circled her domain, avoided it. It is far more true to say, Idris, that the Crone and the Tullagh Sé stand at the *center* of all our stories."

It is a heavy truth Corann speaks. I had not seen it before. "What do you know of her?" I ask.

Corann sits awhile in thought. It is remarkable how active, how restless, is his mind. It travels vast distances while his body sits in repose.

"Perth spoke of a wand bound in human flesh. He spoke of a devouring darkness against which no man could stand. He spoke of fear." He fixes me with a look, but the words are not lost on me. Perth spoke of fear. Perth, who saw the passing of three hundred winters, who roamed the sacred groves of Tír Ársa, who raised forests with a few scratches in the soil. That Perth was afraid.

There is no more question of a battle of strength or sorcery. I had not grasped the full scope of the Crone's power. If Perth was afraid, then—

But who would not fear the Keeper of Death's Door? My next thought is inescapable, and almost unbearable.

Zinerva.

The Crone granted her entrance into the Underworld. That is not surprising. But how often does she grant an exit? How many have escaped that dreaded gate?

"Why should the Crone allow Zinerva to return from the Underworld?"

Corann shifts. He crosses his legs in front of him and rests his palms on his knees. "The druidess Sheridan, who was my teacher, said that Clodagh was a thrall of the Crone. Sheridan believed it was an offense against wisdom for a healer to dance with death."

"They were enemies? Sheridan and Clodagh?" I ask.

"Mortal," Corann replies.

"What message did she bring from the ancestors?"

Corann shakes his head. "I will answer you once more, Idris, but only once. No one tells the tale of Clodagh's initiation.

Either it was done in secret, or the message she brought has not endured."

There is quiet between us, though I see the thoughts flit across Corann's forehead. If anything is clear to me it is this: Zinerva is another Clodagh. If Sheridan spoke truly, if Clodagh is a thrall of the Crone, then Zinerva is the same. What if she slavers after the kind of power that Perth held? He was the supreme druid. He was ovate and bard as well, for in those days the roles had not been sundered. And the Antae trusted him completely. They would have followed him to death.

Will they follow Zinerva into death? Corann's hands are bound. For who can stand against the Keeper of Death's Door? And what value are my words against the wisdom of one who has returned from death?

"Tomorrow," Corann says. "Tomorrow you will tell me your visions."

I WAKE ABRUPTLY FROM A DEEP SLEEP, the first of this journey. I seem to travel a long way up before I understand what has wakened me. A cry is riding on the wind. It is despondent, full of woe, the cry of one who cannot be comforted, who cannot know comfort. The banshee.

I cannot help but rise. I walk past the sleeping Corann and peer from the mouth of the cave. The clouds are a tattered cloak, ragged hems trailing over the Tullagh Sé. The snow has stopped. It lies innocently on the hills, glimmering in the moonlight, as though it had not spent the last day trying to bury me.

The cry comes again. It is terrible to hear. For all its familiarity, I cannot accustom myself to the sound. It grates against my ears and my heart, and I am overcome with the desire to see the wretched, fearsome creature. Now my cloak and tunic and pants are dry, I am not so cold. I leave the shelter of the cave and follow the keening.

The hush around me is profound, the silence after the storm. All the activities of nature, of creature, of man, are muted and stilled. It's as if the snow presses a hand to our mouths and says, "Quiet now. Listen." I do listen. I must. The banshee's cry parts the silence like a blade and echoes over the silent hills. A shiver runs down my back.

I pass the ancient yew where I saw three visions. Beyond it are elder, a few hawthorn, and bramble. Beyond those, another yew. This one is smaller, a little less ancient. The broken moonlight on the snow casts a soft, silver light into the branches. I can just make out the trunk, with its wide, sinuous bands. There is an odd bulge at one side, rising from the roots and twining with the trunk. I almost think I see it stir.

I do.

It does.

All at once, the banshee's cry ceases. Several tortured bands twist away from the trunk. They catch the light, and I see that they are not wood, but—but what? Wool? It is hard to say, and my eyes are drawn upward, to a blot of darkness that has turned toward me. It is a head, I think. A face. Thin strands of lank hair hang from either side of a black circle. Two eyes burn softly, like lamps in a fog. I can see no mouth or nose, only a small, contorted neck.

I am bewitched, entranced. I can no more move than if I were carved in stone.

A pit of darkness opens beneath its pale eyes, and another wail surges out. Hearing it now, in the banshee's presence, I feel again the fear of death, that devouring terror I met in my vision in the birch wood. *The hills are haunted. The hills are hers.*

The banshee looks away and dissolves into the darkness. I turn on my heel and run for the cave.

Corann still sleeps, and I am careful not to wake him, though my breathing is heavy and the noise of the blood rushing in my ears seems loud enough to wake all the creatures of the Six Hills. When I close my eyes, I see the face of the banshee. It is long before I find the solace of sleep.

I tell Corann of my visions, beginning with the dream journey into the realm of the Shí on the first day of the year. The old druid listens carefully when I tell of the tree with branches and leaves like iron. From there, I attempt to clothe my birchwood vision in words. But how do you capture fear? It sits in the belly, crawls over the body, invades the mind. Words cannot contain it. It is always wriggling out of them, shedding them like a too-tight skin.

I tell Corann of the three visions at the yew. The village, the lovers, the tree. Again, the tree. He asks me to describe the village in greater detail. This, too, is difficult. It was a flash, an impression. I felt the loneliness of that place, the desolation, more than I noted the size of the cottages or the positions of the drystones. One thing was clear, though. A ridge of white stone ran along the edge of the village. It veered off, I think, once it passed the last of the cottages.

When I finish speaking I wait for Corann to reply. I hope he has some understanding of these visions, or that his visions will help to illuminate them. Some minutes pass while Corann rubs the tips of his fingers together. I have seen this before, during the more trying phases of my training, when he could hardly bear to recite another story or listen as I repeated it. He is agitated.

The energy builds, until tiny veins of lightning sprout from his fingertips, branching from one finger to the next and one hand to the other. The light flashes on the walls of the cave, glances off the ceiling. It intensifies, snapping the air into tiny fragments, until, with one tremendous crack, the light goes out. Corann and I are alone with the fire.

I want to ask about his visions. He has sat in birch and elder and hawthorn groves. He was with me under the yew. What has he seen? For once, Corann saves me the trouble of choosing a question.

"I begin to fear that, for me, the well of knowing has run dry.

"There was a time when salmon leaped from the rivers, when hazelnuts dropped from the trees, when the still surface of the water revealed the mysteries of earth and sky. Now I sit beneath a yew that saw the coming of the Antae and the pursuit of the Fir Bolg, and my eyes are darkened." Corann looks into my eyes. "I have seen nothing in any of the groves," he says.

No visions? None? I have watched him rest his head, night after night, on a mound of ash leaves. I have waited while he breathed the incense of the rowan. Have all his efforts failed?

"You have seen the coming of calamity," I remind him. "That much you drank from the well of knowing."

He sighs. "But it has no shape, no name."

His frustration rises from his body like steam. The world is out of balance, and he does not know why. It hurtles toward destruction, and he cannot stop it. It troubles me to think that I should see visions when Corann does not. I am the Ollamh, Keeper of the Word. But I am nothing to Corann. If anyone can restore the balance, it is the Druid of Blackthorn.

Corann smothers the fire. He is anxious to be going. He is not at ease in these hills. Who among us could be? I say nothing of the banshee.

The sky is clear. No sign of coming storms. We tread through deep drifts of snow, keeping between the hills, winding south toward the bog. Around us the hills are white, with here and there a whisper of green. There is birdsong, and once I catch the gray puff of a squirrel's tail as it scurries into the branches of a holly tree. I notice more and more hollies as we go. Their leaves are a deep, waxy green, with sharp edges. Their red berries stand out like drops of blood against the white snow.

I take a bit of salted beef from my satchel and nibble at the end. I have not conserved my food like I ought. The strain of travel, the gnawing cold, have driven me to my meager store again and again. I have tried to hold off, to ignore the demands of my stomach. But they have mastered me. This is my last slice of beef. I take another bite, only one for now, and lick the traces of salt from my lips. I sip a little water and hurry to catch up with Corann. As always, he makes rapid progress, even in deep snow.

The day passes. I follow Corann in silence as his eyes sweep the trees, the ground, the sloping hills. What does he think to find? Perhaps this new terrain gives him some hope, for the well-worn paths, the familiar groves, have divulged nothing. I am glad of the clear sky and the shelter of the hills, though it is strange to think of the Tullagh Sé as sheltering. In truth, they are menacing. Yet we have faced no imminent danger thus far. I wonder if the puka peered in through the entrance of the cave last night, if he called to us while we slept.

The sun is low in the sky and the shadows are long when we come to a clearing in the midst of three hills. We entered between the third and fifth hills, and now the fourth rises just ahead. But in the clearing before us is a circle of holly trees. In the center of the trees is an altar.

Corann stops, his hands resting lightly on the end of his walking stick. He glances around the circle of holly. His eyes settle on the stone altar. He reaches beneath the folds of his cloak and takes his hazel wand in hand. He steps within the circle. One step. Two.

The snow on the hollies is undisturbed. The sky is blue over our heads. I am wide awake, in command of my senses and surroundings. I see no enemies. I do not know why I should be afraid. In daylight. With Corann.

But there is deep darkness here, in the sparkling snow. It spills from the altar, spreads over the clearing, laps against the holly trees like waves on the seashore. My throat thickens. The tang of fear is on my tongue.

Corann approaches the altar. It is a wide, rounded stone,

high as the joints of Corann's thighs. Its surface is smooth, with thirteen small depressions forming a circular border. In each depression is a stone, fitted to its place. There is no snow on the altar. It is clean and dry, though the coloring of the stones is strange.

Corann raises his wand in his right hand.

He lifts a little border stone with his left.

I know at once that this is wrong. I have never laid eyes on this altar, but it must be a very ancient place of worship. It is sacred to someone, to something.

Corann sets the first stone aside and reaches into the hollow where it made its bed. He lifts a white feather, examines it, sets it back in its place, and returns the stone. He lifts another and sets it to the side of the hollow. He takes something between his finger and thumb and lifts it, squinting. It is hard to tell if it is a chip of wood or a fragment of bone. The edges are jagged. Corann replaces this as well. In the next hollow is a scrap of bark. Birch. Corann lifts it, shows me. Strange. Birch is the tree of the bard, and I have seen none since we entered the Tullagh Sé.

He lifts another stone, sets it aside. But this time he does not touch the thing in the hollow. He looks at it a moment, leans back. He glances at the surrounding hills. Quickly, he replaces the border stone and strides out of the clearing.

"Let us be gone from this place."

I ask the question. I must.

"What was in the last hollow?"

"Skin."

He is skirting the grove with rapid strides, hurrying south. It does not seem a quick enough retreat. That was human skin in the last hollow. Corann would not have blinked an eye at a scrap of deerskin or a strip of hide from a sacred bull. Someone lost his flesh on that altar. Was it Dermot? Could the former Bard of Blackthorn have come to grief in this profane place?

Now we have trespassed in the Crone's domain and disturbed her sacred altar.

Perhaps the banshee cried for me.

THE JOURNEY OUT OF THE TULLAGH SÉ takes a night and a day.

We pass the night without a halt, and in spite of the cold, in spite of my weariness, I am glad. Even in the darkest hours, Corann makes no use of druidic fire. I do not know if he fears the Crone's wrath or if he feels no need of the fire. Yet the stars are cold and distant, and there is no moon. I set my face to the rippling shadow of Corann's robes and tread through rivers of snow.

Corann leads us out of the valley and along the southwestern edge of the hills. It is a steep rise, and it makes for awkward going. I walk with a hobbling gait, my right knee bent, my left leg straight. But now we are out of the deeper snow, and we move along at a better pace.

I nibble salt beef and sip water. I try to imagine that the darkness that washed over my skin in the holly grove is far behind me, that we have left it contained in that profane circle.

I try to gather up all the terror of my vision in the birch grove, all the horror of the banshee's cry, and stuff it inside the circle of trees. I cannot. For we have only been to the pulsing heart of death. We have not seen its gaping jaws. And its hands, oh, its hands stretch far to the west, all along the banks of the Adder, down to the village of Blackthorn, to all the villages of Baileléan, and out into the sea. Since the Bloodmoon, it has cast its shadow over all of us. What happened that night that gave death such unhindered access to the upper world?

I feel our journey has been wasted. Corann has seen no visions, and my visions have only raised more questions. I begin to wonder what is happening in Blackthorn. Were we right to leave the village in Zinerva's hands? My thoughts run in circles until I can bear it no more. I turn for comfort to the tales stored in memory, rehearsing the long passages describing the battles of the Cogath Tornech while Corann and I keep a tenuous balance on the snow-covered slopes.

We emerge from the Tullagh Sé. On our left hand, to the east, the sixth hill rises. It is broad and dark, higher than the others. Ahead of us, to the south, is the Adder, and beyond it is the creeping bog. It was fertile country once, but the bitter water from the Adder has changed the soil. A few isolated marshes have spread, and every year they eat up more of the land south of the hills. The village of Eyebright, far to the west, is all but overrun. Their maze of drystones has done little to slow the progress of the creeping bog. As yet, Bolghrain is untouched. But who knows what another year will bring?

The red light of sunset falls on a ridge of white stone. It runs east to west, like the hills, then makes a southward turn beyond the ruins.

"Corann!"

He turns and follows my gaze to the deserted village that lies in the shadow of the ridge. The sod roofs have collapsed. The shells of cottages, five times four perhaps, are scattered over the bog. Some of the drystones have sunk halfway beneath the murk, leaving only two or three visible layers of stones. Here and there, a wall has collapsed or leans precariously against its brothers.

But I saw this village as it *was*. In my vision, the ridge was not bathed in blood as it seems now. The windows and doorways were full of cheerful firelight. The grass was green, and spotted with primrose.

"This was Ban Lurgan," Corann says. "The village of your vision?"

It is not really a question. He speaks as though he knew.

"One of the first to be abandoned after the Bloodmoon," he says.

Two thoughts rise in me, and they are bound together. There was truth in my vision, and I have been quick to see it confirmed. That is heartening. But Corann, too, has seen a vision. Is this broken, sinking village a picture of the devastation that is coming to all Baileléan? Is this chance glimpse of Ban Lurgan also a glimpse into the future of Blackthorn?

I am longing to be back in the hillside hut, to climb the stile and join Deirdre and the others in the work of the village. It is long since I spoke with Calder. And Muriel. I have only to think her name and my stomach drops. My throat catches. She is far from the ruined village, far from the Crone's altar. But not far enough.

"We'll stop here tonight," Corann says.

He finds a seat under a lone rowan in a patch of sloped ground that the bog has not touched. I sit opposite him, and take the last remnants of the salt beef from my satchel.

"Save it," he says.

I put it back and rest my head against the small trunk. The sun drags its light, ray by ray, into the western sea. The bog sinks into twilight. The stars show their faces. And I think of Perth, who disguised himself during the early days of the Cogath Tornech and laid a magical feast for his enemies. They ate and ate, while the sun sank and the moon rose, and the moon sank and the sun rose, and still they were not satisfied. At last, they went away empty, for there was no pith or substance in the food of enchantment. Perth's enemies found no strength for their next battle.

They went away empty.

Corann insists that the land south of the Adder is impassable. The bog's shallow pools are easily avoided, but they draw the eyes from the abandoned cooking pits and the deeper hollows nestled behind hummocks of sedge and moss. It is an ill-favored land, an insult to the eye. Even the clinging fog has a brownish, unwholesome look. The snow does nothing to improve it, for the clean white flakes have no time to settle. They melt and darken in the turbid water.

So we keep to the narrow strip of ground between the Adder and the hills. Sometimes the Tullagh Sé rise without pause from the lip of the river. In those places we climb, making a slow path through deep drifts of snow, and work our way back down to the water's edge.

My thoughts are consumed by a gnawing hunger. I stretch the last few bites of salt beef over two days. At night, we melt snow over the fire, and I boil a few oats I scrounge from the corners of my satchel. Corann is generous with his store of provisions. On the third day, he offers me a small dried branch and urges me to chew it. Knowing Corann, this is likely some ancient remedy for hunger. I work the stick until my teeth ache, and still its virtues remain a mystery. I chuck it into the river.

We search out no groves. We do not pause to meditate when we pass a rowan or yew. We make for Blackthorn.

One night, the fourth since we reached the southern edge of the Tullagh Sé, Corann does not stop to make camp. We hurry along the Adder while a thin moon rises and sails through a sea of stars. The night is far spent when we catch sight of a cottage. It lies on the southeast corner of Blackthorn, right at the river's edge. It is Engl's house, and candlelight shines through the open shutter.

Corann walks to the window and peers in. I wonder if he means to speak with Engl, but he only studies her a moment and moves on. I step behind him, leaning around the open shutter to see what lies within. Engl is curled on her side, one arm around the baby. They seem to be sleeping. The candlepot sits just out of reach.

The child is not healed. He is too thin, his face too flushed. But neither is he dead. Relief washes over me. There is some comfort in returning home to find that one thing, at least, is no worse.

I hurry along behind Corann as he makes his way through the village. The shutters are closed at Sloane and Etain's cottage, but Corann works a little magic and opens them. Whatever it is he sees inside, he seems satisfied, for he moves on to Calder and Shannan's cottage. I follow close, peeking into an open shutter at Corann's side. Calder sleeps on his side with Shannan tucked against him. A mirror, polished smooth and etched with gold, lies on a small wooden table in one corner. Beside it is a bouquet of gorse. The yellow flowers look back at themselves out of the gold mirror, and the couple sleeps on. We find Llyr sprawled on his bedroll, his long arms and legs flung far beyond the limits of the sheepskin. Murdoch sleeps peacefully on the other side of the cottage.

Corann is especially quiet when he approaches Barra's cottage. Here, again, he uses a spell to open the shutter. There is a soft glow from the banked fire. It casts a gentle warmth over the broad, bearded face of the chief. Vaughn, Pixie, and Brennan sleep in a tangle of arms and legs and sheepskins.

I am ashamed to look in on Deirdre and Muriel. To see Muriel sleeping would be . . . I cannot. But for a moment I cease to be a bard and become an eye, thrust into the dark of night, studying Corann's every movement. He returns without a word, and a sigh escapes my lips. They are well.

One cottage remains. But Corann does not venture near the

dwelling of the ovate. The owl waits at its perch on the roof. It swivels its head to left and right, stopping to study Corann, to study me. Corann turns a last, satisfied gaze on the slumbering people of Blackthorn and makes his way to the hut in the hillside.

I have never been so glad of a dark, smoky hole.

# 11

The wheel turns toward Snowmelt. According to the ancient ways, this is a time of inspiration, a time when poets divine and prophesy. Yet I have returned from a great journey with a vision of death, a cry of death, an altar to death. The village, the lovers, the iron oak—these are fragments. I cannot offer them to the people of Blackthorn.

I rise early and walk in the grove while the moon sits wedged among the branches of the blackthorns and the stars wheel incomprehensibly over my head. I am determined to fulfill my role. I must find some word to offer my people. I descend into the depths of thought and being. I wait—for words, for visions, for fire. Nothing comes. I carve the ogham sign into a blackthorn, as Corann marked the other groves where we sought the inner flame.

At midday I sit by the fallow fields, hoping the sun's meager warmth will unveil the mysteries of the blight. I lie down by the Adder, by the brink of running water, until the sound of its rushing fills me, until I am the water, leaping, splashing, hurrying to the sea. But instead of insight, I find confusion. The world is a current of bitter water that empties into the Blue Sea, Gormára.

Wherever I go, I feel Barra's gaze upon me. Our chief is not a man I can despise, but my impotence almost makes it so. He believes my words are as potent as Zinerva's. They might be, perhaps, if I had any words to speak. But what am I to say when Snowmelt comes? What am I to tell these people?

The hours I do not give to meditation and searching, I spend with Deirdre and Calder and Sloane, clearing the winter debris from the grove and the fields. Deirdre watches me; the weight of her questions presses against me. It has been so ever since my return. But she will not ask, and I do not offer. I understand, now, why she was reluctant to speak of her vision.

We clear scraps of moldering gorse from each pasture, piling it in carts and stacking it against the hill on the eastern edge of the village. Sloane works at my side. In the tight confines of the smaller pastures, our elbows bump together, yet he never looks my way. There is a bandage wrapped around his head, soaked with blood at a spot above his left eye. I wonder where he went and whom he fought.

We gather fallen branches from the rowan near Barra's cottage, more from the ash tree near Calder's cottage. I catch a glimpse of Shannan through the window. She is gazing into her mirror.

We wheel the carts into the blackthorn grove and gather the branches broken by the snow. We are careful to pinch the broken ends, to avoid the thorns, but it is no small task. Sloane works with such ferocious speed that I begin to wonder if he does not long to feel the bite of a blackthorn. Deirdre's hands are long, Barra's broad and meaty. It is a wonder we come through unscathed.

I am so relieved by our success that I do not see Zinerva standing in the doorway of her cottage. She watches as we carry our load to the hillside.

"The Crone comes for her firewood," she says.

I stop, the handles of the cart in my grip. The others stop beside me, to hear the words of the ovate. Her faded orange shawl stretches over her thin arms. The owl sits on her shoulder. Her hair is changed. Thin braids sprout from her head and mingle with the threaded strands. A haze of yellow hair surrounds them.

Zinerva looks toward the hill. Her eyes, under heavy lids, cut me a glance.

She turns to Calder. "Very soon I leave to gather herbs. But I will come to the lambing, to tend the ewes."

Calder drops his head. "Thank you, Ovate."

The owl flaps to the roof, and Zinerva recedes into the cottage, and I am breathless. I keep my words close until we reach the hillside. Even then, I am afraid to speak while Sloane is near. He is wild, and I do not know his loyalties. I wait until he has emptied his cart before I voice my questions.

"What does the clearing of the winter debris have to do with the Crone?"

Calder removes his cloak and drapes it over his arms, wrapping his hands in its folds before lifting the blackthorn branches from the cart. Deirdre piles the branches: rowan on gorse, ash on rowan, blackthorn on ash.

Calder finishes his load and turns to me. His is a merry face, with round cheeks blooming out of a long gray beard and twinkling blue eyes. There is a yellow flower, gorse, pinned to the shoulder of his tunic.

"It is one of the old sayings, Ollamh. Nothing to bother with. They say the Crone gathers her firewood at Snowmelt."

He speaks the words without fear or foreboding, as though the Crone is nothing but a fancy. He knows better. But why has Corann never told me? We walk in silence day after day, enter the horror of the Crone's sacred grove, and he says nothing of what the Keeper of Death's Door will do at the next turning of the wheel. I grind my teeth. How like him! He will argue, perhaps, that I have failed to ask a well-packed question. And I will answer with a volley of questions. I will ask and ask until I stumble upon the right one.

I set the cart on the ground and beat a path to the hut. Corann is not inside. Of course not! He is not in the grove either. I skirt the hill, heading north. Nothing. I sit outside, my back against the door of the hut, and pound my fist against the snow.

I wait for his return while the sun sinks into the sea. Clouds scud across the sky. They are pink and gold, then silver and gray, then white against a black sky. He does not come. I surrender to sleep.

My nose is cold, and my ears, but nothing else. I open my eyes to find a sheepskin tucked around me. Dawn is hurrying in from the east. I have slept the night through, and I have slept in relative comfort because of someone's kindness. It is hard to imagine that it could have been Corann. More likely Deirdre or Calder.

I stand and enter the hut. The fire is cold, so I light it with a flint and add three chunks of peat. My breakfast of oats and dried berries is not enough, but since the journey through the Tullagh Sé, I find I cannot complain of it. It is warm and cheering, if meager. I eat quickly, bank the fire. As I have slept in my boots and cloak, there is nothing else to do. At the last moment I remember the lambing. If it has begun, the whole village will soon gather in the pastures. Muriel will be there. I splash my face with a bit of melted snow and scrub it with a wool cloth. I run the cloth over my teeth and return it to its nook, then close the cottage door behind me.

I walk along the edge of the grove and climb the stile. I cross the first pasture, passing the rowan in the cliff and turning west. Barra stands in one of the pastures near his cottage, morning sunlight gilding the tip of his spear. He studies the door of Engl's cottage. Pixie, Vaughn, and Brennan run from pasture to pasture, their red heads bobbing among the white sheep and bounding over the drystones.

Others are coming. Sloane and Etain carry cloths for the new lambs. Deirdre emerges from her cottage with a basket of beaten gorse. Calder has put the four pregnant ewes in separate enclosures, so Deidre spreads a handful of gorse before each of them. Muriel follows her. I cannot help but watch as the sunlight washes over her hair, as she tucks it behind her ear and spreads the fodder with white hands. Her peplos is blue, her shawl a soft green. I watch until Engl joins her, and the two of them embrace. Then Shannan makes a rare appearance. She sits on a drystone at the corner of a pasture and watches her husband at his work.

I turn my attention to Calder. He kneels beside a ewe, offering her bits of gorse. She bleats, rocking back on her side. Her udders are stretched, full to bursting. Sometimes she stands, takes a step or two, nibbles a bit of gorse, and lies back down in the snow. I hear gasps from the assembled villagers when a small white nose emerges, the tip of a red tongue, the square end of a hoof. The ewe bleats again, and another bleat sounds from a nearby pasture. I turn to see Clodagh step out of her cottage. Her green-black cloak covers her shoulders. The hood hangs down, but her gaze follows Zinerva as she walks to the pasture where the second ewe has begun to deliver.

In our enclosure, the ewe stands again, making a circle in the snow. She goes for the gorse, changes her mind, kneels down, and rocks on her side. Two small hoofs jerk into the air as she struggles. Her bleating is hoarse. I see the wide eyes of the fosterlings as they peer over the wall. Barra stands behind them, and Shannan leans down from her seat on the drystone. Muriel, Deirdre, and Etain stand ready with blankets and food. Sloane holds a bucket of melted snow. Engl cradles her baby against her shoulder, patting his back. Calder kneels beside the ewe, shushing her and stroking her nose.

Another hoof. Two black eyes. The first lamb is out, sliding to the ground in a slick, yellow membrane. Its mother jumps to her feet and turns, licking the lamb clean. Her tongue rasps over the little body, starting at the face and working down the sides and legs. We none of us can take our eyes off the lamb. We wait for its small bleat, but it does not move. Calder allows the mother a moment or two to get the blood flowing in the little legs, the small, curly head. It does not even twitch in response to its mother's caresses. Calder stoops over it, rubs the legs, massages the neck. No movement, nothing. The lamb is stillborn.

The people of Blackthorn stare at the lamb. We all feel the same. The birth of the new lamb was a sign of hope, of life invading death. But it was defeated before it began to fight. We are all remembering Madigan's message. We are wondering what it means to embrace death as a friend. We remember that it waits to return our embrace.

There is a sharp bleat in the pasture where Zinerva cares for the second ewe. Pixie and Vaughn and Brennan clamber over the stile and join the ovate. Pixie's voice rings out. "No!"

We understand, even while we hover over the first lamb, that another lamb is gone. Deirdre pins me with a sharp, pointed look and goes to stand near Zinerva. She wonders what Zinerva might have done to the new lamb. She is right to wonder. But the first was born dead without the ovate's interference.

I do not know what makes us linger by the dead lamb as if it might somehow rise. I see tears slide into the ruts of Shannan's wrinkled cheeks. Calder sniffs and wipes his nose with his arm. In Sloane's and Etain's eyes there is empty darkness, and Barra's brow is heavy. He casts a longing glance at Engl as she turns away.

I am afraid to meet Muriel's eyes. My glance flutters to her blue peplos, to the basket on her hip, to the strands of spun-gold hair that play in the wind. Finally, I look into her face. She is watching me. There are questions in her eyes, and something else. Expectation, I think. She waits for me to act.

Shannan, Sloane, Etain, and Engl return to their cottages. I follow Calder to the enclosure where the third ewe is resting. Barra stands at my shoulder. Deirdre, Muriel, and the fosterlings follow Zinerva to the fourth.

We spend the morning waiting, taking it in turns to bring fodder or water to the ewes. We carry a bit more of the winter's debris to the piles on the hillside. We watch the passing clouds. But we eat nothing, we say nothing. We wait for two new lambs to come and comfort us.

At last the ewes begin their labor, one after the other. I sit by Calder while Deirdre watches Zinerva with hawk's eyes. Again we catch our breaths when little wet noses emerge from their mothers, when tiny hooves clear the birth canal, when yellow membranes fall to the ground. Again we stand in mute defeat as mothers lick the damp wool of limp, stillborn lambs.

Barra stands silent beside me. I remember his frustration as we returned from the oak grove on the morning of the solstice. Deirdre pierces me with eyes full of fury, and Muriel's lovely eyes ask me when. When will I act? When will I speak? Can I foresee a future where death does not speak the final word, where death does not hold the upper hand?

We take the dead lambs from their mothers and wrap them in cloths. I go with the fosterlings, carrying the bundles to the clearing in the blackthorn grove. Around the portal tomb, not inside, where the bones of our ancestors rest, we bury the lambs. By the time Barra has finished covering the holes with snow and soil, I have decided. Tomorrow I will take up the gold branch. At Snowmelt, I will speak.

# 12

The swan-feather cloak is heavy on my shoulders. The bells tinkle on the gold branch. The people have gathered on the open ground north of the grove. They sit around a fire that burns with the leaves and berries of the rowan. The air is heavy with incense. The moon rounds toward the full, and the night wind is cold. Corann stands at one side of the assembly, his head tilting to the side, his eyes looking through me into the night. Clodagh stands at the other side, her pale eyes pinning me in my place. Zinerva has gone in search of herbs and medicines. There is nothing now but me and the sacred Word. Barra's eyes are bright, expectant. Muriel and Deirdre watch in focused silence. I have seen nothing that will comfort the people of Blackthorn. But memory and foresight issue from the same fountain. So I begin with memory.

I take a breath, inhaling the scent of rowan, and speak the words of a story I learned years before I came to Blackthorn. It was my mother, not Corann, who first told me of the Lightning Men, and the War of Thunder.

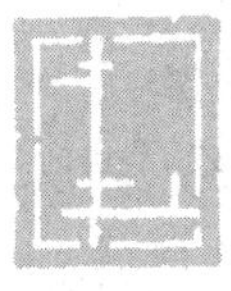*ong ago, in the land of our birth, was the Cogath Tornech, the War of Thunder, when the Fir Bolg coveted the rich land of Tír Ársa and came to make war with mortal men.*

*Now the Fir Bolg were like gods. Their feet were more swift than the stag, their legs as lean and tireless as the wolf. They were lunged like bulls, and their movements were as light and free as a feather. Their hearts were stout, their faces fierce, and their hunger insatiable. In those days, Tír Ársa saw three harvests a year, but for all that, the Fir Bolg still devoured the land. They ate up the wheat and the barley, swallowed the fish in the sea, and drank the rivers dry.*

*The battles of the Cogath Tornech were brutal and brief, and five times ten thousand men might fall at the hands of the Fir Bolg before the sun had climbed its way out of the eastern sea. So Tír Ársa, which had swarmed with warriors and maidens and children, was bathed in blood, and the heads of warriors covered the hills and fields, and all the land was shrouded in the gloom of death.*

The words hang heavy over the people. They know the story of the Cogath Tornech. They know how the Antae came to Baileléan. Yet they wait to hear how I will speak of death. They wait for me to write a new end to the story.

*Now Perth, the great sorcerer, and Madigan, Hero of a Hundred Battles, led the remnant of the once-mighty people to the western reaches of Tír Ársa. They called themselves the Antae, Those Who Remain, and they retreated from the devouring hunger of the Fir Bolg. Yet the Fir Bolg pursued. And no matter how far or how fast the Antae fled, the feet of the Fir Bolg were more swift, their footfalls more light, their strength more terrible. Finally, wearied beyond hope, beyond reckoning, the Antae came to the last hold of Tír Ársa, to the Domain of the Mountain Mother. Thinking the Fir Bolg would abandon their pursuit, Madigan took up the trunk of a yew tree and made it his cudgel. He raised it over his great head and brought it down upon the ground, and again he raised it and let it fall, and the sound was like the beating of a mighty hammer. It rang for a night and a day, till the foundations of Tír Ársa were broken, and a shoulder of land drifted into the Blue Sea, Gormára.*

*For a time there was peace. The Antae dwelt on the eastern shore of their new home, and they called it Baileléan. The land was rich and fair, and the whales spouted in the churning waters, and the seals barked and dived, and the salmon leapt into the fishermen's boats. They danced on the eastern shores, while ritual fires burned and Perth sought for signs in the stars and the great luminaries.*

*It was on a night such as this, when the Antae feasted on the shore, that Perth saw in the distance the flicker and stammer of moonlight on swords and torques and shields, and he knew that the Fir Bolg had not abandoned their pursuit. They had built themselves a fleet of currachs, and they were hurrying over the sea to eat up the rich land of Baileléan.*

*Perth, the mighty sorcerer, warned the Antae. Madigan took up his yew cudgel and let it fall once more, and the rocks convulsed, and the backbone of Baileléan burst from its skin and spread over the land like vessels of blood.*

I see a white ridge, burst from its skin like a backbone, and a broken village lying in its shadow. I pause in my telling to catch my breath. The white ridge is an esker, a stone highway that the Antae used to help them flee from the Fir Bolg. It is a fragment of a larger picture.

The firelight falls on expectant faces. They wait for the Word of the ollamh. Clodagh watches with narrowed eyes.

*The Antae left their fires with the boars still roasting on spits, the salmon still blackening among the coals, and fled to the west. To slow the advance of the Fir Bolg, Perth raised a storm wind and overturned their currachs. Then he used the ogham, the most ancient language of Tír Ársa, to hinder them further. In the soil, he made the sign for the oak. Immediately an oak grove sprang up, broad and timeworn, as though it had always been. And other groves Perth raised, of birch and ash and elder and hawthorn, to hide the retreat of the Antae and slow the coming of the Fir Bolg.*

*Further and further westward they went, running before the wind and hiding in the groves while the Fir Bolg trampled forests and claimed woodlands and meadows, rivers and streams.*

*When the Antae came to the Tullagh Sé, they believed they had found a place of refuge. In foolish desperation, they hoped the Fir Bolg would fear the Crone, that they, the Antae, could appease her, make sacrifice, as they had done with other gods.*

*They were mistaken.*

I have felt the watchful eyes of the Tullagh Sé. When I set these words in the caverns of my memory, it was not so. Now they catch in my throat. I struggle to speak them.

*The hungry grass confused them and led them astray, and some wandered the Six Hills till they perished from hunger and thirst. The puka peered into the caves where they sheltered and called them out into the night. Those that followed were never seen again.*

*No refuge could they find in the Tullagh Sé, domain of the destroyer goddess—Hag, Crone, Keeper of the Door to the Underworld. Many were lost while the night winds brought the keening of the banshee and filled the Antae with dread.*

I see the bands of wool curving out from the trunk of the yew; the wide, shrieking mouth; the round, pale eyes; the strands of thin hair hanging from the dark skull. I see a stone altar in a circle of holly trees. Around the stone are smaller stones, each fitted into a hollow. The altar is stained with blood.

No words will come. My mouth hangs open while the dark inside me expands. It is cold and ancient, and there are no doors that can shut it out.

Keeper of Death's Door.

The Crone holds the keys to the Underworld.

I remember Deirdre's words, her vision of the doorway, the passage. I have known the same dread. It fills me now as it did in the birch grove, its presence growing larger, devouring the empty places. I cannot speak, cannot move. There is no place where death cannot reach. Nothing halts its advance. Everything else is crowded out.

I am choking, and the smoke of rowan leaves and berries is in my face. It burns my eyes.

The Crone is the Keeper of Death's Door.

Where is the door?

When my head clears and my coughing stills, I see a circle of despairing faces. The horror in my mind is mirrored in the faces of Muriel and Deirdre. They know my fear. I turn to Clodagh. If there is any name for the expression in her aged face, for the gleam in her eyes, it is glee.

There is no shame in fear. Yet I am ashamed because the Keeper of the Word can speak no word to vanquish death.

Not one. I remember what Corann said. *The Tullagh Sé are the center of all our stories.* I cannot get around them. Not tonight. I stand over the ceremonial fire while the villagers rise and fade into the blackthorn grove.

The swan-feather cloak is heavy on my shoulders.

# 13

CALDER IS UP WITH THE SUNRISE, milking the ewes. I cannot see the bulging udders without grieving the stillborn lambs. This was their milk. But I kneel beside Calder, where one of the ewes has been tied to a heavy mother-stone, and I set to work. Streams of white milk rush into the buckets, and Calder whistles softly, relieving me of the burden of speech. When the first two are milked, we move to another small pasture and milk the others. Then we carry our buckets, one in each hand, to the cottages, setting one by the door of Barra's cottage. The fosterlings descend on it like a small swarm of flies. They scoop the rich milk with their bare hands and grin as it dribbles down their chins. We take another bucket to Engl. She thanks us heartily, drops a corner of cloth into the milk and pops it into the baby's mouth. She has not named him yet. Since the Bloodmoon, she has lost her husband and three babies. She will wait to see if this one lives. I cannot blame her.

We take a bucket to Deirdre and Muriel. Muriel hears Calder's whistling and opens the door to greet us. I drop my eyes to the ground. Somehow I feel that I have failed her more than anyone. I have seen the expectation in her eyes, the urging. I feel I have nothing to give her, and I yearn to give her everything.

She refuses the milk, and Deirdre joins her at the door and does likewise. They say that Llyr and Murdoch came in last night. The weary fishermen could use the nourishment. Calder smiles his agreement, so we set out for the other end of Blackthorn, balancing our last two buckets as we climb the stiles and squelch through mud and snow. We make a turn, though, before reaching Llyr and Murdoch's cottage. Calder leads us down to the brink of the Adder, where Etain is stacking peat along another wall. They have enough peat to last for months. I wonder what compels her to gather it, how far she has gone into the creeping bog to get it. I wonder what she has seen.

Calder raps at the door. The only answer is a savage roar from within.

"Get away from here, you festering sore of a man!"

Sloane. Calder shrugs his shoulders. He has spent many years in the fields and pastures with Sloane. A man of less patience would have strangled the young man ages ago, but Calder is temperate. He turns to go and spots Etain coming around the corner. Her eyes flit to the bucket, and Calder smiles and sets it on the stoop. Etain returns to her work without a word of greeting or thanks or even acknowledgement. This, too, Calder brushes aside.

We make our way northward, over two more drystones and up to the door of the fishermen's cottage. Llyr answers Calder's knock. His hair is a cloud of white, bound at the forehead with a black cord. His face looks as though an artisan formed it out of clay and pressed the flat of his hand against one side before the clay was fired. The result is unusual—a bit comical, but not unpleasant. The clay is cracked with long years, and with the endless battering of the salt wind. His eyes are piercing. He wears a fishbone on a thong around his neck.

"Any salmon?" Calder asks.

Llyr's face betrays no emotion. "Cod," he says. There has been no salmon for many years.

Calder nods and steps past him into the cottage. He needs no invitation. The two have known each other for three of my lifetimes. Llyr steps back, and I follow Calder inside. Murdoch smiles in greeting, exclaiming when he sees Calder's gift.

"It's been too long!" he says, and dips a cup into the bucket. He raises the warm milk to his lips and drinks, gulps. His tunic rises with his uplifted arm, and the hem is threaded with fishhooks. I wonder he doesn't shred the flesh of his hands on the sharp ends. I have always wondered that.

When he finishes the cup, he drains another and another. His short, brown beard drips with milk. He cups his hand over his mouth and wipes it away.

There is a brief silence. I scan the interior of the cottage. On the walls are scraps of skins, cords for lashing, nets, lines, hooks, oars. A little coracle is propped against the wall below the window. Beside it is a wooden table with two scrawny fish, already gutted. Cod.

Murdoch sees me examining his catch. He smiles, proud.

"First we've caught since Newmoon," he says.

I had not thought it was so bad. I had imagined they sold their fish in Beltrá or Seaswell before returning to Blackthorn. But perhaps they have had nothing to sell.

"First since Newmoon?" I ask. "Two fish in three months?"

Llyr scowls from the doorway. He has propped the door open with a heavy stone. He sits on the threshold, relishing the play of the wind, sniffing for salt. "The Adder poisons everything," he says. "It has claimed the ocean for itself."

"Further north?" Calder asks.

Llyr shakes his head. "The currents wrap around Baileléan, coming from the east. We sail north, and the currents push us south. We sail south, they toss us north. Again and again we return to the waters that pour from the Adder." Llyr leans to the side and spits out the doorway. "The bitter water has made a wasteland of mighty Gormára."

A heavier silence settles over the cottage. Corann says the world has run off its courses. Perhaps it has found a new track, one that rolls along a path of futility, down to a sea of death. I am very low. I sigh aloud. Murdoch takes the bucket and fills two cups. He offers one to me and one to Calder.

"Have you had a drink?" he asks.

Calder and I shake our heads. We raise the cups to our lips while Murdoch gives another to Llyr. The creamy milk is heartening. It puts strength in the bones, I think. The older men seem to feel as I do. I catch wistful, remembering looks in their eyes.

Llyr is first to speak. "Do you remember, Calder, when we sweetened the new milk with honey?"

"At Snowmelt?" I ask. "You had honey left at Snowmelt?"

"There was plenty in those days," Calder says. "And how we would dance!"

"At Snowmelt?" Murdoch asks. We are beginning to sound ridiculous.

Llyr laughs, and the sound is rasping and foreign. Since the Bloodmoon, there is not much laughter. "At every turn of the wheel, there was dancing."

"And feasting," Calder adds.

"If a man stole or killed or dishonored the chief, no punishment was more terrible to him than to be excluded from one of the festivals," Llyr says.

It is difficult to imagine such a time, such a world. At Newmoon there is dancing, and we feast in the spring, but at Harvest we set aside every morsel we can spare. Our ceremonies are solemn affairs. We bring our bitter water and pour it out before the dying sun. We light the sacred fires and send the flaming wheel down the hillside. But to judge it a punishment to be excluded from one of these ceremonies? I cannot imagine it. The world Llyr and Calder knew in their youth was another world entirely.

Calder finishes his milk and sets the cup aside. "My first son was born at Snowmelt," he says.

Calder had four sons, all of them taken by the blight.

"I was at sea when it happened," Llyr says. "But I remember coming home, carrying my coracle over my head, and seeing Shannan standing under the ash tree. 'When will you have that baby?' I asked her. 'I've had him,' she said. And I laughed till the ash leaves shook. I've never seen a woman so beautiful, not before or since, and she just three days past bearing."

Calder cannot reply. He smiles sadly at the floor.

"She was very fair?" Murdoch asks.

Llyr spits out the door again. "Bah!" he says. "You've heard how Egan saw Genevieve dance on the shore while the white waves crashed behind her?"

Murdoch nods. He knows the tale as well as I. But Llyr enjoys the telling. He continues. "Egan made so bold as to ask her hand, and she demanded three times seven cloaks of red and three times ten gowns of green and three times five circlets of gold. And when, after seven years' labor and toil, Egan brought her what she wished, Genevieve flung them into the sea!" Llyr throws back his head and roars with laughter. The sound wheezes and crackles in his throat. "But in the end she kissed Egan's lips and offered him the friendship of her thighs."

Murdoch blushes. Calder and I smile. Llyr is not finished.

"Egan knew nothing of beauty," he says. "If he had seen one lock of Shannan's hair, he'd have forgotten Genevieve in the blinking of an eye, in the catching of a breath, in the pulsing of a heartbeat. There was never a woman so fair!"

Calder's smile has faded, and I hear the unspoken phrase, the one we've all wearied of speaking. *Before the Bloodmoon.* There were salmon before the Bloodmoon. There were spring lambs before the Bloodmoon. Shannan was beautiful before the Bloodmoon.

Calder turns the talk to other things. "When do you go out again?" he asks.

Llyr sighs. "Soon."

Calder rises and grips his shoulder. No more words pass between them. I say a brief farewell and follow him back to his cottage, where two of the buckets have been returned, empty. We scour them with meadowsweet and set them against the wall. Then Calder breaks a cluster of yellow flowers from the nearest gorse and carries it in to his bride.

# 14

Zinerva does not return to Blackthorn for many days. There is another heavy fall of snow, and Calder brings the ewes inside his cottage for shelter. I kneel beside him and work the udders, and fresh milk pours into the buckets. But the ewes give less and less.

Corann comes and goes, indifferent to the seasons and the moods of the sky. Llyr and Murdoch make small repairs to their currachs and coracles and nets. Barra walks the village, making deep, round imprints in the snow with the butt of his spear. Deirdre beats the gorse with her mallet while snow settles on the hood of her cloak. And Muriel . . . Muriel works in the grove.

Since Muriel came to Blackthorn, I have loved this time, between Snowmelt and the spring equinox. For she is often in the grove, gathering bark. She moves from tree to tree, making a small cut in the outer bark and peeling it back. The outer bark is dark gray, and when she pulls a strip from its place and sets it in her basket, the inner bark is the orange of new fire, of sunset. One strip of bark from each of fifty-seven trees. She works in the snow, taking her time, careful to avoid the poisonous thorns. I cannot take my eyes from her. Her hands are white and slender and skillful. Her eyes are the green of spring grass. I am lost in the curve of her mouth, the soft line of her jaw beneath her flowing hair.

It is some trick of nature, I think, that the blackthorns should blossom while the snow falls in torrents. Through a curtain of fast-falling snow, green buds appear and swell on the ends of the twisted branches. Thin, rounded blossoms burst open, their wispy interiors tipped with pink. The frosty mouth of winter kisses the white-petal lips of spring. It is very fair.

Muriel is fairer.

Then I remember. This vision of loveliness works among the snow and the flowers and the thorns, in a grove of trees whose one word to us is a word of reminder. We must die. Death comes to us all, even Muriel. The year races along toward the coming Bloodmoon, the coming calamity, and I have nothing to offer her, not a single word of hope or comfort.

I cannot look at her any longer.

The moon that was rounding toward the full at Snowmelt reaches its fullest span and shrinks to a thin crescent. Zinerva returns to the village, preceded by her owl. She is thin and dirty. The hem of her peplos is crusted with mud. Fragments of dead leaves cling to her orange shawl and her matted yellow hair.

But she enters Blackthorn like a triumphant warrior queen, her satchel overflowing with small branches and bundles of leaves. On the night of her return, there is no moon, and the scudding clouds obscure the stars. The smoke from her chimney is thick and foul. It hovers over the village and lingers the next morning while ravens gather on the edge of the grove.

There is nothing remarkable about an ovate who gathers herbs to replenish her stores. It is the timing of her journey that troubles me. Spring has not settled on the island. Only the gorse and the blackthorns are in bloom.

Where has Zinerva been? Why the look of triumph?

Deirdre comes for me a little after midday.

"Can you make up some tea for Engl?" she asks.

She answers my question before it reaches my lips. "Our healer cannot be bothered."

"You have the new bark?" I ask.

She nods, waiting outside while I retrieve the bowl and pounding stone, the cauldron and spoon.

"You must speak again," she says. We have not even reached the stile. "At the equinox. Continue the story."

"Deirdre—"

"Idris," she says and stops. "Barra despairs. Corann wanders the groves." She is choosing her words with care. These are not complaints, not accusations. She merely states the situation. "We go to the ovate for healing, and she offers us death." Her broad, white forehead is pale. Her mouth trembles. "Speak a word to us, Ollamh."

*Where else can we go for comfort? Who else can give us a word of hope?*

"I have tried." I climb over the stile, stepping into the snow in the next pasture and clinging to the instruments in my arms. She has yet to cross. She stands tall and straight on the other side of the drystone and calls out to me.

"Once."

I turn and meet her eyes.

"You have tried—once," she says.

My anger flares. "I *have* tried once, and failed."

I was shamed, humiliated. And that is not the worst of it. I was proven powerless. What now can I offer the people of Blackthorn? I cross the pasture, heading toward her cottage.

"I have the bark," she says.

I veer back toward the south, crossing two more stiles before I reach Engl's cottage. The door stands open; she is waiting for me. I wonder how long she waited for Zinerva before she gave up and came home. Deirdre follows me inside and hands me a strip of bark. She runs the backs of her fingers over the baby's forehead while I pound the bark and prepare the tea. Engl watches my hands as I work.

I do not remember what Engl looked like in the early years of the blight. But I can imagine her eyes without their deep shadows, her pale lips and cheeks blooming with color. She has a pleasant face. She catches me watching her, and I turn my eyes to the baby. He is wrapped in blankets and nestled in a basket, but he looks bigger than when I saw him last. That is something.

"He's grown," I say.

Engl is distracted, her thoughts fixed on the brewing blackthorn tea. But she acknowledges my words. For a moment, I see a spark in her eye. For a moment, she inhabits the small cottage in a way she had not before. I think I am seeing Engl for the first time.

"A little," she says.

When the tea is finished, I move the cauldron away from the coals and stand. Engl thanks me and retreats into her frantic nursing. I leave the cottage with Deirdre. We cross through a pasture that holds two ewes and a pile of beaten gorse. She turns toward home and leaves me without a word.

Corann is in the hut, scouring the shelves. He comes to the primrose oil and pauses, lifting it, judging the weight. So little remains. He sets it down and moves to another shelf. He finds what he is looking for: a sack of dried berries.

"Elder," he says.

I follow him out to a nearby blackthorn. Corann empties the berries into his palm and raises them to a little knot of twigs and leaves. A nest. It is tucked among the thorns, hidden by white blossoms, safe from owls and ravens. A wren flits to the edge of his hand and lifts one shriveled berry in her beak. She hops to the edge of the nest and drops it in the gaping yellow mouth of a fragile chick. Four others wait to be filled, so

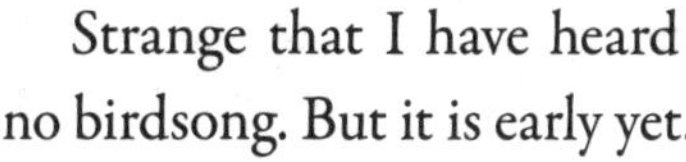

the mother returns, again and again, to Corann's hand.

The wren is sacred to the druids. It is a messenger from other worlds. Its song aids in divination. No wonder Corann is eager.

Strange that I have heard no birdsong. But it is early yet.

Corann exhausts his store of berries and steps away from the blackthorn. He stands and watches the wren, looking as calm and settled as if he were stretched on his bedroll. But I know him too well. Some part of him is roaming.

I have not asked him about Snowmelt, about the death of the spring lambs or the gathering of the Crone's firewood. He has said nothing of my failure to prophesy, and I have only begun to consider the question that rose in my mind when the horror of death stole the words from my tongue. As always, I do not know where to begin.

"Will many come to the celebration of the equinox?" I ask.

His head cants to the side. He studies the wren more closely. That is the only acknowledgement I receive. I have asked the wrong question.

"Should I try again? To speak at the celebration?"

Now my question is acknowledged. He turns to face me, and his gaze does not pass through me. It falls heavy on me. The strands of white hair around his face, the short white hairs in his beard, they seem lit. He is glaring at me. The hair rises on the backs of my arms. The air around me hardens and snaps.

I sense the enormity of the burden Corann carries. Eighteen years' wandering and questioning. Eighteen years of futility. Impotence in the face of impending doom. Deirdre's words return to torment me. *You have tried—once.*

But I am not a child, and I am not a fool. I am the Ollamh of Blackthorn. Two wrong questions I have asked. I will ask another.

"Is there anything I can say that will counter Zinerva's message? Can my words bring any hope at all?"

That is nearer the right question. I know it because the fire in Corann's eyes cools, and a stillness settles on the grove. He does not answer, but he holds my gaze, and I begin to understand what Deirdre was trying to say to me. I am the Keeper of the Word. Mine is the right to speak, and the necessity. It does not matter if my words defy the finality of Zinerva's message. It does not matter if they even soften the blow. I am the ollamh. I must speak.

We celebrate the spring equinox, and the turning of the eightfold wheel. Now day and night are in balance, and the sun moves toward its strength. The blossoms are bright on the blackthorns and the gorse, and the snow is losing its hold.

Our numbers are swelled by a handful of villagers from Kilveagh and Beltrá. Corann wears his grey robes. He has taken two drops of primrose oil and anointed his face and hands. He stands at the edge of the fallow fields, his arms raised to the setting sun.

I hear it again: a murmur among the celebrants. The sound is one of question and dissent, but it is low, and I cannot tell from where it came. I do not turn to catch Deirdre's eye, but I hope she can tell me what is happening, and why anyone should dare to question the authority of the Druid of Blackthorn during the sacred exercise of the rites of spring equinox. Druids have struck men dead for lesser offenses.

When the sun sinks below the horizon, the ceremony comes to an end. But there is more to the celebration, though it is nothing like what Llyr and Calder describe. Since the Bloodmoon, our celebrations are solemn. It is hard to rejoice in the balance of a world that has spun out of balance and rolled off its courses.

We light a fire and share a meal. There is muted talk among the villagers. When the first star appears, I wrap the swan-feather cloak around my shoulders and take up the gold branch. The bright tinkling of the bells accompanies me to the edge of the field, to the place where Corann stood. The people grow quiet. Then another murmur passes through the crowd, and a shiver of rage and fear ripples down my spine. The owl drops out of the darkness and settles on Zinerva's shoulder. I fill my lungs, close my eyes, find the place where I let the story fall.

The words come.

*The Antae could not stay in the groves of the Tullagh Sé. The hills were haunted. The hills were hers. So they fled to the western shores of Baileléan while the Fir Bolg lived off the fat of the land in the east. That land was rich beyond imagining, and the forests writhed with deer and foxes and boar and fowl. And the milk flowed in cataracts, and the fields of wheat and corn and barley grew so thick they were all but impassable. The apples dropped from the trees, and the honey gushed from the combs. And for a time, the Fir Bolg were sated.*

*In those days, Arlan, son of Artek, King of the Fir Bolg, saw a woman of the Antae. Her name was Meréd, and Arlan was enthralled by her beauty. At first sight of her, he proclaimed her "the delight of the ages, the gem of time, the wonder of the world." Arlan had but one thought: to woo her, to have her. The insatiable hunger of the Fir Bolg is the fabric of legend, the spark that ignited the Cogath Tornech, and Arlan's hunger for Meréd was no less. He showered her with gifts: gold torques and fibulae and lunulae and great brass cauldrons and cloaks of blue and gowns of red. He made the flowers grow around her cottage, until their faces greeted Meréd in the morning, and the flowering vines perfumed the night air. He caused the birds to sing at her doorstep and to accompany her as she walked the meadows and hillsides.*

*At last, he called to her from the hidden groves of the Tullagh Sé, and his voice was so deep and so lilting that Meréd could not resist him. She laid aside her fear of the hills and went in among the quiet groves, to meet with the son of the Fir Bolg king.*

*They met often there, in the hills where no one came, and their love was wild and sweet. But the Crone saw all that happened. In their love, she caught a scent of death. She went to Artek and told him how his son made love to a daughter of the Antae, and Artek was overcome with rage. He went to Noch Ingen, the Hill of the Claw, to the place where Arlan and Meréd met in secret. He took the cloak from his shoulders and hung it in the air, and when next Arlan came to take Meréd into his arms, the cloak obscured his beloved. He saw nothing but the empty hills. When Meréd came in search of her lover that same hour, she saw nothing but an abandoned grove.*

*The sorrows of one night were not enough to extinguish their love. But Arlan and Meréd came night after night to Noch Ingen. Night after night, they went away alone, heartsick. In time, Arlan came to believe that Meréd had betrayed him, and Meréd to believe that Arlan had abandoned her for love of one of the Fir Bolg. Each grew bitter with grief.*

*Now Meréd gave birth to a daughter, and though the child was half-possessed of the godlike beauty and strength of the Fir Bolg, Meréd poured her bitterness into her daughter's young ears. She taught her to hate the Fir Bolg, and above all else, to despise Arlan, the great warrior and son of the Fir Bolg king.*

*Arlan's grief he disguised with fury, and every passing*

*year he pressed the Fir Bolg with more urgency, driving them to renew the War of Thunder and push the Antae at last into the western sea. So the Fir Bolg were roused. Great battles raged at Moy Catha, and it was only by Madigan's strength and Perth's sorcery that the Antae were not destroyed.*

*Yet there came a terrible battle between the Antae and the Fir Bolg. The plain of Moy Catha ran with blood, and Madigan, Hero of a Hundred Battles, fell.*

There is murmuring in the assembly. Zinerva's eyes are on me. The owl gives a sharp cry. Sweat breaks out on my palms, my upper lip. My mouth is dry. I am the Ollamh, Keeper of the Word. I must speak.

*That hour was dark for the Antae, but none of them was more desperate for revenge than Meréd and her beautiful daughter, Branna, whose hair was dark as the raven's wing and whose veins pulsed with the blood of the Fir Bolg. Branna had grown into a woman of nineteen, and when her mother sent her to seduce one of the warriors of the Fir Bolg, she chose the mighty Boyd, and he could not withstand her beauty.*

*In the warmth of the wood where the lovers made their bed, Branna drew from Boyd's lips the secret of the Fir Bolg: only iron could hinder them.*

I see a black tree, with leaves like oak leaves, its branches scarcely stirring in a storm wind.

*For the Fir Bolg, it was the stroke of doom.*

*Branna carried the secret to Meréd. Meréd carried it to Perth. And the sorcerer unraveled the mysteries of iron. The Antae made ready for the coming battle. They forged iron swords. They tipped their spears with iron. They wrapped their shields with iron bands. When next the Fir Bolg came to Moy Catha, the Antae were ready, and the gods of the Cogath Tornech, after endless battle and long pursuit, began at last to fall.*

*Meréd stood like a goddess at the back of the battle plain, with a gown of green that fell from her shoulders and a circlet of gold at her throat. She smiled with pleasure as she watched her people defy the invaders.*

*But Arlan caught sight of her, and he stopped in the midst of a sword-stroke. He ran through the heat of the battle, crying her name. When Meréd saw him, she knew by his cries, by the sorrow on his face, that he loved her. She opened her mouth to cry his name, to forgive him and declare her love. But in that moment, Perth caught Arlan and bound him with druidic fire. Branna, who waited at the battle's edge, eager to vent her hatred, rushed to Arlan and pierced him with an iron-tipped spear.*

I pause for breath while the listeners wait, spellbound. Overhead, the stars dance in their courses. They saw the defeat of the Fir Bolg, and to them it must seem but an hour ago.

*Artek screamed and thundered, and the terrible sound of Meréd's grief silenced the battlefield. Each side had lost its greatest champion. The Antae had suffered tremendous losses, and defeat was coming for the Fir Bolg now their secret was revealed. So Artek took the silver cloak from his shoulders and showed it to Meréd. He confessed his treachery, and together they wept over Arlan's body.*

*Perth and Artek made peace. The king of the Fir Bolg, broken by his grief, promised to relinquish the soil of Baileléan and trouble the Antae no more. He swore that the Fir Bolg would never return. Artek would lead them into the Many-Colored Land, where he hoped that their hunger might be sated. He raised his silver cloak and hung it on a breath of wind. His people passed through it and were gone. Beyond hope and yet desperate that his son should return to him, Artek lingered. He would surrender Arlan's body to the Crone only in exchange for a promise that this door between worlds, like all doors between worlds, should stand open one night in the year. The Keeper of Death's Door agreed to the bargain, and the king of the Fir Bolg passed through the silver gate.*

*Artek took the fair Branna as his daughter. With Boyd she passed into the Many-Colored Land, and their children are the Shí.*

*But along with the thousands dead on the battlefield and the son of the Fir Bolg king, the Crone claimed another victim. For Meréd could not bear to be parted from Arlan. She asked that she might be buried with him in the hill that faced the sunrise and the fair land of Tír Ársa. She went living into the tomb to lie at her beloved's side.*

Meréd found the door. She passed through it with the Crone. Where is the door to the Underworld?

*Thus the pursuit of the Antae was ended, and our people found peace in their island home while Perth, the great sorcerer, filled the sacred groves with the wisdom of Tír Ársa, and the lore of trees, and the knowledge of sun and moon, and the turning of the eight-fold wheel.*

*So the wheel turns.*

The story is finished. The people wait for me to move from my place. But I am rooted to the field. I understand what Corann means when he speaks of a well-packed question. He does not merely seek a good question, or a wise one, though that is a beginning. He seeks one question, the ultimate question, the only question that must be asked and answered. What it is I do not yet know. But I am approaching it. I am beginning to see.

I am aware of the wind on my face. I hear the sputter of a log on the fire. I see the watchful faces around me. I move away from the head of the assembly. I want to talk with Zinerva.

Some of the celebrants honor me as I pass. They bow their heads and murmur "Ollamh," and some of them touch the feathers on my cloak. But they hinder me. I cannot move through them quickly enough. Zinerva vanishes into the grove.

When at last they pull aside, scattering through the dark toward their villages and cottages, Deirdre catches my arm.

"Did you hear them?" I ask. "When Corann began the ceremony?"

Deirdre's reply is whispered. "Yes."

"Why do they murmur?"

"They ask for the one who speaks with the voice of the ancestors, the one who has journeyed to the Underworld and returned."

Zinerva.

I try to pull away, but Deirdre holds me, gripping my arm. She says nothing, but I read the warning in her eyes. She is afraid for me. I kiss her white forehead and hurry into the grove.

# 15

Is she sixteen? Seventeen? Younger, perhaps. And her bones are thin, her frame small, like a bird. Yet she fills the grove. I step in among the blackthorns and I know at once where she is. Her presence crowds out everything else.

A thin carpet of snow is beneath my feet, white blossoms around my face. Black thorns reach out to snag my robes, my skin. And I see her, leaning against the portal tomb as though it were the doorway of her cottage. In the dim light, her hair is a storm of dull gold around a pale face. Her eyes are blue. They glimmer with malice.

I feel a quivering inside me. I am afraid. She stands on the bones of our ancestors. She could send me to meet them.

"Why not Meréd?" I ask.

The owl perches on the dolmen and swivels its head to look at me. Zinerva is slow to answer, careless.

"What do you ask, Bard?"

"Why was it Madigan who spoke to you and not Meréd?"

"Who am I to question the ways of the ancients?" she asks.

True. But she is avoiding the question. Perhaps I have chosen the right place to begin.

"But Madigan did not choose death," I reply. "He fell in battle. It was Meréd who embraced the darkness and the eternal quiet of the Crone's domain. She chose to go, to be with Arlan."

Zinerva turns to the owl. She raises a small, white hand, and strokes its brown feathers. "You concern yourself with the wrong set of lovers, Bard."

The wrong set of lovers?

The village by the ridge of white stone. The lovers. The Iron Oak. What does Zinerva know of these lovers? I cannot bring myself to ask, for I know she will not tell me.

A smile spreads slowly over her face. It is a smile of cruelty, of triumph. She is so small, but my heart races. What does she know?

But another question burns in me. A better one.

"Where is the door to the Underworld?"

A soft laugh. "Would *you* go with the Crone into the darkness of her domain?" She steps toward me. "Would you perform the rites? Would you spill the blood and offer it to the Destroyer Goddess?" Another step. "She ruled this land when Perth was a suckling child. She raised the tomb when Corann's father's father's father was not even a thought."

Zinerva stops her advance, pauses. "You stink of fear, Bard," she says. "But you've known nothing of fear until *she* has claimed you."

The owl spreads its wings and rises over the grove. It flies south, toward the village, and Zinerva follows.

I stand in the snow and feel the weight of the swan-feather cloak on my shoulders. The gold branch is clutched in my hand. It tinkles in a warm wind. The grove is full of the musk of the white blossoms.

The answer comes to me then. Where is the door to the Underworld? It is so simple. Meréd asked to be buried in a hill that faced the sunrise and the fair land of Tír Ársa. The hill would have to face the east. The easternmost of the Six Hills. It would have been the first hill the Antae reached when they fled from the Fir Bolg.

I forget Zinerva, forget my fear. If Corann were here I would embrace him! A well-packed question carries its answer on its back as a snail carries its shell.

With the weather warming, I believe it is time for another journey.

I will go to the Sixth Hill.

This time I make better preparations. I wait for grass and soil to emerge from their winter coat, for pale green leaves to unravel on the ash and rowan trees and deeper, oval-shaped leaves to appear among the sprays of blackthorn blossoms. I gather all the oats I can find and eat them sparingly, saving the largest portions for the journey. I beat my bedroll and hang it on the hillside to be freshened by wind and sun. I heap the remaining snow into buckets and bowls where it melts and waits.

I take the long yew staves from their stack beside the hut and sit with them in the small hours of the night, running my fingers over the ogham signs, remembering, rehearsing the stories of our people. In the years of my training, when it fell to me to memorize five times ten lengthy tales of battles and cattle raids, of sieges and navigations, of murders and floods and courtships and destructions, I sat with these same staves in a cave on the northern side of the hill. Corann left me there in darkness, and he blocked up the doorway. It was just me and the staves and the history of our people. In silence, blind to all else, I held to the first lines of the ancient stories (for it is an offense against wisdom to commit more than the first line to writing), and felt my way along the paths of ancient chieftains and sailors and thieves and gods. There was nothing else to cling to—no food, no water. The stories were all that sustained me until Corann came and moved a stone from its place, and the cave was flooded with light, and I remembered the world outside.

Now, as I struggle with a combination of symbols on a very old stave, I am reminded of the great disparity between the Baileléan of our ancestors and the world we know. Since the Bloodmoon, the world is changed. It changes more and more. Can it ever be as it was? These symbols, I think, describe the flowers that bloomed on the hillside while the ring-fort was raised at Rathroe. Wood sorrel and cowslip, pink foxglove and spotted orchids, spring gentian and bluebells. If I saw them as a child I do not remember. In my mind, I see only their shadows scratched on stone. I must look for primrose in the Tullagh Sé. And honeysuckle.

Corann betrays no surprise when I tell him of my plans. Three mounds of flesh rise between his gray brows.

"I begin to think," he says, "that the past must be reckoned with."

I believe I understand. It was in my telling of an age-old story that the questions came.

"We look toward the future," he continues, "and fear it. But it may be that what we call the future is no more than the perpetual beginning of the past."

He looks through me, blue eyes squinting at the stone wall. "It is not so far behind us as we think. It may be it is not behind us at all. What if the past lies ahead of us, blocking our way?"

"Corann," I begin. I pause, swallow. "It is not safe to journey in the Tullagh Sé."

He looks into my eyes. I have asked no question. He waits.

"How am I to defend myself?"

He pokes the fire and sits a moment in thought. "You cannot," he says. "The ollamh carries no weapon. He has only the Word."

A sigh escapes my lips. I yearn for a fuller understanding of the power of the Word, and this is not the path of testing I would choose. Corann understands.

"You leave tomorrow?" he asks.

"The day after."

"Good," he says. "Wait for the full moon." Then he stands, shoulders squared, head erect, and does something he has never done, not even when I received the gold branch. He bows his head, just slightly. "Ollamh," he says. He is addressing me as one man to another, as druid to bard, as friend to friend. The honor is too great. I am undeserving. Tears prick my eyes, and when they fall, I am glad that Corann has left the cottage.

I will not spend my last day in Blackthorn sitting in the hut with my fear and my questions. Nor will I journey to Kilveagh, to see my father and mother. They would not understand. I need tasks to busy my hands, and voices outside my head.

I rise with the sun and pin my cloak at my shoulder. I slip into my boots and eat a bit of porridge. I stop outside the door to listen for the wren song. I hear the harsh cawing of the ravens, and farther off, the sleepy hooting of an owl. But the wrens are silent. I feel a great sadness for Corann.

The first villagers to greet me when I cross the stile are Pixie and Vaughn and Brennan. Pixie's cheeks are round and dimpled. Her hair is parted in the middle. It hangs over her shoulders in two red braids. Vaughn is slight and freckled. His eyes are full of mischief. Brennan's is a face full of sorrow. His eyes and cheeks droop as though he has borne the weight of the world. All three were left behind at the celebration of Newmoon, by parents who despaired of caring for them, who thought, I hope, that their children would find refuge in the village of the druid. Brennan was left a year ago, Vaughn and Pixie the year before. Barra has made a home for them all.

This morning they are checking the bowls, gathering water. Funny how children think of the simplest solutions to problems. It was Pixie and Vaughn who first thought to line the tops of the drystones with any stone that could hold water. They scoured the village for flat stones with hollows and depressions and then spread them along every wall in Blackthorn. After the snows have melted, whenever there is rain or dew, the bowls hold little treasures of clean water. Sometimes the children raise the stones to their lips and drink. Often, they collect the water in a bucket and carry it around the village, to see if anyone is in need.

"Are you going away?" Pixie asks. Word of my journey has spread to everyone in Blackthorn. I would expect no less of the Antae. Pixie wrinkles her nose and looks up at me.

"I am."

Her eyes narrow. "Into the haunted hills?"

"Yes," I reply. Vaughn and Brennan come closer. For Vaughn, that means he dangles over the drystone, stretching his neck and turning his ear toward me. Brennan takes a small step in my direction. He tries to look as if he is not listening.

"Will Corann stay?" Pixie asks.

"I don't know. It's likely he will come and go as he always does."

"Wandering the groves," Vaughn says.

Brennan puts a hand to my tunic and peers up into my face. His cheeks sag, and there are purplish ruts under his eyes. "You will leave us with the ovate?" There is no fear in his voice, no edge of panic or desperation. His question has a ring of resignation, of finality. I do not like to hear very old or very broken men talk in such a way. For a child to speak so . . .

I stoop down in front of Brennan. "Calder and Barra and Deirdre and Muriel will help to keep a watch over Blackthorn."

There is no change in Brennan's face. He is not convinced. His hand falls from my tunic.

"Do bluebells grow in the Tullagh Sé?" Pixie asks.

"I don't know."

"Calder drew me one," she says. "He drew the shapes of other flowers, but I liked bluebells best." She studies me. I think she is judging my worth. "If you find one, will you bring it to me?"

"I will try." I give her braid a little tug and tousle Vaughn's hair. Brennan has retreated to the other side of the drystone.

I stop by Llyr and Murdoch's cottage, but I know they are at sea. They would not waste such fine weather. The shutters stand open, and the interior of the cottage is a confusion of nets and knives and wood shavings and fishhooks. I smile to myself. There must be some consolation in sailing the open sea, even when it yields no fish. I would like to sail with them, someday.

I did not intend to stop at Sloane's cottage. If he is not out working with the cattle, he is shut up in a fortress of stone and sod. He does not like visitors. But Etain is cutting peat beside the cottage. She catches my eye and holds it, and I think she wants to see me.

I make my way over the stiles and stand in uncomfortable silence while Etain slices the thick greenish slabs of peat and sets them to dry in the sun. It is hard to know where to begin. Etain surprises me by speaking first.

"How far will you go?" she asks.

I take a steadying breath. Is this truly what I mean to do? "To the Sixth Hill."

There is a flicker of hope in her eyes. Her face shines, and she looks on me with what I can only imagine is a kind of adoration. "Do you fear the banshees?" she asks. "They're not alike, you know."

I cannot make sense of her words. There is one banshee that cries over the coming of death, that roams the Tullagh Sé. I have seen its eyes. I have known the horror of its lament. Who is this other?

"Etain, I know of only one banshee. What have you seen in the bog?"

She shakes her head. "You can't see anything in the bog. But I've heard them. Two cries. Are you afraid?"

I meet her eyes, wishing I had another answer to offer. "I am."

She nods once, and the glow of her face is unchanged. She bows her head slowly. Her shoulders drop, her knees bend. It is a heavy salute, a great honor. "Ollamh," she says, and the weight of her hope hangs on that word.

I hurry out of the enclosure.

I spend an hour with Calder and Shannan, sharing their small meal of oats and dried berries.

"Shannan once made a fine nettle soup," Calder says. *When there were nettles. Before the Bloodmoon.* "A man could go in the strength of that soup for days."

Shannan smiles. She touches the hair at her temple, smoothing it.

“What else?” I ask. “Tell me more of the time before.”

Calder’s head falls back. He sighs, glad of the excuse to indulge in memory. “You don’t see them now, but some of the cooking pits were big enough to boil a wild boar.”

Wild boar. My eyes grow wide. I wonder, did it taste like beef?

Calder chuckles. “Corann loved wild boar, but he preferred it roasted on a spit.”

I laugh aloud. It is strange to think of Corann savoring food.

“There were games,” Calder says. “Did you know that? All the land south of the Tullagh Sé was dry. At the Feast of the Fertile Earth and at Harvest, there were foot races and horse races. The young warriors fought with swords and tried to best one another at marksmanship.” He shakes his head, sighs. A sadness darkens his merry blue eyes. “They were good days.”

I nod, finish my cup of milk and my handful of berries.

“You are prepared?” Calder asks.

“Yes. And no.” I look at the old man, the round cheeks, the long gray beard, the gentle, weathered hands. “I am determined to go.”

He smiles and comes to me, gripping my hands and kissing me on both cheeks. “You’ll return before the feast?”

“I mean to.”

“Take this, then, for courage.” He hands me a little branch of gorse. It is bright with yellow blossoms and pale purplish buds.

My throat closes, and I cannot speak the words I wish to speak. I can only smile at Calder and Shannan and pass out of the cottage, out from under the shade of the old ash tree.

I make one more stop today.

Deirdre is tending a fire in the pasture, burning a pile of gorse. Nearby are the remains of two other fires. Muriel scoops ashes from the piles that have cooled and carries them into the cottage. No doubt another fire burns inside, and over it a kettle bubbles with fat. They are making soap. They'll mix the gorse ash with the fat and spread it in a shallow bowl. When it cools, they'll cut it into pieces and share it with the villagers. We'll all be clean for the feast.

I stand beside Deirdre, watching Muriel as she comes and goes. I want to tell Deirdre about the other lovers, about Ban Lurgan and the altar and the Sixth Hill. I look at her, studying the brown freckles on her nose and cheeks, the set of her chin, the quiver in her lips. She refuses to turn away from her work.

I do not need her to explain. Her feelings rise from her skin, blending, changing, like the sky at sunrise. She is angry that I am leaving and proud, too, that I should risk so much. She is afraid for me, for herself, for the people of Blackthorn. She fears that I will not return, and if I do, she fears the answers I will bring. She is glad of her choices and full of regret. She is brimming with passion and power, and yet she is not the bard or the ovate or the druid. For now, it is her lot to wait and tend the fire.

"Watch her, Deirdre," I say. "Watch her for me." I do not speak her name. There is no need.

She says nothing. I have laid an impossible task at her feet, but what can I do? Deirdre will see what no one else does. Deirdre always sees.

Muriel comes out of the cottage. When she sees me, she makes no bow of respect, no mention of the ollamh. Instead, she looks into my eyes.

I did not know that I was poor until I saw her. I have not eyes enough to see all I yearn to see, nor strength enough to seize the tenth part of all I desire. I look into her eyes, and I am in torment, because I cannot watch the wind caress her hair. I drink in the sight of her spun-gold hair, and I grieve because I cannot watch the graceful movements of her hands.

She knows I am going. She raises her hand, gesturing for me to wait. She disappears inside the cottage, then hurries out the next moment. She stands close to me, very near, and takes my hand. She places something in my palm and closes my fingers around it. It is a little bundle, something dry. I will look at it later. For now, I look at Muriel. She must read all my soul, all my longing, in my eyes. I don't know how it could be otherwise. I am overcome with an urge to run, to bound away from the cottage like a stag. But she leans in, her hand against my arm. Her breath is warm on my face. Her lips graze my cheek, and I feel as if I have been scorched with fire. Heat courses through me.

Too soon, too soon, she pulls away and returns to the cottage. She closes the door behind her.

Let the Crone rise up in all her terror and glory! Let the Hag come against me! I will make war with the fire in my blood and the hammering of my heart. Let her challenge me now, and I will make an end of death.

I stride out of the pasture. My fingertips burn with fire and sorcery.

# 16

I SET OUT WHILE THE MOON IS STILL HIGH. It is round and silver-bright, and heartening. Muriel's gift is tied around my neck. An amulet of foxglove, to ward against hungry grass. I know it is foxglove only because of Calder's scratchings. I cannot guess where Muriel might have gotten it, or how long she has kept it.

Many hours I have spent in thought, considering which path to take. The creeping bog makes a misery of any journey on the southern slopes of the Tullagh Sé. And I do not wish to skirt the northern edge of the hills as Corann and I did after the winter solstice. I think I must travel *in* the Tullagh Sé, fearsome though it is. I dread the watchful eyes of the Crone, and I do not know what would stir her to anger most: to linger in her domain or approach her altar or set my feet on the soil of the Sixth Hill. Wherever I turn, there is danger.

I climb a steep ridge by moonlight and enter the woods and groves of the first hill. I have brought a bedroll and a satchel and another sack for collecting flowers. If I can find them, that is. If any remain. I have brought no ash leaves, no fragments of rowan for making incense. I seek no guidance from stag or hind or fox. I leave it to Corann to read the signs of earth and sky. Mine is the path of the Word.

The moon sinks, and the stars make a last bright plea. Ahead of me, through numberless branches now heavy with leaves and buds, through the rising and falling of five towering hills, over the eastern edge of Baileléan, the sun begins to rise. I set my face toward its light as it scales the heights of the heavens. I walk through sun-dappled grasses. Green ferns brush their curling fronds against my legs. The air is warm and sweet, and the rhododendrons shake their huge purple fists. Twice, I find a patch of meadowsweet, and I tuck the blossoms into my sack. Meadowsweet eases pain. It keeps the milk from souring in the buckets. My heart lightens at the thought of returning to Blackthorn with such a gift.

When the sun is high, I stop in a little glade and sit with my back against the trunk of an ash tree. I have walked through a night and half of a day, and after a small meal, I find I am drowsy. It is hard to be anxious when the sun is so bright. I spread the sheepskin over my legs. My head falls back against the tree and my eyelids droop.

I remember the years of long ago, when I ran in the birch woods of Kilveagh. Our cottage was warm. It smelled of oats and peat. I remember how my mother leaned over the kettle, stirring the porridge, how she taught my sisters to sew. I remember my father's hands, how steady they were when he cut a bit of rot out of an abscess in my foot. He wrapped the wound and walked beside me to the old ash tree. He gouged a hole in the trunk of the ash and tucked the rotten flesh inside. Next morning the ash had sewn itself up, and my foot was healed. I was filled with astonishment.

But my father said, "The ash took it. It took the hurt into itself."

I remember how I wept, but my father pointed to the tree. "See there?" he said. "Not a mark on it." And there was none. I traced the bark of that tree in the place where my father had wounded it. I walked around the tree to see if the wound had spread. I ran my fingers over the bark until they were raw. But the ash was whole, and I ran home on a sound foot, without any pain.

After the Bloodmoon, they tried putting bitter water into the ash trees. It did not heal the sick. The water drank their vigor. They wasted away. There was nothing to cut out and put into the trees. So no one gave anymore thought to the ash.

My sleep is deep and quiet, and I wake in the early morning with a sense of gratitude. It is good to have a bedroll. It is good to sleep after hard walking. It is good to build fires with birch bark and flint, to eat porridge in the open air while the dawn presses up against the dark.

The Tullagh Sé is beautiful in spring. I can see why the Antae were eager to shelter here. There are meadows that catch the sunlight like bowls. As the sun climbs the sky, the golden light sloshes over the edges. In one of these I sit and listen to the buzz of hornets and bees. I watch the clouds curl golden edges toward the light and race over the hills to the western edge of the world.

I cross a ridge of stone and pass into the trees of the second hill, and there I stop, gaping at what must surely be an apple tree. The scent of the blossoms tickles my nostrils, and I find, in the midst of my wonder and delight, that tears stream from my eyes. *Tell me of a time when the cattle spread over the hills like drifts of snow, when the warriors were more fierce and the women more fair. Tell me how the honey dropped from the comb and the otters played in the rivers and the air smelled of apple blossoms.* I remember the hazel grove north of the Tullagh Sé where Corann searched for nuts. "There are no nuts," he said. "The trees no longer flower." But the apple tree flowers. I wonder, will there be apples in the autumn?

Not far from the apple tree, I find a cluster of primrose. I wrap it in a cloth and add it to my sack. In the next clearing, there are dozens of clusters. I hurry to each of them, like a great, clumsy bee, and pull roots and leaves and flowers from the ground. Primrose will soothe a toothache, cure gout, close a stubborn wound. If this good fortune continues, we might have enough to make a little oil, and Corann can anoint himself properly for the ceremonies of the eight-fold wheel.

One day passes, and another. My steps are light, and my heart is glad. Then the rain comes. It batters the hills, and I am drenched to the skin. My hair clings to my face. I struggle down the eastern edge of the second hill, sliding in mud, grasping at shrubs, banging my legs against scattered stones. There is no easy crossing from the second hill to the third, only a narrow, overgrown valley where the mud runs deep.

I push through the valley, beating aside the scrub with a stick. The mud cakes my legs to the knees. The rain will not relent, and here there are no trees to shelter me. I think how Teague, the Bard of Bolghrain, saw the waters of the Adder rise so high that he fled his cottage and dove into the river and swam to the sea. He fought the currents with nothing but the strength of his arms and the fury of his legs, until he came to Beltrá, to answer the summons of Weylin of the Shield. After that journey, Teague stood for three days and told tales in the chieftain's hall. He asked for no water, no food, no sleep, and his voice never faltered.

I sigh and sit back against the valley wall to rest, wishing that a bard could call druidic fire. It would serve me now, for I need to find a place to sleep out of the rain. I close my eyes a moment and wait while my breathing slows. The rain drips from the ends of my hair, splashes on my nose, runs in little rivulets down the corners of my mouth.

When I open my eyes again, I spot it. A cave. In the rise of the third hill, facing south. I stand and fight the sucking mud, clambering up the hillside, clinging to roots and grasses and the trunks of low trees. With a final tug, I pull myself inside the cave. It is earth, mostly, and neither very tall nor very deep. I cannot stretch out on the floor in any direction, so I curl against the wall and sleep.

I hear it calling in my dreams. I stir, rising from the depths of slumber. It calls again. The voice is deep, grating, full of wind and gravel. I do not know why it should move me so, why I yearn to answer and follow.

I crack my eyes, studying the opposite wall through narrow slits. To my right is the mouth of the cave. The rain has stopped, and the hills wear a thin veil of starlight. Behind a dark figure I can see a curve of the moon. Slowly, I turn to face it, my lids fluttering open, my mind clearing. It stands on two legs. Its arms are spread across the opening of the cave. Where the moonlight touches its shoulder, I can see that its skin is black. It is powerful, built like a warrior of old. Ridged, black horns grow from the sides of its head. They are nearly as broad as its face, and wider than its shoulders.

There are tremors in my muscles now—uncontrollable quaking in my arms and legs. My sopping clothes cling to me. I cannot catch my breath.

Its mouth is enormous, the upper and lower teeth long and pointed. They meet in a jagged yellow line. For so large and terrible a body, its eyes are nothing. Pricks of red in a black face. It calls again.

"Come away. Idris, come away. Come away! Leave the weeping world behind. Come where no sun can scorch the ground, no wind can stir the air, no voice disturb the eternal quiet. Come away, Idris. Come away."

The puka. I am consumed with the urge to rise and follow,

to go with him into the darkness. His broad, muscled torso blocks the entrance. There is nowhere to run.

I gather my knees against my chest and cling to them. I have no weapon but one. I close my eyes and mouth the words, the vigorous, sun-drenched passages of all the stories I can call to mind.

*. . . He looked on the sway and flicker of the green bank . . .*

*. . . The clouds packed the upper world with stir and color . . .*

*. . . There the lovers met, in the meadow where the sunlight drowsed . . .*

*. . . The wide water lay wrinkling and twinkling below them . . .*

*. . . The trees crowded in together, massed in the morning haze . . .*

It is hard to say how long I sit just so, picking through hundreds of stories, scouring the past for words of light and comfort. At length I fall asleep.

I wake to sunlight and birdsong. The mouth of the cave is empty, and I am limp with relief. I step out on the hillside and climb the steep rise to a level place where birch and elder grow. I take a scrap of birch bark from my satchel and light it with a flint. There is plenty of fuel for a large fire. A spark catches, and I build it up, adding branches of birch until the fire roars, until the heat is unpleasant. I unpin my cloak, pull off my shoes and tunic and pants, and set them on the grass beside the fire. I feast on porridge while they dry.

The clouds are piled in wooly mounds. Feathery white blossoms adorn the elder trees, and the birches are bright with new leaves. But I cannot savor the beauty of this place. Fear has set its bony jowl into my heart. I resisted the puka, and for now, he is gone. But every day I draw nearer the door to the Underworld. The worst lies before me.

When my clothes are dry and the fire has warmed me through, I dress and plunge into the woods of the third hill.

As I go, I remember my dream from the first day of the year, how the Shí moved on the corners of my vision, and a strange light fell over leaves and branches and stones and hollows. The Shí do not walk the soil of Baileléan, for they left it to the Antae. But we breathe the same air, and there is some bond between the worlds, some kinship I cannot explain. As I journey east, it presses against me, the weight of these two worlds. In Baileléan, I walk three paces between trees, yet I sense that I have traveled great distances, that in the Many-Colored Land I have crossed enormous reaches of time and space. In Baileléan, I step onto a boulder. In the Many-Colored Land I stand on a finger of rock overlooking a wild and beautiful country. There is more gold in the sun, more silver in the moon. The air shimmers with wonder and dread. Then I step from the stone and my feet are met by grass and moss and the crumbling remains of fallen trees. The soil of Baileléan.

Artek and the Fir Bolg passed into the Many-Colored Land through the silver door of Artek's cloak, and the Fir Bolg king made certain that, for one night each year, the gate should be open. He hoped that by some miracle his son could return to him. But the Crone made the better bargain. For who among the Antae would dare enter the Tullagh Sé to find the door?

Some of the old tales, the most ancient tales of Tír Ársa, tell of other gates and other realms beyond the Many-Colored Land. Some say we pass into the Many-Colored Land through clay. But Murron passed through water. Some stories tell of

The Land of Wonder, which can only be reached through fire. The last and greatest of all journeys, the journey to the Land of Promise, can only be made through iron. These realms, so far removed from the soil of this earth, are stacked one upon the other, always ascending. If the Many-Colored Land—one step, one breath, one veil beyond us—is so dreadful and beautiful and unpredictable and overpowering, I cannot fathom what lies in the lands beyond. Yet it is pleasant to think on as I push deeper and deeper into the Crone's domain.

# 17

Another day in the woods of the third hill. I pass the cave where Corann and I sheltered from the storm, but I do not sleep there. I do not want to wake and find the puka blocking the mouth of the cave. I do not want to hear its call.

I follow the narrow valley between the third and fifth hills, keeping well clear of the holly grove. I pass the ancient yew where I saw three visions.

Another day and a night on the fifth hill. Then, I do not know what compels me, but I leave the Tullagh Sé and camp on the open ground north of the gap between the fifth and sixth hills.

I wake with one thought. *Today. Today I climb the hill that faces the sea. Today I will find answers.*

A sliver of moon slides behind the western hills. The sky warms on the curve of the eastern sea. I have no appetite. I sling my bedroll over my shoulder and remember the bunch of foxglove that hangs at the base of my neck. It is fragile, but I cannot resist touching it and thinking of Muriel. The amulet has proven its worth. I have traveled almost directly east, and no hungry grass has led me astray. In my satchel is the branch of gorse Calder gave me. I see now why he thought it a fitting gift. Gorse is a remedy for hopelessness. It is given to one who despairs of life. I take it from my satchel and study the faded yellow blossoms. I see the village of Blackthorn, the stands of gorse that line the drystones and brighten the hillside. I see the people of Blackthorn, and strength comes into me. I set out northward, in the shadow of the Sixth Hill.

It seems to me that if Meréd asked to be buried in a hill that faced the sunrise, then the door to the tomb must be somewhere in the eastern face of the hill. That is where my feet are carrying me when a startling change in the landscape alters my course. On my right hand, all through the morning's sojourn, the groves of the Tullagh Sé had rustled and murmured over my shoulder, over my head, rising high to the summit of the Sixth Hill. But all at once, the trees and groves disappear. I step back from the shadow of the hill. Ten paces, twenty, trying to get a clearer view.

My mouth hangs open. The Sixth Hill is two hills—one wooded, one bare. It is as though each was parted down the center and two of the halves driven together by some ancient, unfathomable power. With my eyes, I follow the line of trees to the top of the mighty hill. To the right are woods and groves, their leaves green in the morning sun. To the left, the hill is bare. Low, green grasses fall from summit to plain in a rounded arc. Corann would delight in the balance. It is perfect, exquisite.

I return to the base of the hill and look to the right and left before choosing to climb along the centerline, beside the wall of trees. The way is steep. At times I catch hold of roots and stones and use them to hoist myself up. Once I reach for a handhold and come away with a lizard in my fingers. Its skin is green, dry. When I flick it to the ground, it wriggles away, unconcerned with my ascent. The same thing happens further up, and when I look closely, I see that there are many lizards on the Sixth Hill. Their small backs arch and twist as they scurry over the smooth grass and vanish in the undergrowth beyond the line of trees.

A hawk's cry shatters the quiet overhead. A warning. It circles the summit of the hill and wheels off, eastward. Not for the first time, I wish that bards were warriors. The sacred Word seems a paltry shield against ancient evil. I would rather hold a sword in my hand.

At length, I reach the summit of the hill. I stop to rest and sip from my water skin, but I do not linger. I am unaccountably eager to stand in the center of the hill and see the eastern shore of Baileléan. The view is captivating. Looking down the bald side of the hill, I see a green patchwork of meadows and groves that stretches all the way to the coast. The Blue Sea, Gormára, is wild and lovely. The wind cuts the waves into jagged white shards, but they do not protest. They seem, rather, to clap their hands for joy. The sun on the water is sharp and bright. I hear the call of seabirds.

Suddenly, out of the stillness of the morning, over the silence of the smooth, green hill, comes the banshee's cry. I turn on my heel. A white form disappears into the trees. The cry comes again, long and high and mournful.

The trees that guard the western half of the hill form a wall of leaf and bark and shadow. I do not want to go in among them. They are watchful, forbidding. But the cry continues, and I remember Etain's words. There are two banshees. I pause to listen. This is not the same cry I heard by the yew tree, when the round pale eyes stared out from the darkness. The lament is the same. It is woven with the same grief. But the voice is different. This cry issues from another throat.

I plunge into the woods, following the cry.

I stop.

The tree of my visions stands before me, towering high, high over my head. A few paces behind me, the sunlight is bright on the bare side of the hill. But here . . . here is the summit, the true center, the crown of the hill: an immense black tree, with rounded veins of black bark and branches that rise higher than the surrounding trees. Its roots are broader than I am, and they twist from the trunk and plunge into the earth like monstrous snakes. I stretch my hand to touch one black leaf. It is hard. Iron. My curiosity carries me farther. I press the leaf, trying to break it. But it is not brittle. It bends.

The tree is alive, made of living iron. It seems to grow larger while I stand and watch.

The banshee's cry comes again, and I follow the sound to the opposite side of the Iron Oak. There are bushes of rhododendron and honeysuckle. Their leaves and blossoms sway in a light wind, and they bump against something. It looks like a line of curving bones beneath white skin. I move around it, trying to see it from every angle. At the base of the spine is more smooth flesh and . . . toes. A pair of feet are pulled close against the back, and now I see arms, bundled on either side of the spine, and a head of dark hair.

This is not a banshee. It is naked, helpless. My eyes close while I sort through tale after tale, seeking an answer to the mystery of this woman's existence. It is not Meréd. She followed Arlan *into* the tomb and *into* the Underworld. Besides, that was hundreds of years ago. And she could not have wandered from her village and lost her way. North and south and east, there is nothing. Blackthorn is the nearest village to the west, and it is a six days' journey. Is she one of the Fir Bolg, left behind when Artek and the rest went into the Many-Colored Land? Even then, this is the Crone's domain. She has no right here. How did she come to this place?

"My name is Idris," I say. "I am Bard of Blackthorn." I wonder if these words will comfort her. If she knows anything of the Antae, she will know that a bard carries no weapons.

There is a slight tremor in the white skin. I wonder why she does not run. If she fled into the groves, I would not be able to find her.

I slide my bedroll from my shoulder and untie it.

"Here," I say. I step closer and lay the sheepskin over her back. There is a little movement. White fingers search for the edges of the sheepskin and take hold. She pulls the covering around her shoulders.

"I have a little food and water," I say. I crouch down, balancing on my toes, setting the satchel on the ground and rifling through it. When I look up, she has uncurled. She sits to the side of a wide gap in the trunk of the Iron Oak, her knees pulled against her, the sheepskin around her shoulders.

I am caught unawares by her beauty—her long, delicate feet, her graceful hands, the curves of her legs, the skin like milk, like moonlight. Her face is startling, with eyes like emeralds and a fierce, white brow. It is strange to say, but she is too lovely. She is the kind of woman no man touches for fear of her. Her beauty makes her unreachable. I tear my eyes away and extend my hand, opening my fingers to her. In my palm are rowan berries.

She shows no interest. Instead, she retreats into the gap in the trunk. The hollow in the tree is like a small cave. Does she live there? And why? What binds her to this place? I remember the altar, the dark stains, the skin. Is she a captive of the Crone, one marked for sacrifice at the next Bloodmoon? How does she live?

I sigh. I discovered a vital question—Where is the door to the Underworld?—and it carried its answer with it. I traveled to the farthest end of the Tullagh Sé, and here, now, where I thought to find answers, I find more questions. Perhaps, if I give her time, she will speak.

I return the berries to the satchel and stand. There are shrubs and wild herbs surrounding the tree, and some flowers, but the grass is low and worn. Some places are bare, with the brown earth exposed. These form circular paths that weave and twist around the oak. But they never go beyond the cover of the iron branches or the shade of the iron leaves. In one spot I find a flat stone with a depression on one side, like those the fosterlings use to line the drystones. It is damp. She has used it to collect water, I think. Beside the damp stone is a spot of bare earth where a sprig of keck, a bunch of honeysuckle, and two green berries are neatly displayed. A meal. This is her food. How does she live on such scant fare?

I circle back. The woman has come out of the tree, but she must have left the sheepskin inside. She stands as I imagine Genevieve must have stood when Egan came to win her. There is pride and strength in her bearing. She is naked and overwhelming, and I cannot look at her.

I see it by accident, as I turn my eyes to the ground. A thin band of iron circles her neck. A root. She is bound to the tree, and the skin around the iron band is red, swollen, chafed.

"Who are you?" I ask.

She stares at me. No answer.

"Why are you captive here?"

She moves to the edge of the iron canopy, to a little worn path, and places one white foot inside it. She walks the wide circle under cover of the oak, and the living iron moves with her. When she comes to the place where she started, she turns and retraces her steps, unwinding the iron band from the trunk. She stands before me again, wordless, beautiful.

"How long have you been here?"

No reply. She reaches to the iron band around her neck and digs at it with her finger. One side loosens slightly. The other pulls hard against her neck. She makes a small noise, a stifled groan. I rush to help her, to comfort her, to—she throws out her slender white arm and repels me with such force that I lose my breath. I fall to my knees, gasping and coughing.

What am I to do? I cannot leave her here, yet I have nothing to offer her. This was the day I was to find the door to the Underworld. How long can I wait? I was to be home for the Feast. I move to sit against the trunk of an ash tree and stretch my legs in front of me. The captive sits and watches while I eat my berries and salted beef. Her look is curious, but after a time she goes about her business. She walks her paths. She eats her meal of keck and honeysuckle. She stands in the shadow of the wood, looking out at the fading sunlight. She curls in the hollow of the trunk and sleeps.

When I sleep, I dream of lovers, of a village by a ridge of white stone, of the Iron Oak.

All the next day I keep watch. The captive drinks dew and rainwater. She eats the herbs and berries and roots she can reach, and somehow, I do not know how, it is enough. The blood of the Shí must run in her veins, or she'd have long since died from hunger and exposure. It is clear she has no need of me. But I grieve for her bondage, for the bite of the iron against her skin.

In the evening, the captive sits facing east. No moon will rise tonight, but the stars assemble behind wisps of gray cloud. She watches through a tangle of branches. Her smooth white skin shines in the dark.

I sit beside her, at a little distance. In the dirt, I trace the ogham sign for holly. She looks down, studies the sign, and returns her attention to the sky. I wipe out the mark and trace a holly leaf, all curves and thorns, with a cluster of berries at the bottom. I point to the drawing, and she looks down. Her eyes narrow.

"Crone," I say.

She casts a glance over her right shoulder and turns to me. "Cailleach," she whispers.

Cailleach. An ancient name for the Crone. She knows.

"Do you know anything of a door? In the hill?"

No answer. I smudge out the drawing of the holly leaf and scratch a doorway in the dirt. It is just an arch with a hole beneath it, but she understands at once. She turns and leans to the side, gesturing around the Iron Oak, into the woods.

I nod, and the captive turns back to the stars. The red skin on her neck is bright against the lovely white shoulder.

I sleep again and wake in the gray dawn. The captive is collecting dew, brushing it into the stone bowl with a long, white finger. I mean to leave, but my conscience pricks. I gather my things and set them on my shoulders. I kneel in front of her to offer an ancient promise, a binding oath. She will not allow me to take her hands.

"Whatever you ask," I say, "you will have, if it is in my power to give."

The words feel empty and foolish. What do I have to offer her? What would she even ask? Yet she watches me closely as I set off into the woods.

I have the sense that I stray from the bright center of something.

# 18

THESE WOODS ARE NOT LIKE THOSE of the other hills. The groves are more dense, the trees more ancient. Every stone and branch is burdened with mosses and lichens, and but a few ragged sunbeams find their way through the canopy. It strikes me as I go that the door to Meréd's tomb faces westward, into the dark of the woods. Meréd wished to see the sunrise and the fair land of Tír Ársa, but this is the Crone's domain. The hills are hers.

Lizards dart through the undergrowth. One dashes under my foot as it falls, and I feel the crunch of its bones. Worse than that, I begin to hear voices. These last days, I have passed the hours of my journey with the memories of stories and songs. But now a host of voices gathers, multiplies. Each shrub I pass adds another cry, each branch another murmur, each blossom another whisper.

Between one breath and the next, a fog rolls in. I wave my

arms before my eyes, lest the trunk of a yew or an elder should stop me short, lest something worse should devour me. Again and again, my feet are caught in tangles of bramble and brush. But there is no thought of stopping. My head throbs with the tumult of ten thousand voices.

The hill begins its downward slope, and I struggle for footing. I grasp for handholds among the branches of the trees. Rough bark and thorns tear at my sleeves, scratch the skin of my arms. The fog creeps inside my cloak and tunic. I am cold, dripping.

The hillside drops away. There is nothing to cling to, only mist and voices. I fall.

A square of dark soil rises to meet me, interrupting my descent. I come down hard on my feet, jarring my knees and my back. My head knocks against a wall of stone and I slide to the ground. I lie still, aching.

The noise of the voices has risen to a roar—thousands upon thousands. They make pleas. They confess treachery. They shout indignations. They mutter fears. I struggle to my knees and press my forehead to the damp earth. I shove my fingers in my ears, but it does no good. The voices will not be silenced.

I brace my hands against the wall of stone and stand. I open my eyes, wait for them to clear. I am facing west, looking over scattered groves into the heart of the Six Hills. The Crone's altar is near, just a few hours' journey westward. I know, before I turn, what lies behind me. This is no crude cave entrance, no hole where foxes and badgers shelter from winter snows. The stones beneath my hand are hewn, cunningly fitted. Slowly, I

turn, until I am looking inward, toward the east, into the heart of the Sixth Hill. There is a door of stone.

Where is the door to the Underworld?

*I saw a door in a hill, and a black passage beyond.*

The voices scream around me now. I am lost in a storm of voices.

Two steps, and I stand before the door. It is circular, with traces of markings worn smooth by time—but it is broken.

A thick iron root has burst through, cracking the stone into three jagged pieces. I touch the root. It is hard, cool. My fingers trace its path until the root is narrow enough to bend.

The Iron Oak.

I take one of the broken stones in both hands and push it to the side. Dust coughs from the darkness. My hands tremble as I move the remaining stones and clear the doorway. A narrow passage cuts into the hill. It is not large enough to stand in. I must crawl.

*I was carried along the passage and into a kind of tomb. My body ached with the cold of that place.*

Deirdre saw this passage, when she met Clodagh in the blackthorn grove. But she was carried into the tomb in a vision, and I must scramble through the dark while the narrow walls press against my shoulders and the voices shriek in my ears. The air is stale, and bitterly cold. My movements are so clumsy that I nearly fall on my face when the passage comes to an end. At the last moment, I catch myself and pull back. I manage to get my legs under me, to drop down into the tomb. When I land, I understand what Deirdre meant when she spoke of a place with no more room for darkness. My vision in the birch wood returns to me, yet its power has increased ten-thousand-fold. An elusive vision of Death has become palpable, present. I seem to feel its fingers on the scratched, bleeding skin of my arm. They move to my back, raking slowly upward. I feel its breath on my face. There is no room for darkness here. There is room for nothing but Death.

I mean to cry out, but I cannot even whimper. I can scarcely draw breath. There is no space. Everything is crowded out.

A flicker of clarity. A longing for druidic fire. A memory.

I reach into my satchel and fumble for my flint. When my fingers find it, I snatch it out and drag it against the wall. I light a scrap of birch bark, and suddenly there is a little space. Just a little. Wherever the light falls, I can move. I can breathe.

I can see.

The cavern is a chaos of broken stones and running water. The roots of the Iron Oak dangle from the ceiling and branch over the walls. I see two long, rough-edged stones lying side by side. On each stone is a set of bones wrapped in moldering garments. One skull wears a golden circlet, and the shaft of a broken spear protrudes from its breast. Arlan. The other wears a gold torque, and in its breast is a stone dagger. Meréd. And this was her end! To follow her beloved she took a dagger into her own heart. I should have known the Crone would not allow her to enter the Underworld so easily as walking through a door.

Beyond these stones a raised pool juts from the south wall of the chamber. Iron roots have broken its bounds, and its border stones are scattered. Water bubbles up from deep in the earth and spills over the edge of the pool, flooding the floor of the chamber. The spring that feeds the Adder! The water runs out of the cavern through unseen channels and forms a river of bitterness and blight.

All this I see while the voices scream around me. They beat against my head like cudgels. I stumble over a broken stone and fall, and the fury of the voices increases. My torch shines on the lip of a deep, black pit. Water drains into it, and I hear the sound of its descent. It falls until it has forgotten its voice, its lap and babble and rush and roar. It falls into the mouth of Death. There is a sound like whirling wind, and ten thousand times ten thousand voices cry.

The door to the Underworld.

My torch burns out.

I am alone in the darkness.

A rush of cold breath caresses my neck.

I crawl back from the mouth of the pit and stumble over broken stones. I run my hands frantically over the wall, searching for the passageway. My fingers curl around the edge, and I drag myself up. The voices fill the narrow passage as I scrabble along, cutting the palms of my hands and bruising my knees.

I tumble out of the broken doorway, gulping clean air and sunlight. In an instant, the voices are silent. Then another voice, full of wind and gravel, calls to me.

"Idris, come away. Come away!"

Two flickering eyes, pricks of red in a black face, peer down the passageway, looking out from the inside.

I can only run.

The journey from Ban Lurgan to Blackthorn is a six days' journey. I make it in four.

I am thirsty, always thirsty. But I gather dew like the captive, and I run where I can, and I hardly sleep. How can I sleep when death yawns before me each time I close my eyes? How can I rest when ten thousand times ten thousand voices haunt me? By the time I reach Blackthorn, I am spent. My body is sick with thirst and weariness. My mind is plagued by terror and dark visions.

I have moments of clarity. Deirdre wipes my brow with a cloth. Muriel raises a cup to my lips. The drink is bitter. Blackthorn tea. They are trying to calm me.

Calder's voice mingles with a sweet-smelling smoke. Corann puts oil on my eyelids and mumbles incantations. At last, there is the sharp, reviving sweetness of hedgerow wine. I come fully awake.

"Idris."

Corann crouches at my side. We are in the hut. A half moon shines through the window. It is split down the center, like Half-Bald Hill.

"Idris," Corann says again.

"Is everyone well?" I ask.

He hesitates.

"Who?"

"Etain."

"What's happened? How was she hurt?"

"Blackthorns," he says. "She burns with fever, and the wounds will not close."

"There is primrose in the sack. Take it to her!"

"I have." He places a hand on my shoulder, pressing me back against the bedroll.

"No change?"

"It's early yet," he says.

"Corann, what day is it?"

"Tomorrow is the Feast of the Fertile Earth."

"Already?"

"Yes," he says. He gives me another drink of wine and sets the cup aside. "You have found answers, I think."

I have, but I cannot speak of them now. "Have you?"

Corann is silent. He banks the fire and spreads another sheepskin over me. It is late, and I read his weariness in the deep lines of his forehead. He goes to the door.

"Corann."

He huffs a sigh and turns to me.

"Will the wren sing to you in the morning?"

"No," he says. "But I will sit and wait for it all the same."

# 19

THE WHEEL TURNS. Today we celebrate a fertile earth that is no longer fertile.

Before the sun has shown its face over the Six Hills, hundreds have arrived. The women swarm the blackthorn grove. Outside the Tullagh Sé, there are only a few stands of hawthorn in Baileléan, and they are many days' journey from here. So young women and old women bathe their skin in the dew of the blackthorns. They hope to make their bodies fertile. Many times over the years I have watched Engl enter the grove and bathe herself in dew. This morning, I do not see her.

Deirdre and Muriel are there. And Shannan has come. I stand against the cliffside to the south of the hut and watch as she collects drops of dew on bony, wrinkled fingers. She balances the tiny drops with care, lifting them slowly to her face. She spreads them over her cheeks, moving upward, running her fingers along her cheekbones and sweeping her hair up from her temples.

After the ritual bathing, the women, young and old, pluck bouquets of blackthorn blossoms (how long they linger!) and pin them to their cloaks. According to the wisdom of the ancients, the blossoms will bring them husbands. But the older women and the married women wear their bouquets unabashed.

I glance at the wren's nest and wonder where Corann has gone. He is likely preparing the fires. This morning I rifled through my satchel and found the primrose and meadowsweet missing. He must have exhausted the primrose oil when he anointed his black robes for today's rites. I hope I gathered enough flowers to glean a few more drops of oil, enough to make salve for Etain's wounds.

The women leave the grove, scattering to join their families and the villagers with whom they traveled. They're keeping to the north side, mostly, where the ground is drier, but some are spread over the western slope, around the oat and barley fields. Barra and Sloane and Etain have taken such care with the fields while I was away. I feel a pang for the lost moments of sunlight and sweat, when we walk side by side and press the seeds into the cool earth. Deirdre is often there for the sowing. Muriel, too. It is a sweet time. But I have spent it in journeying, in rain, in caves, with darkness. While the hope of harvest went into the ground, I saw the face of Death.

"Ollamh."

Barra stands beside me. How did I not hear the man's approach?

"Chief."

"It does my heart good to see you up and well," he says. "We feared for you."

How many meanings are secreted among those four words! *We feared for you.* Not Barra only, but all the villagers. All but Clodagh and Zinerva. And we did not only fear for your journey, but for the weakened state in which you returned. We were afraid of what you might bring home. We were afraid of what you left us with. We are filled with fear. Always.

Strange. I sense Barra's fear, sense the calcifying dread and despair of Blackthorn and all Baileléan. But my fear has altered. It is tempered by something. Wildness, I think.

"How are Engl and the baby?" I ask.

Barra shifts his weight and moves his spear to his left hand. He studies his feet, coughs. "As they were."

"The fosterlings?"

"Full of mischief," he says. "As they were." His face softens.

"Today we feast the fertile earth," I say.

Barra makes no sound of bitterness or sour humor. He could. There is something ridiculous in the determination to celebrate the turning of a wheel that rolls us furiously toward death.

"Will you speak?" he asks.

"No." I feel certain that this is not the time. Besides, I am still weak. To stand before the Antae in the swan-feather cloak and speak the sacred Word is a heavy undertaking, an exhausting task. I have another part to play in this celebration.

"I will play," I say.

He makes a low humming sound in his throat, a sound of

satisfaction. He nods and angles his large frame through the stile. He walks across the pasture, leaning on his spear.

When the sun has risen, I go to Sloane and Etain's cottage. I rap at the door, and Sloane flings it open. He is ready to bare his teeth at whoever has come to disturb him. But when he catches sight of me, he calms and steps aside. I enter.

Etain is covered in sheepskins, and the fire is built up to a choking heat. Sloane paces the floor, wearing a groove in the packed soil. I do not blame him.

Some years after the Bloodmoon, when a spring of clear water was discovered near Rathroe, Sloane and his father went to see if they could bring some home. It was a two-days' journey, and when they arrived, the men of Rathroe had built a second, larger ring around their fort. The spring was enclosed within it. Sloane's father asked if they could buy some of the water to take to Blackthorn. The men of Rathroe said they could, but they set an extravagant price, far beyond what simple farmers could pay. Sloane and his father were filled with rage. They reacted with violence and received it in turn. The way Sloane tells it, his father killed five times seven men before his head was broken by a cudgel. Sloane was a boy of ten at the time, yet he killed a man of twenty before the men of Rathroe descended on him. They beat him cruelly and sent him home, a warning to anyone who might come in search of clean water. He stumbled into Blackthorn with a strip of his cloak wrapped around his head. I remember the rivulets of dried blood that marked his face. When he reached his cottage, he found only Etain. Their mother had abandoned them. I have never seen either of them smile.

I kneel beside Etain. The wounds are in her forehead, along her hairline, at one side of her face. There is swelling, and greenish-purple skin around the punctures. A yellow pus has filled the deepest wound. She burns with fever.

"Corann brought a primrose salve?"

Sloane nods. "Morning and evening, Corann said, and I try to put it over the wounds, but she screams."

Corann has done all he can, then. It is a horror and an outrage that the ovate is not here in this cottage, watching over Etain. Yet I would not wish it. Zinerva is no healer.

"How?" I ask.

Sloane growls. His eyes burn with tears. He will not stop pacing.

"I don't know. She was in the grove, carrying branches for the bonfires."

I want to comfort him, but Sloane is not fool enough to be deceived by empty assurances. Etain may well die. We can only watch and wait. "You have water?"

"Yes. Deirdre and Muriel have brought some of their supply. And Calder."

The fosterlings, too, by the look of it. The open windows are lined with shallow stone bowls full of rainwater. I stand. The light swims before my eyes. My legs are unsteady. I grip the seat of a stool and wait, gathering my strength. There's no use trying to calm Sloane, and the heat is making me faint. I stumble to the door and take my leave.

Outside, the air refreshes me. I walk the western edge of the village, while the sea sparkles on the horizon. I follow a wandering drystone to a place apart from the crowds of celebrants and sit in silent thought. Whole epochs of time have passed since the spring equinox when I spoke of the War of Thunder. I have aged in body and mind. And how far I have journeyed and how much I have seen! Yet the hills of Baileléan are unchanged. The blackthorns raise twisted fingers to the sky. Barra walks the village and leans on his spear, Sloane's face is full of rage and ferocity, and Corann has gone out when I needed to speak to him.

*. . . Like the lapping of the gray waves that are never the same and never different . . .*

One question I have answered, and still I have no hope to give the Antae. We are all that remain of a mighty people, and I am the least of us, a smudge of shadow beneath the broad, luminous sky.

It isn't much of a feast. Nothing to the thirty-days' feast that Angus of the Mighty Arm spread before the Antae when he took Aislin to wife. To every guest, Angus gave a cup of gold filled with the sweetest mead. The cups were enchanted, and for thirty days the mead did not run dry. And each man had his own roast boar and each woman her own roast deer and each child his own roast pheasant. There were barley soups and nettle soups and herb-roast fish. There was cream and butter and thick brown bread and nuts and apples and berry pies. My mouth waters at the thought.

We have three sickly cod. A gift from Llyr and Murdoch. Some of the attendants have brought rabbits. Another man boasts of venison, but it's a dog he turns on his spit. At this feast, we praise the fertile earth, indulge in a few bites of greasy meat, and drink the dregs of the hedgerow wine.

Twin fires are lit at sunset. We make a show of passing the cattle between the fires. For fertility, we say. I remember lambs lying still in the snow.

Traditionally, it is the time of open pasturing. Before the Bloodmoon, the cattle roamed the hills and feasted on the summer grasses and herbs. Now there is so little for them to eat, they simply return to their pastures and wait for their portions of gorse.

I think the gorse is thinner this year. Where the village was wrapped in a cloak of yellow flowers, now it is only spotted with them. The smaller shrubs will bloom at harvest time. I hope. But what will we feed the cattle next summer? Am I a fool to imagine that another summer will come to Baileléan?

When the remnants of the feast are cleared, the music begins. Devlin has brought his bodhrán. Three others carry claves and flutes and drums. We gather around the twin fires north of the fields and play. I begin on the eagle-bone flute. It makes a sound like singing, like sighing. The Antae dance around the twin fires, and those who hope for fertile lands and fertile bodies pass between the fires. So everyone goes.

There is a pause while Corann performs the rites. Zinerva stands near the grove and watches. This time I am free to watch as well. Eyes shift toward Zinerva. Feet shuffle. Corann speaks of the rising strength of the sun, how it warms the seeds we sow and brings forth fruit. The people are uneasy. Zinerva speaks no word, makes no sign. When Corann's arms fall from their adulation of sun and moon, I blow the dord. The tension dissolves in a whirl of dancing, and Zinerva fades into the grove. I start up a rhythm on my bodhrán, and the other musicians follow. It is a driving rhythm, full of the pulsing of blood, the spinning of earth and sun, the pounding of rain. Muriel joins the dancers, and I beat the bodhrán in time with the racing of my heart. Her peplos is blue, and she wears no cloak. Her arms are white and bare in the firelight.

I play while the half moon rises and soars above us. I play while it falls. Some of the celebrants sleep, but others refuse to abandon the old ways. Even with so little food and drink, they insist on dancing until sunrise. In the gray before dawn, I take my instruments and return to the hut. Corann will not be there. He will wait by the twin fires until the sun has risen and the last man has taken his bedroll and gone away.

I pass a few hours in sleep. When I wake, Corann sits on his side of the fire, his eyes half-closed, facing me.

"Are you ready to tell me of your journey?"

I sigh, groaning as I push myself up. I would rather eat and drink. I would rather forget. I cross my legs and rest my hands on my knees. I am ready. Yes. But my lips part, and the horror of the tomb returns to me, and I cannot speak.

"You have been with the Crone. You have seen her."

I breathe, gather moisture in my mouth, swallow. "I have seen Death."

"Little difference," Corann says. "You found the door."

He leans forward, eager for my answer.

"In the Sixth Hill," I begin. And I tell him of the puka, of the captive, of the Iron Oak and Half-Bald Hill. I tell him of the tomb, the bones, the pit. I tell him of the water, the spring that feeds the Adder. I tell him how the Iron Oak has opened the doors of death.

The telling is terrible, as I knew it must be. When I talk of the narrow passageway, of the voices, I think I cannot continue. Corann gives me a sip of hedgerow wine, the last drops from the bucket. It is reviving. It carries me through the flight from the tomb and my journey home.

It is a relief to have it out, to share the knowledge with one who can carry it. What's more, the telling has raised new questions.

"You said that Perth feared the Crone's power, that he warned you against dealings with her?"

"Yes, in the inner groves," Corann replies. "He was wise to fear her."

"Since our people left Tír Ársa, there have been no stories of journeys to the Many-Coloured Land or the Lands of Wonder and Promise. Perhaps in Baileléan, there is only one door to the Lands Beyond. And if that door is closed—"

Corann sighs. "There were never many tales of journeys to the Lands Beyond. But the doors between *all worlds* stand open at Newmoon."

"So says Clodagh."

Corann's eyes snap at the words, but there is truth in them.

"The story of the Cogath Tornech ends with Perth and Artek making peace. But the Crone played a part in that bargain."

Corann stares at me a moment. "You know the part she played. The Crone took the dead and the body of the Fir Bolg prince and the fairest living woman of the Antae. The Fir Bolg passed into the Many-Colored Land and the Antae had peace. And one night in the year—just one—the doors between realms would stand open. It was always so, even before the War of Thunder."

Artek made a gate, but he did so in the Crone's Domain. He must have feared that she would close it. He must have known she held that power. Otherwise, he'd have struck no bargain. While his son passed through the door to the Underworld, the Fir Bolg king entered the Many-Colored Land through a different door on the same hill. Three worlds. Two doors. One hill—one seat of primeval power.

Perth would not have returned to the Tullagh Sé, not even to pass into the Lands Beyond. As Corann has said, he feared the Crone. Yet I saw no door to the Many-Colored Land on Half-Bald Hill. Is it only visible at Newmoon?

A heavy sigh empties me of questions. "There is but one door open to the Antae, flung wide and pinned in place by the roots of the Iron Oak."

Corann's eyes burn, and I see shame and frustration etched in the lines of his face. "Perth would have maintained the balance."

I hate to see him so. He is breaking under the weight of an impossible burden. My anger kindles. "What balance?"

The atmosphere in the hut stretches taut. "Before the Bloodmoon, there was life and there was death. The wheel turned, driving one into the soil as it drew another up."

Now the wildness I have brought home from my journey shows its face. I would not have challenged Corann before. My fear has made me audacious.

"What sort of victory is that?"

I meet his eyes and thunder rumbles in the tight confines of the hut. Time slows while Corann holds my gaze. I see him wrestle with the old ways, with Perth's teaching, with year upon year upon year of seeking for wisdom that never comes. The world is out of balance, and Corann longs to restore it. But what good is a balance between life and death? It is a fleeting balance at best, if Death always speaks the final word.

Corann begins to read that truth in my eyes. Perhaps his heart has whispered it to him during his long years of searching. At length, he turns away.

# 20

The summer days are warm. The blossoms wilt on the blackthorn branches and drift to the ground. To the south, the creeping bog spreads, gaining new footholds every hour. The sedge is limp and gray-green, and it gives off a sour smell. To the west, the land rolls to the sea in waves of gentle green. The wind taunts the grasses and warps the branches of solitary trees.

My thoughts turn often to the east, where a captive sits in the dark under the branches of an iron tree. She is singing, perhaps, the only song she has ever heard—the cry of the banshee. She makes her bed at the doorway of death, while the sea breezes play over the bare hill just a step beyond her circle of bondage.

Corann assures me that the captive must be one of the Shí. She has strength beyond that of mortal women, or she could not have survived in that place. If she is being kept for sacrifice, he says, such a ceremony would not be performed until Newmoon, when the Crone is at the height of her power.

And who would commit such an atrocity? My heart is quick with the answer.

Clodagh would.

Zinerva would.

I have made the sacred oath. Whatever the captive asks, I will give. But what do I have to give? The question torments me. I no longer spend hours in meditation, for I can find no quiet within me. The silence has filled up with questions, with voices. The dark is full of the fear of Death.

So I work, weeding the fields with Deirdre and Muriel and Sloane and Barra while the fosterlings bring bowls of rainwater to quench our parching thirst. Always we pray for more rain.

Sometimes I sit with Etain, dabbing her forehead with salve while she winces and jerks. She trembles with fever, and dreams, and raves. Some days, I can get a little water down her throat. More often, she clenches her teeth and every muscle in her body goes rigid. Sloane grows thinner and wilder.

I feed and water the cattle with Calder. We wash the sheep in the Adder, letting the bitter water carry away the mud that cakes their wool. Afterward, we herd them back to their pastures and shear them. I sit with Deirdre and Muriel and Shannan and help with the carding of the wool.

Corann comes and goes, but what he seeks I do not know. At the next turn of the wheel, we celebrate the summer solstice. It is the most sacred druidic rite, the greatest exhibition of his power and authority. I wonder what answers will come when the sun rises on the longest day of the year and rides in its glory over Baileléan.

I keep a close watch on Zinerva. It is rare that she leaves her cottage in daylight. But once I catch her bending over a copper cauldron, studying the still surface of the water. I wonder why she takes the trouble. Hasn't she found the answers she sought?

I wait for Zinerva to leave, to travel the villages of Baileléan and rouse the people against Corann. But this is folly. She does not have to. The word has already spread abroad. This girl conquered death. For those who dwell in the shadow of death, there is no greater hope, no clearer guide. On many days it seems to me that Zinerva has already won.

I begin to long for a visit to Kilveagh. I would like to see my father and mother and walk in the birch woods again. I have missed the flapping of the round, green birch leaves and the groaning and swaying of the white trunks.

I leave at sunrise, taking nothing but a dab of primrose salve and a water skin. The journey is not long. Before the sun has reached its zenith, I'm ambling through the birches, remembering the summers of my childhood. Those days were slow and sweet, and after I milked the cows and tended the garden, I was free to roam the woods. I learned the calls of larks and swallows and wrens and martins. I built ring-forts of tumbled stones and gathered berries in autumn. I knew little, then, of druids or hunger or sorrow or death.

My father's cottage comes into view, and at the same moment my foot splashes into a puddle. I stumble, and turn my gaze to the ground. When Corann and I came in the winter, we went no farther than the birch grove. I did not see how the creeping bog had spread over my father's land. A narrow tongue of the Adder runs down the north side of the first hill, and it has poisoned the ground of Kilveagh. The marshy soil clings to my boots and slows my progress. There is no more garden beside the cottage, just a few limp weeds and clumps of grayish grass. And water. Many shallow pools of bitter water.

"Idris?"

My father appears. He has heard my boots squelching in the mud.

My greeting sticks in my throat, for it is hot and tight. My father has aged. He looks a different man from when I saw him last. The lines around his mouth and eyes have sprouted new lines, and those have sprouted still more. A network of furrows and wrinkles marks his face. The skin under his eyes is thin and gray.

"Father."

He takes my hands in his and grips them tightly. He kisses me on both cheeks and pulls me into an embrace. "Come in! Come in!"

My mother rises from a heap of sheepskins and comes to me. Her back is stooped, and I am careful with my welcome. She touches my face and smiles. Her eyes are wet and sparkling.

I have been away too long.

We sit around the fire in contented silence. We are glad to be here in this cottage together, and for a time, that is enough. My mother offers me a bowl of dried sloe. My father shares water from their little bucket. I ask after my sisters, but there has been no word. Both met their husbands at the Feast of the Fertile Earth and moved to villages north of Rathroe. That was years ago. Likely they struggle as we do, for there is nowhere in western Baileléan where the Adder's tongue does not reach.

We fall silent again, but the contentment has passed. My father and mother have fallen on difficult times. Is it any wonder? They do not wish to burden their son with their troubles. I can guess that there is not enough water, that their health is failing, that they do not see many years ahead of them. They will not come to Blackthorn. I have asked. They love the birch woods too well, and that I understand. Besides, there is nothing better waiting for them in Blackthorn. We, too, know hunger and thirst. We, too, wall ourselves up against the relentless spread of the creeping bog.

They will have heard about Zinerva. They may even have heard of my journey east. But what is there to say of that?

What is there to say at all?

We make a few efforts at conversation. Here and there, we share a word about the weather, or the coming solstice, or the rumor of a new chief in Beltrá. My mother asks about Muriel, and I hardly know how to answer.

"You should build her a cottage in Kilveagh," my father says. His eyes shine out of his thin, wrinkled face. "Just think of autumn."

He has forgotten himself. He speaks of a forgotten time, before the Bloodmoon, when a man could marry and build a house for his wife and father children and hunt and farm and drink the clear, sweet water of the Adder. He speaks of a time when a man lived a life before he surrendered to death. The words pain me. He prods a deep wound.

"I'd like to rest," I say. I am not tired, but the pretense of talk is wearing.

My mother apologizes for keeping me up, and my heart is pricked. My father brings me a bedroll and banks the fire. I lie for hours with my eyes closed, listening. I hear my father's shuffling feet as he goes to retrieve a block of peat for the morning's fire. I hear the soft rasping of my mother's comb as it slides through her hair. They are careful not to disturb me. My eyes burn behind their lids.

Next morning, I talk of returning. I had not intended to stay long. I should not be away from Blackthorn. I think of Zinerva, of Etain, of the work that remains to be done in the fields, of the preparations for the solstice. My mother nods and smiles, but she will not be satisfied until I have eaten a small breakfast.

When I stand and sling my waterskin over my shoulder, she rises with me. She places one hand on either side of my face and holds me. The light of her love, her pride, is warm on my face. I blink back tears, kissing her cheeks and the backs of her hands.

My father waits at the door. He smiles and pats my shoulder. I think at first that it is merely an affectionate touch, but he guides me, steering me toward the old ash. It is a beautiful tree—tall and straight with full branches forming a smooth, rounded canopy. The leaves are small, each with a single white vein running through the center.

My father strokes the gray bark on the trunk. "It is good that the trees endure," he says. "They are not so soon poisoned by the bitter water."

Yes. It is good. We depend on the trees, the gorse.

"They are ancient," he says. "Some were already mighty trees when the Antae first set foot on this land."

True. Tree-lore is central to our beliefs and traditions. *The tree is the supreme teacher. Its roots are planted in the invisible past. Its branches rise to the heavens, holding the potential of the future in the seeds that have yet to fall.*

"Do you remember the abscess?" he asks.

How could I forget?

"Yes, Father."

"Since the last Newmoon, I've come to the ash every evening and made a slit in the trunk. I've tipped a cup of the bitter water into the veins of the tree."

"The next morning?"

"The tree is whole."

"But the land is not."

"Ah, it's too big a blight for one tree," he says. "Still, the ash is hale as ever. Every drop I've given it, it's taken."

It is good that the trees endure. *The tree is our supreme teacher.*

My father turns to me and grips my arms. Tears slide over his wrinkled cheeks. His voice trembles. "I would take this blight if I could. I would drink up a river, an ocean, of bitter water, so that you could come and build a cottage and live in Kilveagh with your bride."

He keeps his hold on my arms while the wind rustles the ash leaves. Behind us, the birch wood is filled with birdsong.

"Oh, my father." I kiss his cheeks and he wraps an arm around my shoulder. He pulls away before I can say more. I watch his back as he shuffles to the cottage.

In the birch wood I find the log where I sat in meditation, where I saw a vision of Death. I drop my water skin to the ground and sit down and weep.

# 21

WE HAVE COME TO THE SEASON OF THIRST. There is rain, but it is never enough. Day and night we are thirsty, and the skin on our lips is cracked. Calder no longer spends his days in the pastures. He rests in the cool of his cottage and tends the cattle in the evening. In the early morning, he scours the gorse, searching out the brightest cluster of blossoms for Shannan.

Engl keeps to her cottage as well. The baby is growing. We are all grateful for that. But his fevers return, and late into the summer nights, Engl's candlepot winks from the open windows. Etain has not recovered. I think of the abscess and the ash, but the wound is in her face, and I cannot bring myself to cut her. Not with the cure so uncertain. During my visit to Kilveagh, she came very near to death. So Sloane told me. But Muriel and Deirdre sat with her through the night, spooning a syrup of elderberries and birch gum into her mouth. She has been a little stronger since.

Barra has met with Corann to discuss the solstice celebration, but he spends most of his strength on the oat and barley fields. The soil is not what it was, and the barley does not thrive. Pixie and Vaughn and Brennan follow close on Barra's heels. Wherever they go, they share their bucket of rainwater.

Corann thinks of nothing but the solstice. He has passed many days in meditation in the oak grove west of Kilveagh. He gathers tallow from every possible source, storing it for the midnight vigil. He presses the last of the primrose leaves and gleans a few drops of oil. He takes his white robe all the way to the sea to wash it. I'm not sure the water is any better there than what he could find here on the bank of the Adder, but Corann is doing what he can, what he believes is necessary to prepare for the rites. I think he hopes to meet Perth in the inner groves.

I travel with him to a stretch of land west of Eyebright where the ground is drier. The rites must be performed in a place where we can see the sun when it first touches the horizon. Our view cannot be blocked by the Tullagh Sé. So we journey south, out of the shadow of the Six Hills. We dig a broad circle in the ground. Inside it, overlapping the boundaries of the circle, we dig another symbol, three-sided, to represent the power of sun, moon, and stars. We roll stones to the three points where the symbol meets the outer circle and clear the ground in the center of the site.

Everything is ready.

It is a three-quarter day's journey back to Blackthorn. A sliver of moon has risen in the sky when we ford the Adder and climb the stiles. We are weary, and eager for rest. Tomorrow we will not sleep.

"Corann! Idris!" A voice halts us as we cross the third drystone. It is Murdoch. He is running, waving his arms. The fish-hooks threaded through his tunic glint in the light of Corann's lantern. My first thought is charged with fear. *What has happened?* But Murdoch's face beams. He looks like the fosterlings look after they've drunk their share of honey mead. "Come, please!" he says, and leads us to his cottage.

A fire burns inside. Llyr stands at a low table, leaning on his staff. His head is cocked to the side, and his bushy white hair frames his face. "Corann," he says. How much he speaks in that solitary word! His voice is full of wonder, of his shared history with Corann, and their shared sorrow. "We've found it," he says.

He steps back from the table, and I notice a bundle of cloth. Apart from the bundle, the table is empty. It looks as if it has been cleaned. The wood surface gleams. Corann takes Llyr's place beside the table. He stops, looks at Llyr. Then he pinches a corner of the cloth between thumb and finger and flicks it aside. He lifts another corner, and I lean in to see what it is they've found.

"At last."

Corann breathes the words like a prayer.

I see silver scales and a small, narrow mouth, sharper than a cod's mouth. Around the fins and near the belly, the skin has a pinkish cast. I've never seen a herring with that coloring.

This is a salmon. They have found a salmon, a creature as old as time, and one acquainted with past and future. This creature gives knowledge, gives wisdom, and they have found it on the eve of the summer solstice.

Corann stares. He is hesitant to touch it. He has waited so long. He glances at Llyr, and Llyr spreads his hand, palm up. "It is yours, Druid."

With a deep sigh, Corann pinches the corners of the cloth and covers the fish. He is careful not to let his fingers graze the scales or fins. This is a sacred being. It must be handled with the utmost care.

Murdoch grins. He stands with his head high and his chest out, rocking from his heels to his toes. Llyr's eyes shine. He watches Corann with a look of love and satisfaction. They have brought something of value to the people of Blackthorn. Their joy overflows.

Corann places the salmon carefully in his satchel and bows to each of the fishermen in turn. "Llyr, Murdoch, you bring the blessing of the ancients to our people. I thank you." I have never heard him speak so to anyone.

They receive his thanks in silence, and we go. The remainder of our journey is brief, but the air around Corann snaps and sparks. He has such hopes.

Before I open my eyes, I smell the smoke of the peat fire. I cough, for the smoke is thick in the hut. When I sit up and look to the window, I see that Corann has covered it with a sheepskin. Even the smoke from the fire that burns below the salmon might offer insight and wisdom. Corann will not waste it.

He sits beside the fire, beckoning the smoke toward him with the waving of his hands. I listen for the sizzling sound of fat dripping into the embers, but Corann has put a bowl beneath the salmon. He will catch every drop. The spit is propped on two forked branches. From time to time, Corann turns it. I pull a corner of my cloak over my mouth and breathe through it. Before long, my eyes are raw and gritty, but I cannot leave the hut. I do not think I have ever seen a salmon. It is almost as though one of the ancients has come in the flesh to sit in our hut and share our meal and impart his wisdom. It is not a thing to be missed.

Corann lifts the spit from the flames. He sets the salmon on a copper platter. He takes the bowl of drippings and pours it over the salmon, shaking the bowl until the last drop is emptied. He takes his knife in hand and moves it over the platter as if he is not sure where to make the first cut. He chooses the eye, popping it from its socket with the tip of the blade. He waits a moment, letting it cool. Then he sets it on his tongue and draws it into his mouth. He closes his eyes. His body is still, poised, ready to receive the word of wisdom and knowledge. At length, he chews the eye and swallows. Next, he makes a cut in the center of the salmon. He eats a slice of the pink flesh—scales, bones, and all. Again he sets it on his tongue and waits before chewing. He swallows slowly, and takes another bite.

Piece by piece, he eats the salmon. It is not a feast. The fish is only a hand's breadth between head and tail. But it is an extended meal, a sacred rite in itself. When he has eaten all that can be eaten, he takes the larger bones and fins and places them in the fire, inhaling the smoke of their burning. He scrapes the oily residue from the copper platter with his fingers and anoints his face and arms.

I watch, saying nothing. When Corann stands, I do likewise. When he opens the door and pulls the sheepskins from the window, I gulp great breaths of clear morning air. When he walks to the edge of the blackthorn grove, I follow him. Yet I cannot think what question to ask. Who can find words for such an occasion?

Corann stands below the wren's nest. It is empty now. The chicks have learned to use their wings, and they have flown away. Corann turns to me, no doubt sensing my anxious curiosity.

"It may come during the vigil," he says. "Or with the sunrise."

So he has heard nothing. After eighteen years' searching, he has eaten the salmon of knowledge and gained no word. It may yet come. Tonight's vigil is the most sacred of the solar year. But I am glad that Corann did not eat the salmon in sight of the village, with Zinerva standing by.

"We leave at midday," he says. "Make ready."

In the years before the Bloodmoon, and even the first years after it, the people of Blackthorn, and those from other villages who joined the celebration, traveled just south of the Adder for the summer solstice. There was a wedge of land between two tongues of the river where the symbols were dug. It was green and pleasant. As the journey was brief, no one in Blackthorn was prevented from coming, and the preparations were simpler. Now we spend the day battling the bog and the buzzing flies. Engl cannot bring the baby so far and stay away so long, and Shannan is not well enough for the journey. Sloane has stayed behind to tend Etain. It seems an empty celebration, and it has not yet begun.

We reach the sacred site. Some few have come and spread their camps around us. They do not come very close. They must not interrupt the vigil or endanger the sanctity of the rites. So they seek out the drier bits of ground and build their fires.

Corann prepares the solstice fire. We have brought gorse branches and birch and peat. The fire must last until dawn. I am glad of it, for the smoke keeps the flies away. But I dread the coming fast. I long for a draught of cool, clear water and a thick slab of salted beef.

After the Bloodmoon, when the water first turned bitter, some said that those who took ill were victims of the joint-eater. They wasted away, it was said, because the joint-eater devoured all the nourishment from their food before they could eat it. But for a man to be rid of the joint-eater, he must consume a huge quantity of salt beef without drinking any water, then lie down by a stream with his mouth open. It was said that the joint-eater would grow thirsty and jump into the stream to drink. What a cruel and false hope it was! Men and women poisoned by the bitter water ate the salted beef and waited by the bitter stream, refusing to drink, until their thirst killed them. A man can drink the bitter water or drink no water at all. The end is the same.

There is a little water in my water skin, but it must wait until after the noon rites tomorrow. The hours until I can feel the water on my lips, on my tongue, yawn before me. During my first sojourn in the Tullagh Sé, I turned my thoughts from hunger to the battles of the Cogath Tornech. Now I turn my thoughts from thirst to a question that has been taking shape within me.

What will I seek in this midnight vigil?

The Crone reaches the height of her power at Newmoon. The druid's powers are greatest at the summer solstice. And Corann has eaten the salmon of knowledge. Never have his hopes of restoring the balance been higher. He will descend into the inner groves and seek the wisdom of the great sorcerer.

Do I join him in his descent? Would our combined energies guarantee an audience with Perth?

It matters not, for Perth will speak only of balance, and I do not wish to hear it.

No. I am the Custodian of the Word. It is a Word I seek. All Baileléan lies under the glam dicin, the words that curse, that wound. I seek a Word that blesses, a Word that heals.

I take my seat on a ceremonial stone at one corner of the three-sided symbol. Corann takes the stone at my left. He is eager, agitated, yearning for visions and revelations. Zinerva takes the stone on my right. Her orange shawl is pulled taut across her collarbones, and her hands lie open in her lap. She faces Corann, but her eyes cut to the side, glinting. The owl perches on her shoulder. It swivels its head from left to right, scanning the bog and blinking its round eyes.

Though we began our journey at midday, the sun rides over the heavens in such glorious strength that it is not yet dark. The gold and purple sunset is slow to fade into the western sea. When darkness falls and the silver stars rise in the east, we begin our vigil. Bard, ovate, and druid must wait through the night for the sun's return.

The vigil is not long. Four hours in the dark. For awhile, I watch the stars wheel overhead. I wonder how the realms above us can seem so wide, and those within us wider still. I watch the fire, searching for signs and omens in the arc of the flame, in the spit and crack of the branches. I study Zinerva. Her body is rigid. Wisps of yellow hair blow in the light wind, and her eyes twitch beneath their lids. Corann is still. No doubt he waits in the inner groves.

I go to seek a Word. I close my eyes and breathe a sigh so deep it feels as though my body has turned inside out. I descend, slowly, through mists and darkness. I am afraid. I know what is coming. The voices. I fall into them, and I am immersed. The voices are an ocean, and I drown. They clamor, scream, wail, entreat. They long to be heard and they know they will not be. Their despair consumes me. Yet I fall further, through fleeting visions of storm and battle, through memories of feasting and flowers, through the yellow canopy of a birch wood, through the spreading branches of a tree of iron, to the summit of a hill. I look around. The woods are troubled. There is a whirring of wings, a sound of birds driven into reluctant flight. Farther on, beyond the trees, the hill is bare. A red moon hangs heavy in the sky, and the colors of the world are changed.

Again I fall, through earth and stone, into a darkness as old as time. There is no room for me here. I will be crushed by this expanding presence. How can it grow? What more can it devour? Yet it goes on. Flesh and bone and rock and tree and wind and sky are blotted out.

I have come to the end. I have entered Death's domain, and there is no returning. My body is wracked with tremors. My teeth rattle in my head. My hands, my arms, my legs—they are useless. I yield. I fall.

I fall through darkness. I fall into the bowels of the earth, into the mouth of Death.

I gasp, dragging air into my lungs as if for the first time. Something has interrupted my descent, stopped it so abruptly that my bones ache. I am surrounded by light, suspended by light. It is something like druidic fire. No. It is nothing like.

It is . . . it is . . .

Words fail me. This . . . something . . . wraps me like a sheepskin on a snowy night. It warms me like a fire. It calms me like a draught of blackthorn tea. But no! It is like none of these things. It is vibrant. It throbs and presses like roots, like new vines. It pulses like blood in the veins, bursts like blossoms in spring. It roars like thunder, blinds like lightning. It scorches, scalds; it heals. It is brighter than sunlight and more constant. It does not change like the moon. It is . . . it is . . .

I am jolted awake. Fragments of cloud drift on the eastern horizon. They are silver, pink. The sun, so newly set, has risen again. It boils up from the eastern sea. It hurls its light over Baileléan, rays of red and yellow and gold flung toward the western sea, coursing over wood and meadow and hill and bog. It has come.

I look down. I am crumpled on the ground with my hands and knees under me. I am trembling. Zinerva watches me out of the corner of her eye. Corann looks to the east, to the brilliant sunrise, but he is the same as he was when I descended. I have gone far and returned. But I did not descend into death. I have not journeyed through the Underworld as Zinerva did. I have not met with the ancients. They are shadow and dust, and their wisdom has not redeemed us.

No. I have had an encounter with something, something for which I have no name, nor even a proper image. None of our stories tell of such a thing. Not one even hints at the possibility of something so violently opposed to Death, something so unutterably, undeniably, unalterably *alive*.

Corann is performing the dawn rites, but I cannot rise. Zinerva takes my place. As Corann needs them, she hands him the dust, the oil, the burning branch. He completes the rites, and he and Zinerva return to their seats.

My forehead is pressed to the ground. I remember how pale Zinerva looked, how weak she was, after her journey at Newmoon. Did she feel like this? I know neither hunger, nor thirst. From my outermost skin to the innermost depths of my being, I am still. There are no voices, no darkness, no fear. In their place is a radiant peace. Is this the Word I seek? The sensation is new and strange, so unlike the absence of battle and conflict that we usually describe as peace. Again, words fail. This is larger, deeper. This light, this thing, invades me, pervades my being. It is as wide as eternity.

Corann puts a hand on my back, and I find I am able to rise. The sun is overhead. It is time for the noon rites. I do not understand how it happened, how the hours rolled along with such ferocious speed while I lost myself in stillness. The solstice fire has gone out, and the air is heavy and damp. Midges and flies buzz over the marsh. I stand beside the druid and the ovate and raise my arms to a sun that has risen to the height of its glory. Yet I look beyond it. Another light has captured me.

# 22

Deirdre walks beside me on the return journey. Muriel walks at a little distance, but I think she listens in.

"You had a vision," Deirdre says.

"No," I say. "It was something else."

"Zinerva has watched you since you fell from the stone."

"I fell?"

"You don't remember?"

"I was falling . . ."

"It *was* a vision, then."

"No!" Deirdre, who always knows my mind, who sees my thoughts so clearly, does not understand. How could she? I do not understand. "It was not a vision. It was—"

"You met with the ancients?" she asks, in a whisper.

"No."

"You saw the coming days?"

"No."

"You received a sacred Word?"

"No."

She is frustrated. Her footsteps fall faster, heavier. She kicks at a clod of wilted grass. But I am basking in this new light. My eyes are dazzled. In this moment, I do not see what it is that plagues her. "What is it, Deirdre?"

"We've passed the summer solstice, Idris."

"Yes." I know the cycle of the year, the paths of the stars and the great luminaries. This rising and waning has always been. It is the way of things. But she speaks of the coming Bloodmoon. If the last Bloodmoon brought bitter water and blight, what will this one bring?

"Now the sun's strength wanes, and the wheel turns back toward the dark half of the year." She grabs my wrist, yanking my arm and turning me to look at her. Her eyes burn. "And still you see no visions. Still you receive no word."

I open my mouth to explain, to tell her something of my encounter, but what can I say? There is no tale of our people to guide me. There are no words to capture what I have seen. And if there were, what comfort would they offer Deirdre, or any of the Antae? They are not an answer to our questions.

Deirdre releases my arm with a jerk and we continue our slow journey through the bog. The ground is pocked with holes, and we must be careful of our footing.

"Is it the Crone you fear?" I ask. "Or Zinerva?"

"Zinerva, Clodagh, the Crone. All three are dryads of Death." She clenches her hands into fists and drops her voice. "Idris, Llyr and Murdoch heard whispers in Seaswell of a woman who ate the leaves of the wild cherry."

The leaves are poisonous, deadly. "Where did she get them?"

Deirdre casts a meaning glance toward the ovate, and I remember Zinerva's bulging pouch, her triumphant return to Blackthorn.

I watch Zinerva as she picks her way through the mud and the scattered pools. It is true that she and Clodagh are one and the same. They use the same methods, seek the same ends. And if both are thralls of the Crone, then it is as Deirdre says. But I begin to think that they are not the enemy. If the three were to vanish, if the wind were to carry them to the farthest reaches of the Blue Sea, still our world would languish. All that we know, all that we love, all that has sustained us, everything grinds to a halt.

Who, then, *is* the enemy?

It is the right question, the necessary one. I grow closer now, nearer to that single question that must be asked and answered.

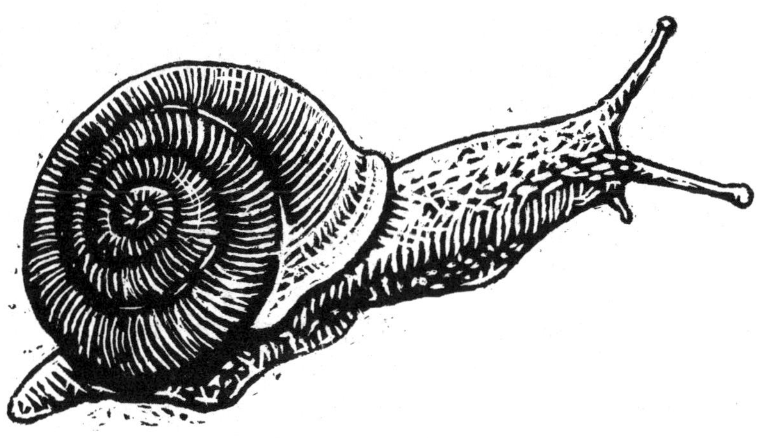

I think I must smile, for Deirdre gives me a look of confusion and scorn and hurries away. She joins Muriel. They travel ahead of me now, and I can watch the golden strands of Muriel's hair as they swing at her back. For a moment, I am transported to the ash tree. I see my father's tears and hear his voice. *I would take this blight if I could. I would drink up a river, an ocean, of bitter water, so that you could come and build a cottage and live in Kilveagh with your bride.*

Corann has foreseen the coming of doom. His agitation, the growing sense of urgency in his every action, suggests that doom comes swiftly. He searches the sacred groves. He listens for wrensong, he eats the salmon of knowledge. He waits for visions and wisdom that do not come, not even at the summer solstice. If Corann had received a word from the ancients, he would have spoken it at the noon ceremony. But he walks at the head of our company, and his white robes drag through the mud. His gait is not as sure as it once was. He leans on his staff.

The Bloodmoon approaches. And what is it I have seen? The world is wide and terrible and teeming with beauty, and there are things for which we have no names. I do not know my place. I cannot find my footing.

We are not three days returned from the celebration of solstice before Engl is back at the door of the hut. She no longer speaks when she comes. I know why she is here and who has refused to help her. I pound the blackthorn bark and prepare the tea. She looks at me a long time after I have finished and the tea is hers. In her face I read unspeakable weariness. There are shadows under her eyes, shadows in her eyes. She clutches the baby against her and searches me. For what? She does not look through me as Corann does, but into me. I open my mouth to ask if she is well, if there is something more I can do for her, but she is gone before the words come.

More and more, my thoughts turn to the captive and the Iron Oak. I have sworn the oath, and it hangs between us, the words stretched thin over the long rising and falling of the Tullagh Sé.

*The Tullagh Sé are the center of all our stories.*

The days pass in heat and thirst. I lie on the grass and watch the clouds pile up. They darken and drop their rain, and I receive it like a blessing. I lean against the rowan in the hillside, to watch the villagers come and go. I tend the cattle with Calder. I sit on the slope below the fields and study the paths of the glittering stars. I journey to the shore to bid farewell to Llyr and Murdoch as they sail into the Blue Sea, Gormára. I stand on the western edge of the world while the wind whips salt into my hair and the sea birds cry. The waves hurl salt mist into my face, and, thirsty as I am, the taste is good on my tongue.

I think on tombs and enemies and captives. I consider the wisdom of the ancestors and the mystery of balance. In fancy, I pass the bright gates of the Many-Colored Land. I remember the pleas of the voices in the pit. Yet always, undergirding every thought, is that fierce light, more ancient than ancient. I do not know what is happening to me.

One morning, while the sky is gray and cool, Barra comes to the hut. The force of his knocking jolts me from sleep. But he is not angry. His brows are knitted, his face troubled. He motions for me to follow him.

He leads me through the blackthorn grove, to the fields. The oats are ripening, and their heavy heads begin to droop. We pass them and go on to the barley fields. Even in this light, I can see that the stalks are yellowing. The long, thin leaves are splotched with brown. Barra stands at the edge of the field and takes a spike of barley from the stalk. He extends his hand and shows me the kernels. They are black, with a thin, whitish fur between them. I step into the field, cupping other spikes in my hand, checking here and there. They are all the same.

"The whole field?" I ask.

Barra sighs. "At least the oats do better in wet soil."

A whole crop of barley lost. I look up, searching the village for yellow blossoms. The last of the winter and spring gorse has faded, their blossoms weeping to the ground. The late gorse has not bloomed. I wonder if it will. If the creeping bog claims the gorse, we have no soap, nothing to nourish the soil, no bees, no honey, no fodder for the livestock.

"How many of the cattle will we slaughter at Newmoon?"

Barra passes his spear from his right to his left hand. He looks out toward the sea, then turns to me. "If there is no gorse, we will slaughter them all."

How long will that meat sustain us? With no barley, no

honey mead, just oats and berries and an ever-shrinking supply of salted meat. I read the same questions in Barra's face. Our time runs short. We have nowhere to go. What will be left of the Antae after another turning of the wheel?

"I will speak tonight, Barra. Will you prepare a fire?"

The chief's face brightens. He stands taller. "I will, Ollamh," he says, and bows to honor me. I remember Etain's look of adoration before my sojourn in the Tullagh Sé and Engl's searching gaze in the hut. What do they see in me that gives them hope?

I take a sip from the bucket in the hut. The fosterlings have replenished it with a little rainwater. I eat nothing, carry nothing, wear no cloak. I hurry along the western edge of the first hill, heading north toward the cave where Corann took me as a boy.

A short journey brings me to the opening. It faces northward, away from sunrise and sunset. There is a pile of stones near the entrance. I carry several loads inside, and stack the stones across the opening. Row on row, all the way up, walling myself in. When the last stone is wedged in place, I take my tunic from my shoulders. I tuck the edges of the cloth into the gaps in the uppermost stones.

Now the cave is black. The air is close, musty. I settle myself in a familiar spot, though I feel nothing of my boyhood fear. I have come with a purpose—to receive a sacred Word. I close my eyes (a foolish action, but one of habit) and descend into a state of quiet. My body is calm, relaxed. My mind is clear. I am hoping to capture something of the presence I felt at the summer solstice. If I can give this ancient, vital, pulsing, blazing stillness to the people of Blackthorn, perhaps, as Corann says, we can set the world back in its courses. Perhaps we can avert calamity.

But the hours pass, and my thirst makes itself known. The dark in the cave grows deeper, more settled. The light eludes me. No Word comes. I begin to wonder if this presence is so ancient that even the old ways cannot touch it. Perhaps it does not come to the inner groves. Perhaps it cannot be contained in sacred words.

Hours pass. The cave is close and hot. Sweat beads on my forehead and stings my eyes. It coats my chest and arms and gathers at the backs of my knees. I feel a rising panic. What am I to say when I stand before the fire tonight? Barra will have already spread the word. Does the fire already burn? I yank my tunic from the mouth of the cave and pull it over my head. I push through the wall of stones. Outside, the sun is setting. The western horizon burns. Behind me, in the east, the stars are rising.

I hurry to the hut. My first thought is of water. I raise the bucket to my lips and drink, blessing the fosterlings as the rainwater revives me. I wrap myself in the swan-feather cloak and take the gold branch. At the last moment, I remember the dirty cave, the long day's vigil. I dip the corner of my tunic in the water bucket and run the cloth over my face to clean it.

I close the door behind me and walk through the grove. The gold bells tinkle, announcing my arrival. I do not know what I will say. Bard of Blackthorn, Master of History, Ollamh, Keeper of the Word. What word can I give?

Barra has built the bonfire near the barley fields. He stands at the head of the fire, tossing the diseased barley into the flames along with the wood and peat. Calder is there, standing at Shannan's shoulder. Engl has the baby in her lap. Sloane has come, and the fosterlings. Llyr and Murdoch are back from the sea. They sit beside Deirdre and Muriel. Corann sits on a stone and leans forward on the handle of his walking stick. Zinerva sits under a blackthorn tree, her owl perched in the branches. Her look is suspicious, and full of questions.

I move to Barra's place at the head of the fire. Those who were standing are seated. They look at me, all of them, waiting for a word of hope. I glance again at Zinerva. What does she know of the coming calamity, of the Bloodmoon? What has she foreseen? She cannot know everything. But she knows more than I. Something about lovers, another set of lovers. Not Arlan and Meréd, but . . .

*NOT SO MANY YEARS PAST, when the water was sweet and the fields in flower, when the chiefs of the tribes met in feasting and celebration and the days were full of dancing, there was a man of the Shí called Dughall.*

I do not know this story. This is no recitation, for the words do not spring from memory. They rise to my tongue the moment before I speak them.

*Meréd's daughter, Branna, and Boyd of the Fir Bolg had made a home in the Many-Colored Land. For their children, the Shí, it was a realm of delight. Yet Dughall was restless. In the towering mountains and sprawling forests of the Many-Colored Land, he found nothing to marvel at. In the faces of the women of the Shí, he descried no beauty. He had heard of the charms of Meréd, of Arlan's passion for her, and he longed to look on the women of the Antae.*

*Now the Fir Bolg had made peace with the Antae. They'd sworn that they and their descendents would never again set foot on the soil of Baileléan. But Dughall knew of the gate, the door that opened but once in the year, and he cared nothing for the promises of his fathers. At Newmoon he seized his chance. He passed through the door and found himself at the summit of a hill. Not far off, beyond the cover of the trees, the hill was bare, and the stars shone.*

*Dughall set out in search of the Antae. He left the hill and found his way to a village built in the shadow of a ridge of white stone. The people were gathered for the celebration of Newmoon. Dughall crept to the drystones as the fire burned and watched while the rites were performed. A woman of the Antae caught his eye. She was fair as the Shí and fairer, and when she removed her blackthorn crown and flung it into the sacred fire, Dughall was inflamed with love. When the sun rose on the first day of the year and the door to the Many-Colored Land shut fast, Dughall did not return to the Shí. He had made up his mind to win her.*

*The woman's name was Iona, daughter of the village blacksmith, and well she knew the tale of Arlan and Meréd. At first sight of Dughall's face, she trembled, and the fear of death fell upon her. But it is a hard thing for a mortal woman to resist the wooing of the Shí. In time, Iona forgot her fear. She forgot everything but her consuming love for Dughall, and he, his consuming love for her.*

I cannot help but look at Muriel's face. It shines in the firelight, and there is a wonder and an eagerness in her eyes that I would like to drink up. Apart from Zinerva, whose eyes are lit with malice, the villagers look on in amazement. For though I do not see into the coming days, I am looking into a past that was hidden from us. Even now, I do not know the end of the tale. The words come as I draw breath, no sooner.

*Iona's father was not glad of this new lover. Morning and evening he warned her against Dughall. He took to hiding scraps of iron under her bedroll, in the hem of her peplos, the soles of her boots. The poor blacksmith feared the power of the Shí and he feared to lose his daughter. But a man must eat and ply his trade. He could not be watchful every moment.*

*So it happened that Iona came to be with child. Since the blood of the Shí ran in the child's veins, and since Dughall could not bear to be parted from Iona, he risked the wrath of the king of the Fir Bolg. He waited until*

*Newmoon, when Iona was heavy with child, and again he seized his chance. He hurried to Artek and made his appeal, and Artek's heart was moved within him. He remembered Arlan's love for Meréd, and the terrible consequence of his treachery. Artek's anger and hardness had cost his son's life, and he had no wish to cause such grief again. He granted Dughall leave to bring Iona and the child into the Many-Colored Land, to dwell among the Shí.*

*Dughall hastened back through the gate and down the hill to the place where Iona was waiting. The sky was dark. Thick clouds sat low, like the lid on a pot. On the edge of the horizon, a red moon rose. Lightning lit the curving black hollows of the storm clouds, and the air crackled with dark magic. Dughall took Iona's hand and led her up the hill, but by then she was near to delivering. Her pains came, slowing their climb, and Iona was very weak.*

*At the summit, she fell down and cried out. Dughall knelt beside her and called for help—from the Shí, from the Antae—but his voice was lost on the storm wind. Iona bled, and the soil drank her blood, and Dughall cried the more.*

*When the child came, it was bluish and still. It made no sound. While Dughall held the babe in his hands, Iona passed into death, and in his terrible grief, Dughall determined to follow her. He searched the satchel she had carried with her, knowing the blacksmith's ways. He hoped to find a scrap of iron sharp enough to end his suffering. Instead he found a little iron charm fashioned in the ogham sign for oak. It was useless, and Dughall flung it away.*

*The night was far spent. Dughall's time was short. He lifted Iona in his arms and carried her body to the realm of the Shí. The child he left behind, thinking it dead.*

I pause in the telling. The blood pounds in my head.

The captive.

*But a promise had been broken. The children of the Fir Bolg had trespassed on the soil of Baileléan. And the Veiled One, drunk on the blood of new sacrifice, seized her chance. This was the seat of her power, and the sun had not yet risen. She took up the forgotten ogham charm, spoke the words of an ancient curse, and thrust the iron into the soil. It came up, a small shoot. Its trunk grew wide and its branches climbed while lightning split the sky. Roots plunged deep into the belly of the hill while a red moon set.*

*So a tree of iron barred the door to the Many-Colored Land. And none could contend with it.*

There is not a sound from the people of Blackthorn. The settling of the fire, the hiss of the flames, the sigh of the wind—these are the only sounds. Zinerva's face has changed. She wears a look, almost, of satisfaction. If the blackthorn were a gilded throne, she could look no more queenly. I do not know what victory she has gained. Nor do I know what victory I have gained. To unravel a mystery is a sacred undertaking, and I have done it. But I am not one step closer to freeing the captive. The door to death stands open, and my people have no hope.

I turn from the fire and leave the villagers with their silence and their questions.

# 23

In the following days I watch Zinerva. I have feared her as the enemy of Blackthorn, and all Baileléan. I have seen her as the Hand of Death, the Mouthpiece of Death, for those who come to her find only despair—in poisonous words and poisonous leaves. But it is they who come to her.

Llyr and Murdoch return from a voyage with news of chaos at the ring-fort of Rathroe. They say the people murmur against the Druid of Rathroe, that they clamor for a word from the one who has conquered death. We are not the only ones who watch the turning of the wheel, who fear the coming Bloodmoon. Murdoch says they met a fisherman at Beltrá who told them of failed barley crops up and down the western coast. In Seaswell, Eyebright, Bolghrain, Kilveagh, and Moy Catha, the oats, too, rotted in their stalks. Only a few villages will reap any harvest at all.

The Antae look on the blight and the bitter water, and there they find the supreme enemy.

If the water was sweet . . .

If the Adder was cleansed . . .

If the land was restored . . .

But if tomorrow the water ran clean, if the bog dried up and the fields yielded increase, if not a man of the Antae suffered hunger or thirst, still we would walk the path of death. If Clodagh and Zinerva were swallowed by the sea, if the Crone left the Tullagh Sé and never returned, still the dark of the Underworld would yawn before us.

Corann comes and goes. He looks at me strangely, as though his thoughts are unsettled. I do not think he despises me, for Corann is not a jealous man. But he has haunted the sacred groves. He has eaten the salmon of knowledge. Yet I receive the vision and the Word. It must chafe.

He will not abandon the old ways, not when he has held to them so faithfully, not when he has spoken with Perth. I catch him gazing toward the east, and I know he is thinking of the door, the hill. The world before the Bloodmoon was Perth's world. But in seeking to restore it, Corann hopes in vain. He asks the wrong question.

There is balance in day and night, in summer and winter. I do not know if that is good. We live some years in the light of the sun. We work and love and weep and dance. Then we go down to darkness. There is a kind of balance in that. But I want none of it.

Zinerva rises from the seat of death and sits on the capstone of the portal tomb. She delivers the message of the mighty warrior, Madigan. She savors the words as she speaks them. We must embrace Death, she says, as a friend, as a lover.

But Death is the great enemy, the last enemy.

I would wish that Death could die.

In that, there is no balance.

In the days before the harvest celebration, I work in the fields with Barra and Calder and Deirdre and Muriel. Sloane has come, and Etain follows, walking slowly. She is pale. Her wounds are partly open, and the skin around them is tinged with red. But she is up and moving, and it seems certain now that she will recover. She stands on the edge of the field with Deirdre and Muriel while the men cut the stalks of oats and load them into sacks. We pass the sacks to the women, who tie them shut and beat them with mallets. Muriel and Deirdre leave most of the tying to Etain, I notice, while they bring the mallets down onto the sacks with a will.

I have one row to myself. Calder works at my left, humming as he goes. Sloane is to my right, and Barra beyond. We come to the end of the field and start again, claiming new rows, cutting and bagging, handing our gleanings to Deirdre and Muriel.

The fosterlings come mid-morning and bring their bucket of rainwater. We are glad of the drink and the chatter.

"You didn't bring me a bluebell," Pixie says.

I laugh. I had forgotten her request. "I couldn't find one," I reply.

"I liked your story," Vaughn says. "I never heard that one before."

"Nor had I," I say.

Vaughn's jaw hangs slack. His eyes are large as gulls' eggs. "Do the Shí look like us?" he asks.

"Much like," I reply, remembering how I turned my eyes from the captive. "But brighter, harder."

He gives me a serious look and nods understanding.

"Is it true we're the only village with a harvest?" Brennan asks.

He's overheard conversation among the villagers. The news Llyr and Murdoch brought has weighed heavy on everyone.

"I do not think so, Brennan."

He studies my face. If he were older, I would warn him against incredulity. It is a weighty offense to question the word of the ollamh.

"Off with you," Barra says. He thanks them for the water and shoos them from the field.

We take up our scythes and continue, stopping at midday to chew handfuls of the oats and sip a little water. The harvesting is finished before sunset, though the winnowing remains to be done. I glance at Deirdre as we leave the field, wondering when her anger will cool, but she refuses to look my way. Her white forehead has burned in the sun. Muriel is not so pale as Deirdre, but her face is bright as well, whether from exertion or sun I can't say. I long to run the tips of my fingers across her forehead and over her temples, to push the damp hair from her face. The foxglove amulet hangs in the hut. I took it off when the days grew so warm that I no longer wore a cloak. I was embarrassed, afraid she might see me wearing it and guess my heart. Is it possible she does not know it?

In my dreams, I see Deidre and Muriel. They stand with hands clasped, on the shore of the blue sea. They are not the same, and they are. The wind tosses their hair, and between them the strands mingle—Deirdre's brown and Muriel's gold.

I rise to waking, ashamed that thoughts of a woman should so consume me when the Bloodmoon approaches.

There is a faint glow from the fire, the familiar stink of peat. I hear a voice at the window. It is low, scarcely a whisper. I wonder if Engl has exhausted her store of blackthorn tea. I turn on my bedroll and look out.

The stars are eclipsed by a face, by broad, ridged horns of black. A summons rasps through long, pointed teeth.

"Come away, Idris. Come away."

I turn and whisper. "Corann." He stirs and pushes himself up. He squints at me. I turn to the window, but the puka is gone. There is nothing there. Only a glittering belt of stars girding the endless dark.

Next morning, I hear another voice at the window. It shocks me from a troubled sleep. I gasp and startle, plunging the fingers of my left hand into the embers.

Sloane watches me. "You didn't hear my knock," he says. I look over at Corann's place. His bedroll is against the wall, and he is gone.

"What is it?" I ask.

"Etain."

I search the shelves for the bottle of primrose oil, but Corann has taken it. Or it has run out.

"Please," Sloane says. I abandon any thought of breakfast and follow him to his cottage.

Etain lies on the floor. There is no color in her skin. Her breathing is so shallow, I can scarcely discern any movement of her chest. I look at Sloane.

"Yesterday she was well, or near enough."

"I know. She spoke of the winnowing before she slept." His voice wavers, catches. "I cannot wake her."

I touch the skin around the wounds on her forehead. It burns. The blackthorn poison rages through her body. No primrose salve will save her.

I look again at Sloane. The horror of death is on his face. His eyes are pools of sorrow. The tears spill over. "Please, Ollamh," he whispers.

She is too far gone. She slips into darkness. Fast now she falls. I set one hand on her burning head, one on her chest. If only I could interrupt the fall, stop her descent. If only the light that caught hold of me could catch her, too.

I feel a strange warmth in my hands. A profound calm settles over me. It is bright, living. It laps against the darkness like a rising tide. Every moment there is more light, every moment more life. It crowds out the dark until there is no room to fall.

Etain opens her eyes. Sloane makes a sound, a strangled cry. My hands fall to my lap.

Etain sits up. "Ollamh," she says. She lowers her chin to her chest, slowly, in a sign of extreme deference. When she lifts it, the look of adoration has returned.

Sloane squeezes into the narrow space beside her, taking her face in his hands and kissing both her cheeks. He weeps and laughs for joy.

I go and stand by the door. I do not know what has happened. What have I done? I study my hands, turning them over, searching for markings, changes. There are none. The fingers of my left hand are pink, still singed from the morning's clumsiness. They are unaltered, but it is as if these hands are no longer mine.

Sloane and Etain come around the fire. They do not touch me, but they are eager to show their gratitude. They offer the last of their oats, their water bucket, a stack of peat. I refuse them. I do not know how to receive their thanks. Etain is well and whole. There are no puncture wounds along the line of her dark hair. But I have done a small thing. I have only raised my hand against the coming flood and spared Etain a few brief moments of life.

They release me at last, and I run from the cottage to the broad stone on the slope west of the fields. I stretch out on its solid warmth and sigh until my body eases into its bed. The morning sky is clotted with clouds. Some are lit by the rising sun, and these are jeweled, ornamented with gold. Others are dull and gray. They pack the western sky and hold the heaving sea in check.

Corann would read the clouds. He would make a study of the shining ones, the dark ones, how they glide through the upper world. That is the old way. For hundreds of years, Perth sat in sacred groves, teaching the mantic works and the lore of trees. Was there truth in any of it?

I have no strength for great questions now. The clouds are my covering, the rock my bed. The distant roar of the ocean lulls me to sleep.

I wake to the drumming of oats. Deirdre and Muriel have begun the winnowing. Etain is with them. It surprises them when I sit up on the stone and turn their way. They pause, make a slight bow in my direction, and carry on. I do not know what Etain has told them, but whatever it was, it does not slow their work. Deirdre dumps a sack of beaten oats into a bucket on the ground. She holds the sack high, so the wind has time to catch the chaff and blow it away before the oats reach the bucket. Muriel pours the grains from the bucket onto a cloth. She stretches it taut between her fists and jerks it. The grains pop into the air and fall back onto the cloth, while the wind takes the last of the chaff. Etain takes the grains from Muriel's bucket and pours them into smaller sacks, to be distributed among the villagers. It is not the easiest of the three tasks, for the buckets are heavy and any spilled grains must be found and returned to the sacks. There can be no waste.

Etain shows no sign of fatigue. She works as quickly as the others.

I sit in wonder and watch. The winnowing is beautiful. The girls raise their white arms and the golden grains fall. The wind stirs their hair and carries the chaff to the ends of the earth. On and on it goes. The grains fall like rain, and the wind blows.

CORANN HAS ASKED ME TO MAKE THE WHEEL for the harvest celebration. It cannot be made from blackthorn. That is a mercy. But the rowans are scraggly, and I do not like to break branches from the ash. I walk the village and the surrounding land, studying the gorse, searching for branches sturdy and flexible enough to make the wheel.

The summer is passing. The slopes should be bright with yellow blossoms. But the winter and spring gorse have faded. Their branches are brittle. The smaller, late-blooming gorse has not blossomed. I stoop beside a plant no higher than my knee. Mud oozes over my boots. This plant has a few drooping leaves, but not one bud. I squeeze the stem where it disappears into the soil. It is soft, spongy. I give it a tug, and the whole bush comes out of the ground. Its roots hang limp.

The bitter water has changed the soil. The bog devours the good, green land. The late gorse will not bloom.

On the eve of the harvest celebration, the banshee's cry rides the winds of the Tullagh Sé. My thoughts return to the captive, and I wonder what song she sings tonight. I am comforted to know that she is one of the Shí. She is heartier and more fierce than any of the Antae. But I have given the oath, and I begin to think my time runs short.

I make the wheel out of the brittle branches from the spring gorse. I feared the spongy branches of the late gorse would not burn, though they would have been easier to shape. It is hard to weave a smooth circle with branches determined to snap and splinter.

Barra comes to the hut to talk of preparations. He is nervous about the harvest celebration. The very thought of theft runs so contrary to the ways of our people that he thinks it unlikely any of the attendants would steal our oats. But with so many failed harvests, men grow desperate. Barra would not build a ring-fort around Blackthorn to keep the Antae out. I stand with him. We are part of our people. Our fate is theirs. Would we add battle and bloodshed to plague and blight?

Corann says little, either to me or to Barra. He has not asked me about Etain. Nor has he spoken of the summer solstice or the Bloodmoon. I do not know what thoughts occupy his mind. It may be he has heard the rumor that the Druid of Rathroe comes to Blackthorn. It is a troubling rumor. What would cause the Druid of Rathroe to leave the safety of his ring-fort? Has their spring run dry? Does he come to stir up strife?

I spread my bedroll and go out for a chunk of peat. The air is balmy, and the sloe are ripening on the blackthorns. I am looking over the grove, my mind whirling with thoughts of the coming day, when I see her. Engl stands in front of the stile. As always, the baby is in her arms, covered with a cloth.

I cannot think why she hesitates. I do not mind making the tea. I motion for her to come in. She comes closer. I reach for the latch, and she stops me. There is something in her face I have not seen before.

"Ollamh," she says. The word is almost a question. She cups one hand behind the baby's head and the other behind his back. She extends her arms, holding the child out to me. I shake my head. She has not come for tea.

"Please, Ollamh," she says.

I want her to leave. I want to send her away with a pot of blackthorn tea. She cannot ask this of me. I cannot heal. Whatever it was that cured Etain, it was not me.

"I will give anything you ask."

No! Give me nothing. For I can promise nothing. This power does not come at my call. I cannot control it. Do not ask this!

*Once*, Deirdre said.

*You have tried once.*

"I do not know what I can do for the child. Let me make the blackthorn tea."

Engl's shoulders sink. In her eyes I see the weariness of countless vigils in the flickering light of the candlepot. I see cauldron after cauldron after pot after cup of blackthorn tea. I see fevers that come without warning or reason. I see three babies buried in the portal tomb. I have nothing to offer, yet how can I refuse?

I take the baby in my hands. My movements are stiff. I fear I will harm him before I begin.

What am I thinking?

Begin what?

I look into the child's eyes. He looks back. It is not a weak, wandering gaze. It is fixed, intent. I shift him so his back rests along my left forearm. Now my right hand is free. I run the backs of my fingers over his small cheeks. They are red, splotched from fever. His chin is tiny, a soft hill of pink flesh beneath a wet, red mouth. I run the edge of my thumb over his lips, and he twitches. He opens his mouth, tries to raise his head toward my thumb. I pop it into his mouth and he sucks with surprising force. I laugh at the odd sensation.

What did I do for Etain? I made no conscious choice, performed no rite. I touched her, and something went out of me. Yet what came out I did not call. I cannot control it. It answers to none of the old ways. What can I give to this tiny boy?

The pull on my thumb intensifies. The baby sucks as though he draws honey from my fingertip. He drinks until the sensation is unpleasant. But what is there to drink? When I start to remove my thumb, he opens his mouth and lets it go.

I don't know what to say, how to admit defeat to this weary mother. I take the baby in both hands and give him back to her.

"I'm so sorry, Engl. I would take his fever if I could."

She ignores me and studies the baby. She lifts his wrappings and examines his body. She presses her cheeks to his, right to right and left to left. She puts her mouth to his forehead in a lingering kiss. She looks into his eyes.

She looks at me in disbelief, in wonder.

Then she lowers her head and breathes a single word. "Ovate."

A thrill of fire, of fear, runs up my spine. I raise my hand to stop her speaking. She must not say such a thing. She must not question the power and position of the Ovate of Blackthorn.

She glances over her shoulder, toward Zinerva's cottage. I know she understands my warning.

She lowers her head and repeats the word softly. "Ovate."

She sets the child against her breast and turns, climbing the stiles with careful steps and returning to the cottage where the candlelight flickers in the window.

By sunrise, the village is surrounded. Ten times fifty visitors, more. They gather in groups or spread sheepskins on the slope. Some of them poke at the rank soil of the barley fields. Others, knowing nothing of sloe, pluck the berries and put them in their mouths and spit them on the ground. They will not sweeten until after the first frost.

Corann has cleaned and aired his black robes. But there is no primrose oil, not a drop, with which he can anoint himself. He was snappish this morning. When I offered him breakfast, he only said, "Where is the wheel?" I sent him to the place outside the hut where I had propped it against the yew staves that hold the history of our people. He came back a moment later and declared it was gone. I searched through the crowds and found nothing. Until I saw the wheel rolling along one of the drystones near Barra's cottage. The fosterlings. It was difficult to convince them to surrender it. They thought that a vital component of a sacred rite could be their plaything for a few hours yet. But Corann has it now, and he can spend the day in preparation.

I walk among the people, picking up scraps of conversation. Most of them do not know my face, and I do not carry the gold branch, so they speak freely. The talk is of poor fishing, failed crops, vanishing gorse. The blight has reached its final stages, and there is scarcely a habitable piece of ground in Baileléan. Many of the people talk of slaughtering the cattle at Newmoon. There will be little or nothing to feed them through the winter, so it must be done.

I move from group to group, passing circles of men in bright tunics and bunches of women in peplos in faded hues of blue and red and yellow. All their talk runs along the same course. They come to the slaughtering at Newmoon and bump up against the unknown. They grow silent, fidgety. They make predictions about the Bloodmoon.

"The moon will run red with the blood of the cattle," some declare.

"It is our blood that will flow," others say.

Then, in whispers, with hasty sidelong glances, they talk of The One Who Conquered Death. They ask about her appearance, hoping to catch a glimpse of her. They wonder if she has received any new word from the ancestors.

"Will it be Perth this time?" they ask. "Or Weylin of the Shield?"

Some make bold enough to ask whether or not she will speak during the rites of harvest. Of course no one can answer that question, but there are whispers here and there, little reassurances that the Ovate of Blackthorn will preside at the Newmoon ceremonies this year.

Zinerva will preside at the celebration of Bloodmoon.

Strange that the thought does not frighten me. Had I heard the Antae speak these words at Snowmelt or the spring equinox, I would have been afraid. Now I wonder why no one sees Death as the enemy. Once we were a thriving, audacious people. Now we talk of the weather and wait for our end.

He does not appear until the fires are lit. If he meant his arrival in Blackthorn to cause a stir, he has succeeded. The Druid of Rathroe wears black robes. He strides to the ceremonial fire.

Corann pauses. I think every man in Blackthorn holds his breath. I have never seen two druids share the performing of the rites. Is this how it was done in the years before the Bloodmoon? Druids are not men of war, but this seems a dangerous game.

Something happens in the space between the two men, in the firelight between the black robes. It feels akin to waves crashing on shore, or storm clouds colliding. The fires are dimmed by the disturbance. They falter, hesitate. Then Corann steps aside. The Druid of Rathroe begins the rites. The fires leap behind his upraised arms.

No. This is not as it should be. Why does the druid not perform the rites at the ring-fort? Why should he come to Blackthorn and usurp Corann's authority? I am not the only one who is angered. Barra stands on my right hand, clenching his spear with such ferocity that I fear he will splinter the shaft.

Others, too, are uncertain. They have not seen this done. The comfort of ritual has been superseded, replaced by questions and doubt.

Partway through the rite the Druid of Rathroe makes a small gesture to Corann. He steps aside, and it looks as if he means to share the ceremony, to divide the performance of the rites equally. I feel the easing of tension, the muffled release of sighs. Hundreds of the Antae watch while Corann offers thanks to the earth, lifting a handful of precious grains and dropping them into the ceremonial fires. Am I the only one who wonders if this is the last harvest celebration?

Corann makes the signs in the earth. He takes the wheel in hand. In a moment he will light it and send it tumbling down the slope toward the sea. It symbolizes the turning of the year, the descent toward darkness.

But the Druid of Rathroe stops him. Corann holds the wheel in one hand, a flaming branch in the other. The Druid of Rathroe steps in front of him and speaks.

"Three times I have seen a vision," he says. "I saw it first in the clouds, and second in a spring of clear water. And because I was troubled in mind and body, I sought to confirm the vision by wearing the skin of the white bull."

I did not know they had a white bull skin at Rathroe. The ancients thought it a great aid in divination. What has he seen?

"I have seen the coming of doom," he says, "a fiery descent into a pit of darkness. We, the Antae, have endured war and flight. We have battled the Fir Bolg, and they have fled from our swords and spears. We have seen days of prosperity. We have feasted like gods on the good of the land, and our songs will endure till the end. But our time is passed. Eighteen years and more we have watched the river poison our people, watched the bog devour our farmlands. Now the last crops fail, and the last of our cattle go to slaughter."

He raises his staff and points it at Zinerva. She stands quietly among the blackthorns, watching him.

"Through the Ovate of Blackthorn, the ancients have spoken. Madigan, Hero of a Hundred Battles, urges us to embrace our end. He has found peace, he says, in the dark and quiet of eternity." The Druid of Rathroe tosses his staff into the fire and takes the wheel from Corann's hand. "The Druid of Blackthorn means to keep to the ancient ways. He would light this wheel and send it rolling to the sea. In that, he is blameless. The year descends, it is true. But we all descend. Those who remain must find the courage to hear the word of the ancients, to descend to the Underworld and find peace beneath the soil of Baileléan."

He thrusts the wheel into the ceremonial fire. It catches. He raises it high so that everyone can see. Then he brings it down around his head. It is just wide enough to wrap his shoulders. His black cloak catches fire.

We stand frozen, horrified. The Druid of Rathroe walks to the blackthorn grove. He passes Zinerva and vanishes among the trees. I turn, searching for Corann. He follows the Druid of Rathroe, but slowly. Who can oppose the druid, or stop him in his path? He is no less than a king among men.

I push through the crowd and follow Corann into the grove. It is not hard to find the Druid of Rathroe. He burns with furious light. He is a pillar of fire. We follow him to the clearing, where he crawls inside the portal tomb. Flames leap from his cloak and blacken the capstone. The silence is the worst of it. There is nothing but the roar of the fire. No one speaks. No one weeps. We watch while his body shudders and stills.

I spot Zinerva in the crowd. Did she choose to be the Mouthpiece of Death? Her words drove the Druid of Rathroe to madness. How many others hold those words in their thoughts? How many others begin to envision their descent? The Druid of Rathroe called it courage. He was mistaken. This stinks of despair.

Corann cannot complete the rites. There is no wheel to roll down the slope. I do not think anyone notices. Some approach the capstone to watch the fire burn out. Others return to the ceremonial fires to watch them die. Every eye is wide, every mouth agape. No one speaks.

Night has fallen on the Antae, the last remnant of the mighty race that once dwelt in Tír Ársa. Our eyes are darkened. The road to death stretches wide before us. And the door stands open.

A PROFOUND SILENCE SETTLES OVER THE PEOPLE of Blackthorn. I can only imagine that the others who attended the harvest celebration carried the silence home to their villages as well. We are suspended in a waiting dread. No one hums or whistles. No one gathers in the pastures to talk of the weather or the cattle or the autumnal equinox. The air ripples with the last blast of the summer heat. There is never enough rain. Last year's supply of salted beef runs out. And the wheel turns.

In the mornings, I walk the blackthorn grove. Three times nineteen tortured trees. Trees that remind us of the necessity of death. I wait for them to convince me. So far, they have failed. I see waxy green leaves and ripening berries. I see life forcing its way out in season after season, conquering heat and snow. I see white blossoms opening to shield us from thorns. *The tree is our supreme teacher.* So says Perth. So say the old ways. Are they wrong about everything? Was there any truth they understood?

Zinerva sets out from Blackthorn one morning with an empty satchel over her shoulder. She says she goes to gather herbs in the Tullagh Sé. Soon after, Barra requests a meeting with the druid and the ollamh. He begs to meet in secret, but Corann insists there is no need. When Barra arrives, Corann hangs a sheepskin over the window and passes a hand along the edges of the window and the door. Smoke-like tendrils curl from his fingers and cling to the wall. "No one will hear us," he says.

Barra wipes his brow with the back of his arm. With the windows blocked, the interior of the hut is stifling.

"I wonder if there is any way around the tradition of the ovate's presiding at Newmoon," he says. He shifts his weight, passing his spear to his left hand. In the small confines of the hut, he looks enormous, big enough to lift the roof with his shoulders. Yet his eyes are full of sorrow. I am reminded that he bears a burden not unlike mine and Corann's. He, too, loves his people and seeks their good. He, too, faces an impossible enemy. He is making a last effort to protect the people of Blackthorn. It is a futile effort.

Corann gives him a sharp look. "Why should the ovate not preside at Newmoon?"

Barra balks. Corann has seen everything he has seen, and the druid is no fool.

"What has the ovate done that we should strip her of her office?" Corann asks. He is not looking at Barra. He frowns at me. In his face I see anger and rebuke. "Zinerva completed her training, passed her initiation. She is Ovate of Blackthorn, and no other."

I cannot account for my actions. I did not set out to heal Etain or the child, but that matters little. I performed the office of ovate, and Corann is angered. Even now, even in this, he seeks to maintain the balance.

"What has the ovate done that we should strip her of her office?" Corann repeats.

I watch Barra as he opens his mouth to speak, as he closes it, as his eyes shift with the searching of his memory. He is finding nothing but whispers and rumors. I know. I have searched as well.

"But, the Bloodmoon," he stammers.

"The Bloodmoon comes," Corann says. "And it matters not who stands behind the portal tomb."

"Have we truly come to our end?" Barra asks.

Corann sighs. "The Druid of Rathroe is not the only one to see a coming calamity." He looks at the chief.

"You?" Barra asks. Corann is silent. He studies the ashes in the firepit. Barra turns to me. "Ollamh, what have you foreseen?"

"I have seen backward, Barra, not forward."

"But you have seen more than you tell."

"I see the Iron Oak," I reply. "It bars the gate to the Many-Colored Land and opens the door to the Underworld. I do not know if the tree can be reckoned with."

Corann shakes his head, spitting his reply. "We can no more challenge the Crone in the seat of her strength than we can make war with the moon."

I am quick to answer. "If that is so, then there is no escape from the coming doom."

Corann's shoulders slump. The sound of his sighing fills the hut.

Barra turns to me. "Can you not preside at the Bloodmoon, Ollamh?"

Corann stiffens. "He cannot."

Barra searches my face. His sorrow threatens to overflow. I can see it in his eyes. I can taste the bitter draught. "Can you heal Baileléan?" he asks.

Such words! Such a question! Can I heal Baileléan? I stand with my teeth clenched, staring at Barra. What answer can I give?

After a moment he nods. He squares his shoulders and raises his head. He is gathering himself to leave, without answers, without hope. He has a parting word, though. "Engl's boy is well, you know. She put him up on the drystone the other day and he sat tall and straight as a birch. He waved his arms, laughed. The fosterlings can't get enough of him." He watches me, making sure I have received his words. Then he turns and ducks through the doorway.

I am left alone with Corann. We have not spoken of Etain or Engl's child or the Druid of Rathroe. I am aching to speak with him, to lay out the fragments of my visions and discoveries and see if we two might piece them together. I am eager to hear his thoughts about the harvest celebration, the coming equinox, about Zinerva and the Bloodmoon. There was a time when I waited for him to speak to me as an equal. Now I long for him to speak as a father. I long for him to tell me what lies ahead and what part I must play in the coming days. I long for his assurance that some hope remains.

Corann, my father, what am I to do?

"Corann," I say. He yanks the sheepskin from the window and rolls it hurriedly. He does not look up.

"Please," I say. He takes his walking stick and goes to the door, and I do what I have not done, not ever. I reach out and touch his arm. The heat of his anger snaps against my fingers. I pull back.

The door slams shut behind him.

Every night, now, we hear the keening of the banshee. I wonder what befalls the Antae who dwell at Bolghrain and Beltrá and Moy Catha. What of those at Rathroe who saw their druid descend in flames? The puka returns, and not to my window only. Sloane tells of waking to hear the puka's call and rushing to the window to fight. The puka pulled him through the open shutter and flung him against a drystone. Sloane's head is wrapped in a bloody bandage. "I will not come away," he says. I like the fight in him.

Calder says he woke one night to find Shannan standing at the window with her mirror in her hand. She was leaning toward the puka, entranced by his call. "Come away, Shannan. Come away. Leave the weeping world behind." Calder took the mirror and coaxed her from the window.

Barra says the fosterlings can scarcely sleep for fear the puka will come to them. I wonder if it has called to Deirdre, to Muriel. I go to see them.

Deirdre is beating a pile of gorse. She raises the mallet over her head and brings it down with particular force. Is it because the gorse is brittle? Or is she angry? I miss her—the ease of her company, her keen insight into the workings of my mind and heart. She has seen hard years since she came to Blackthorn. How easy her days would have been if she had chosen to apprentice to Clodagh, as she had planned. Like Muriel, she chose the harder road.

I watch the working of her thin shoulders and arms. The edges of her peplos are damp with sweat. *I would take this blight if I could. I would drink up a river, an ocean, of bitter water, so that you could—*

Could what?

I wait until the mallet falls. I touch Deirdre's bare shoulder and turn her to face me. "What would you do, Deirdre, if there were no blight, no Bloodmoon?"

She blinks, and her brows come together. She opens her mouth as if to speak, then shakes her head. "Do not ask me, Idris. It is a cruel question."

Because there *is* a blight, because there *was* a Bloodmoon, because another Bloodmoon comes.

"You believe the vision of the Druid of Rathroe?"

"It is not his vision only," she says.

I cock my head to the side and search her face. Does she know of Corann's vision?

"*I* have seen the coming of doom, Idris. Etain has seen it. Shannan has seen it. Llyr has seen it. The fosterlings dream that the stars fall from the sky and the world is black and silent."

A long moment passes while the sounds of the village recede. It cannot be. Why have they not spoken?

"It is only you who has not seen the coming of doom. You, the Keeper of the Word, you who speak mysteries and heal the sick. You are bard *and* ovate. Will you perform the office of druid as well?"

"No! That is Corann's place."

"Corann has failed. He searches within the problem for the solution," she says.

"He will not abandon the old ways."

"He cannot, Idris. He knows no other way."

"Why should you imagine that I can do what Corann cannot?"

"You have received the sacred Word. You have unraveled the mystery of the lovers and the source of the bitter water. You have healed two who were dying."

"I have only slowed their journey to the Underworld. I have not delivered them from death."

"Then conquer Death!"

*Only Zinerva has conquered death.* That is my first thought. But it is not so. Zinerva has not conquered death. She has allied with it. Death is the true enemy, the last enemy.

Deirdre reaches out and grips my arm. Her voice is low, her eyes flaming. "The savage, unending hunger of the Fir Bolg was nothing to the hunger of the Crone. She will not be satisfied until all the upper world is devoured by darkness. And when earth and sea are swallowed by death, when the Crone herself is devoured, still Death will not be sated. Its hunger can never be satisfied."

There is no hesitation in Deirdre's voice. She is convinced of the truth of her words. So am I.

"What can I do against such a power?"

Her hand falls to her side. She sighs. "I have watched you, Idris. You are changed. You have seen something none of us has seen. Not the coming of doom. Something else."

I feel a great wave of loss, of sorrow. Why have I not shared my encounter with Deirdre? Why have I not made her understand? She sees the regret in my eyes.

"It's all right," she says.

We stand together in a sweet silence, unwilling to part. After a time, Deirdre wipes a smudge of dirt from my face and brushes bits of dry grass from my tunic. "Idris," she says, "what would you do if there were no blight, no Bloodmoon?"

My eyes dart to the cottage.

"Go," Deirdre says. She gives me a little shove. "Don't waste another moment."

The door is open. Muriel is inside, but she has no task before her. She is not dyeing cloth or making soap or mending. She sits on the floor with her head against the base of the window and looks up at the sky. Her hands are folded in her lap. I savor the light, how it slants through the window and caresses the soft curve of skin beneath the line of her jaw. She startles and turns. She lowers her head, addresses me as "Ollamh," and hurries to stand.

"I am sorry to startle you."

We face one another across the fire pit. Neither of us knows quite where to rest our eyes, or what to do with our hands.

I fumble for a place to begin. "I never thanked you for the amulet," I say.

A quick smile passes over her face. A look of concern follows. "Zinerva has returned."

I wait, having no desire to turn my thoughts to the ovate.

"She works some mischief, Idris, in the Tullagh Sé."

I read the fear in her eyes, and my fear for the captive is rekindled. Corann believes no power can contend with the Crone, no sorcery unmake the magic of the Iron Oak. But I made the sacred oath. I have left the captive too long.

"Muriel—" I begin. She looks into my eyes, and I forget my words. I meant to say—

"Ollamh," she says. "You asked Deirdre what visions she saw when she met Clodagh in the grove."

"I did."

"You did not ask me."

I never thought to ask. Have I offended her? Is there something more I must know about the Crone? Muriel waits for my response. "No," I say.

"You know I first met Clodagh at Newmoon. She came to me in the grove and put her finger here." She presses a finger to the skin above her nose, between her brows. "Clodagh thought to see my mind, to know whether I would serve her well. But I also saw her mind."

I shudder. What evils lurk in the dark of Clodagh's mind? "What did you see?" I ask.

"I saw many things I cannot tell, many things I wish to unsee. But one thing I saw was you."

"Me?"

"Yes. I saw Clodagh's fear of you."

"I had not finished my training then. I was not yet the Ollamh."

Her brows come together in question. "What does that matter? It was not the bard she feared. It was Idris."

"Why should she fear me?"

"You have received the Word."

"No, I—" How can I tell what I have received? It has not gathered itself into a word that I can speak. I do not know if it can. My doubt and confusion must be written across my brow, because Muriel makes a reply. She speaks no words, but what I see in her eyes unravels me.

Barra asks if I can heal the land as well as the people. Deirdre asks me to conquer death. She would not urge me on if she did not believe it could be done. And from the look in her eyes, Muriel believes as Deirdre does.

I have wished it. I have tossed my words into the wind like so much chaff. But I have not asked the question. My friends and my beloved, they have led me to it—the question above all questions, the one that *must* be asked and answered.

Can Death be conquered? Can Death die?

The look of hope on Muriel's face is more than I can endure. Oh, can ecstasy and despair ride the same wave? I fear that they will crush me. My knees give way and I fall hard to the floor of the cottage. What am I to do? What have I to offer the captive or any of my people? Can a man armed only with words make war with the moon?

*Once*, Deirdre said. *You have tried once.*

Muriel skirts the fire pit as I rise to my feet. She takes my hands in hers. She turns them, brings them to her lips, and kisses my palms, one and then the other. Her hair falls against my wrists.

"Idris," she says. "Come back safe from the Tullagh Sé."

I CANNOT SORT OUT MY FEELINGS. I journey to Half-Bald Hill, to the place of my greatest terror. This time, I know what darkness awaits me and how great is the task before me. No, I deceive myself. I do not know how great the task. How is a man to conquer Death?

I pack my satchel with provisions, sling my bedroll over my shoulder, and tie the amulet around my neck. When I scale the first hill and pause to bask in the sunrise, I am reminded of the solstice, of the light, the force, that stopped my descent into darkness. That light is older than Death. I know it without knowing how. And Death will not outlast it. Of that, too, I am sure. I take comfort. I carry that light within me. I wear it like a garment.

I pass through groves of ash and birch and rowan, past flowering rhododendron where bees crawl on every blossom. My sense of the Many-Colored Land is strong. I long to journey there and walk among the Shí, to see what lies farther on. That realm is so near. I think I catch the scent of its pine woods, its wild roses, its salt seas.

I shelter in the cave where I saw the puka. He does not come to call me. Perhaps he is busy in the villages, peering in at the windows. On my fourth day in the Tullagh Sé, I hear the crying of the banshee, and another voice joins the lament. It is unmistakable. When the first voice trails off, the second echoes it and carries the cry farther into the night.

Every day the air grows cooler. The winds change. They blow the stagnant summer heat off toward the south. The haze clears, and the sky is a deeper, lovelier blue. The oak leaves begin to brown, and here and there, a birch leaf has brightened to gold. Ash and rowan are tinged with red.

I stop awhile at the ancient yew and sit in its shade. The same magic crackles beneath the branches, and I wonder if I will see visions. I spend an hour in meditation before I think better of it. This is the tree of memory, and there is no history to guide me now. I have moved beyond the boundaries of knowledge. I have left the old ways behind.

I come to Half-Bald Hill from the north. Perhaps it is weakness, a small comfort in the onrushing unknown. I could have tramped through the woods and groves on the western side of the hill. But I know what lies behind the broken door. I know the terror of the voices, the darkness of the tomb, the horror of the endless pit. There is no need to see that now.

I climb the hill, following the line of trees. Lizards dart and wriggle into the undergrowth and a hawk's cry sounds overhead. I stand on the summit and survey the green land to the east.

In the distance, the sea roars, its waters overlaid with a veil of glittering sunlight that stretches to the eastern end of the world.

Slowly, I make my approach. I do not want to startle her. I circle the tree, stepping over the larger roots and laying my pack against the smaller tree where I camped when last I came. The worn, circular paths are the same. A shallow stone bowl of dew and rainwater rests beside a little mound of berries.

I catch a glimpse of her. She must have been resting in the hollow of the trunk. Now she peers out, watching me. Strange that her beauty should astonish me again. I wonder if the Antae can ever grow accustomed to the hard brightness of the Shí. But then, Iona came to love the sight of Dughall's face, and she was not afraid. I feel my throat thickening toward tears. This woman has never known a mother's love or a father's care. She has known nothing but bondage and solitude. Somewhere on the other side of the gate, her father roams the glorious paths of the Many-Colored Land. Oh, that I could break her bond and fling wide the door!

She steps out of the hollow and stands. I smile at her and kneel down to my satchel. I have brought her a peplos and a cloak. I do not know what she will think of them. She is not ashamed of her nakedness, but she has never been among people. She has never owned a garment of any kind. Before I came to this place and gave her my sheepskin, she had not even a blanket to warm her. I take the garments from the satchel and smooth them. I walk to the base of the trunk, a few paces from her, and set them on the ground. I step back. She approaches, and I study her carefully as she picks them up, fingers the cloth.

Apart from the inflamed skin around her neck, there is no mark on her. If someone were to harm her, would there be any sign? If a blade cut her skin, would it leave a scar? Only if the blade were made of iron. But who could come near her? My last approach was repelled with such force, it stole the breath from my lungs.

She sets the garments inside the trunk. I return to the satchel and dig out a handful of oats. I set them on the ground, just as I did the clothing, and retreat. She pinches an oat between thumb and forefinger and sniffs it. Her actions are graceful, delicate. She puts a grain on her tongue and rolls it around in her mouth. She bites down and breaks it with a soft crunch. One by one, she puts the grains into her mouth and chews them and swallows. She seems content.

I sit against the tree and join her in a meal. The oats are sweet and nourishing. I chew them and sip from my water skin and wonder what path lies before me. What answers will I find on Half-Bald Hill that could not be found in the blackthorn grove? I have no sorcery that can unmake the Iron Oak. I have nothing but an encounter I cannot describe with a force for which I have no name.

I will wait awhile, a little while, and see what comes.

I wake to frost. The chilly morning air is bracing, a relief after the parching heat of summer. Back home, they may be harvesting the sloe. I think of their white hands, of the black thorns. Muriel will be in the grove with Deirdre. Sloane and Etain will come, and Calder and Barra. Perhaps Engl will join them now the baby is well. I wonder if Llyr and Murdoch have hung up their oars for awhile.

There were a few clusters of berries on the rowan trees, some brambleberries north of the village. They can begin to make the hedgerow wine. That will please the fosterlings, though this year's wine will not be sweet. Vaughn and Pixie were inconsolable when they found no honey in the bee tree. I saw no difference in Brennan's face. It bore its usual weight of sorrow.

"Where have the bees gone?" Pixie asked.

"They've gone to find the flowers," I replied.

"But where have the flowers gone?" Vaughn asked.

I didn't have the heart to answer him. The gorse is failing. There will be no honey mead. But at least there will be hedgerow wine.

A thought strikes me. It is so sudden, so unbearable, that the tears start in my eyes. Hedgerow wine takes some weeks to ferment. It will not be ready until after the Bloodmoon. If the people of Blackthorn have seen the coming of doom, will they take the trouble of harvesting the berries and making the wine?

*The savage, unending hunger of the Fir Bolg was nothing to the hunger of the Crone. She will not be satisfied until all the upper world is devoured by darkness.*

Two days I wait at the summit of Half-Bald Hill, while the captive uses the cloak and peplos for bedding and walks the worn paths under the branches of the Iron Oak. I search within the hollow of the tree for some sign of a door, a gate. I find nothing.

I receive no new visions, no answers, no sacred words.

The captive tugs at the iron band that wraps her neck. I had hoped to heal the raw, red skin, but I think the Shí can never bear the touch of iron. To heal her once would be futile. The tree must be destroyed. Anyway, she will not let me near her. I sit on the bare slope of the hill and watch the rising of sun and moon, the wheeling of the stars. I meditate on the story of Dughall and Iona. In my mind, I see the Bloodmoon, the storm clouds, the flash of lightning.

Like Corann, I seek for wisdom and understanding. Like Corann, I wait for answers. He seeks along the old paths, crossing and re-crossing them. But I know not where to seek. There are no paths to guide me.

One thing grows clear in my mind: If Clodagh or Zinerva or the Crone means to harm the captive, she will do it. But she will wait until the Bloodmoon. The spilling of such blood on the night of the Crone's greatest strength! I cannot fathom what such a sacrifice would mean, what power it would afford to the Keeper of Death's Door.

I must find a way before the Bloodmoon.

At the end of the two days' vigil, I bow to the captive and repeat the sacred oath. I shoulder my pack, and climb down the Sixth Hill.

The desolate village of Ban Lurgan is a grim sight. On my last journey, I fled from the tomb in such haste that I took no notice of it. Now I pause by the white ridge and pass my eyes over the collapsed roofs, the walls leaning askew, the drystones sinking beneath the murk. This is the fate of Blackthorn, if I do not find a way.

The journey along the Adder is unpleasant. Foul gases bubble from the mud, and the sodden ground sucks at my boots. After the fourth hill, I climb back into the Tullagh Sé and breathe the sweet fragrance of the groves. I come to the apple tree and find half a hundred red apples hanging from the branches. I take one and bite into it, but the skin gives too easily, and the flesh is brown.

I return to Blackthorn at the new moon, a little before the autumnal equinox. I am comforted to see that the sloe berries have been harvested. Most of them. As always, some are left for the birds. The celebration of the autumnal equinox takes place on the shore, so the villagers prepare for the half-day's journey. Corann keeps his thoughts closer than ever. If Zinerva is to preside at Bloodmoon, this is the last rite Corann will perform. The last rite before the coming of calamity.

I do not know if anyone will dance, but I tuck the eagle-bone flute into my satchel and tie the bodhrán across my shoulders. I pack some of the newly-harvested oats and a bit of rainwater. Deirdre comes to bring my share of the sloe, and when the morning of the equinox arrives, she and Muriel walk beside me on the journey to the sea.

Corann wears his white robes. His uplifted arms are dark against a magnificent sky. Fiery reds and molten golds follow close on the heels of the setting sun. Their train spreads behind us to the eastern horizon. As it goes, it darkens to deep purple, and its hem is pricked with stars.

There is a large company from Beltrá, which lies just north along the coast. I recognize the chiefs of Eyebright and Moy Catha. Many have come from Rathroe, and I wonder if they are remembering their druid while Corann performs the rites. I wonder how the druid's words have infected them. At the spring equinox, day and night were in balance, but the year moved toward a time of greater light. Day and night have found their balance again, but now we move toward darkness.

When the rites are concluded, I am surprised to see men and women pair off. A boy from Beltrá begins a rhythm on the claves. Another takes up his flute. I retrieve the bodhrán from where I left it a little way up the shore, and I join them in the song. The Antae circle the sacred fire and pound the sand and raise their skirts and clap their hands. There is a wildness to their dancing that is not like joy. The longer I watch, the quicker the rhythm, the more frantic the movements of the dancers. Their faces are flushed and damp. Their eyes are savage. They dance as though they will not dance again, as though all their passion, all their vitality, must be expended in this one night, around this one fire.

I am consumed with the bodhrán, enthralled with the spectacle of the dance. But shouts and cries interrupt the song. There is a disturbance on the shoreline. I leave the drum and push through the crowd. Murdoch stands in the water. The waves lap against his knees, and the firelight shines on the fishhooks threaded through his tunic. Sloane is further out, shouting at a man I do not recognize.

"Let her go!" the man roars.

Sloane wades deeper into the water. The man raises a huge, brawny arm and swings it at Sloane. He knocks him in the head, throwing him back. Sloane sinks under the water. That is when I see her. She is pushing against the tide, walking into the sea. Her long hair streams behind her, floating on the surface of the water. The pins at her shoulders catch a final ray of fading sunlight and sink beneath the waves. Her neck disappears. The circle of her head is cut in half, in quarters. She is gone.

Murdoch pulls Sloane to a stand. He puts an arm around him and helps him out of the water. The Antae stand on the shore, looking out at the darkening sky, at the sea, at death. The man walks solemnly from the ocean and joins his family—a wife, it looks to be, and a son.

The scene is illusory. It passes before me with a strange fluidity, an unnerving silence, like a dream or an imagined scene from history. Madigan raises the yew cudgel, while the currachs of the Fir Bolg pause on the crests of the waves. Perth binds Arlan with druidic fire, and the iron tip of Branna's spear sinks into his breast.

Yet the sea laps against my boots, and the wind stirs my hair. Behind me, the ritual fire burns. If I thrust my hand into the flames, it would be scorched.

Zinerva stands on shore, watching with the others. She is so still. But look! Look what her words have done! She need not worry herself with battle or conspiracy. Her presence, her being is enough. Like Death. Death makes no stir. Its arms are spread, its mouth is open. We struggle, we resist; or we run to meet it. It matters not, for the end is the same. Death holds the upper hand. Death speaks the final word.

*Then conquer Death.*

Murdoch drags Sloane to the shore and crouches over him. Etain kneels at his side, and I stand at his feet. Blood runs from a gash above Sloane's eye. It streams down his nose and cheeks.

"Bastard hit me right where I cracked my head on the wall," Sloane says.

When the puka pulled him out of the window, he means.

Etain dabs the cut with the edge of her cloak and tears a strip of cloth to wrap around his head.

"What happened?" I ask.

"I tried to pull her out!" Sloane says. His face is contorted with pain and fury. "He stood in my way. Said I would not insult her courage by stopping her."

"Who is he?"

"Her father," Murdoch replies.

"You know him?"

Murdoch nods, but his eyes are on the man and his family. "He's a fisherman. Lives at Rathroe."

Rathroe. "So she follows in the footsteps of the druid."

Murdoch and Sloane make no answer. They are watching the Antae. One by one, they turn from the western horizon and scatter. There is no more dancing, no sharing of food or drink. The people merely walk into the darkness.

"What will they do at Bloodmoon?" Sloane asks.

# 27

Now the cold comes in earnest, and the leaves of the blackthorns return to their sulfurous yellow. The sloe berries and brambleberries and rowan berries sit in their buckets, quietly souring. The fields are covered in frost. Wool cloaks cover bare, white arms and sunburned shoulders.

I have not forgotten what I saw, or what saw me, at the summer solstice. Beneath the sadness and foreboding, beneath the anxious thoughts that trouble me, there is stillness. It bears me up, and I cannot fall too far. I have a settled sense that when the time comes, I will know what to do. I have asked the ultimate question. It will carry its answer on its back. The path that lies before me has only to be lit, and I will follow it.

Llyr and Murdoch bring word of four deaths from yew and wild cherry. Three villagers have gone missing from Seaswell and two from Kilveagh. Those five disappeared in the night, and in both villages others saw the face of the puka at their windows and heard his haunting call.

*Come away, come away. Leave the weeping world behind.*

Madigan lied. Or Zinerva did. There is no quiet in the Underworld. I have heard the voices that fill that place. It is the Underworld that weeps and wails and begs for mercy.

The gorse is sparser than ever. Blackthorn no longer wears its covering of yellow blossoms, and the village I love no longer looks like home. What branches we can harvest are brittle and dry, and though Barra and I beat them with a vengeance, still the cattle are reluctant to eat.

I linger in the pastures with Calder. He rubs the cows' bony heads and pats their sides. I know he dreads the slaughtering, but he would not have the poor beasts starve. Any other year, we would wait until Newmoon to kill and salt the meat. But the fodder runs so low that we cannot delay.

I ask Calder if he would rather I do the job, but he refuses. He says there's no one they trust like him, that he ought to do it. It is quite an undertaking, though. We run ropes over the branches of the ash that grows by Calder's cottage. Calder slits the cows' throats, and we hoist them up and catch the draining blood in barrels. It is three days' grisly work to drain them all and cut them up. Then we salt the meat and give the hides to the women to clean and stretch.

When the task is finished, and the soggy little pastures hold nothing but a few sheep, Calder invites me to join him in his cottage. Shannan sits by the window, gazing into the polished brass face of her mirror. There is a tiny, faded blossom of gorse in her hair. It is wilted, and the cheerful yellow has browned at the edges. But I marvel that Calder found it, that he continues to search.

Calder steps to my side and speaks low. "It's not so much her beauty she pines after," he says. "It's the life we had. That's what she misses." He hands me a cup. I take a drink without thinking. It is sharp and very rich. Hedgerow wine.

His eyes twinkle over his round cheeks. "I always set my bucket in the sun. Moves things along."

I savor the drink, feeling foolish, childish. We come to the end, and I do not know if it is wisdom or madness that sweetens the wine.

"Calder," I say, "Muriel said that many of the villagers have seen visions of a coming calamity. She said Shannan was one of them."

Calder's face darkens. He leans against the door and sighs. "Yes. My Shannan has seen it."

"Are you frightened?" I ask.

Calder thinks a moment. "Not so frightened as I am of another Bloodmoon," he says.

Yes, that I understand. "There are some in Blackthorn who believe I can do something to stop the calamity."

I wait for Calder's bushy gray brows to rise. They stay put. He is not surprised by the thought.

"What have you seen?" he asks.

"Nothing yet," I reply. "Or nothing that is clear to me yet."

"So you've made no plan," he says. Does he voice his disappointment? Did he hope for more?

"No."

"It is a heavy burden to lay on such slight shoulders," he says. He puts a weathered hand on my shoulder and squeezes.

I had thought to stay awhile and eat, but, apart from the wine, Calder and Shannan have no more than I have—some dried berries and a few sacks of oats. I do not want to exhaust their store. So I say my farewells and walk along the slopes west of the village.

I am waiting for the Word.

Waiting.

Whatever wisdom or madness sweetened Calder's wine now sweetens my days in Blackthorn. I cannot get enough of the ordinary doings of the villagers.

I go with Etain into the bog. She carries a basket on her hip, and I carry a long blade at my side. We search for flats of ground with fewer grasses and stones. We mark them off and cut rows north to south, more rows east to west. We prise them from the ground and line them up at the base of the wide basket. We repeat the task, several times, and once or twice I catch Etain watching me with that look of adoration. If she had pulled me from the brink of death, I would gaze at her the same way. But it is strange to receive such regard.

I give her the blade and carry the full basket to her cottage. I help her spread the squares of peat along the drystone, and those we are replacing, the ones that have already dried, she stacks against the outer wall of the cottage. I offer her the empty basket, and she takes it and makes a deep bow.

One morning, I accompany Llyr and Murdoch to the sea. Murdoch carries a light currach over his head. Llyr holds the oars.

"How long will you continue to go out?" I ask.

Llyr throws me a look of shock and scorn. "As long as the wind blows," he says. "As long as there are seas to sail. As long as there are swells to ride."

Murdoch smiles at the reply. His eyes are sad, but I think the old man's determination has kept him from despair.

When we reach the shore, I hand him a water skin full of hedgerow wine. He nods his thanks and holds the boat while Llyr steps in. He settles down, adjusts the black band around his forehead and takes hold of the fishbone around his neck. Perhaps it is his ritual for embarking. Murdoch follows, and the young man takes the oars and plunges them into the sea.

I watch while the boat shrinks to a blot of darkness on the far horizon. When it disappears from sight, I sit on the shore, feeling the warmth of the sunrise on my back.

I am waiting.

Waiting.

One morning I set out for Barra's cottage. Though the rains drop off in autumn, the fosterlings are not deterred. They check the stone bowls every morning. They walk the drystones between cottages, making games as they go and racing one another to hedges and corners. I came to talk with them, but their play is so innocent, so beautiful, that I lean against the hillside, in the shadow of the rowan tree, and watch them. Pixie's braids bounce against her back, and when they fly over her shoulder, she flips them back again. Vaughn is fearless. He balances on the walls and tumbles off, rolling through the damp grass and weeds. Once he falls against a sheep and sends it stumbling aside. It gives an angry bleat and moves to another part of the enclosure. Brennan hurries along behind. He is never at the head of the group. He never begins a game and never wins one, but he is content to play and to be with the others.

Barra ducks through the door of the cottage. His cloak is pinned at his shoulder, and his spear is in his hand. A look of calm, of pleasure, passes over his face when he sees the fosterlings. For a moment, the weighty troubles of the dying world fade. He smiles. Then he looks out over the village, perhaps planning his day's work. He catches sight of me and, understanding my wish to remain hidden, gives me the smallest of nods and turns toward Engl's cottage. I wish he would go and take that woman into his arms. How many years has he yearned to comfort her? And now there is no more time.

I walk west, past the cottages and the blackthorns. Sloane is burning the remainder of the debris from the failed barley crop. He carries the last load of limp, rotted roots to the fire and sets to work plowing the fields. I watch him furrow the rows, turning the dark clods of earth while the wind snaps his clothes against him. Soon it will be time to spread the ashes. I catch myself. We come to the last turn of the wheel. If the doom of my people comes at Bloodmoon, there will be no one left to spread the blackthorn ashes over the fields. But I suppose I must make the crowns. And soon.

Llyr and Murdoch pass, carrying their currach and oars over their shoulders.

"Any salmon?" I ask.

"Nothing," Llyr says.

"Will you go out again?"

Llyr glares at me and swipes his arm through the air as though my question is a stink he must blow away. Murdoch's smile shines out from the shade of the currach.

At nightfall, I go down to the river. Candlelight flickers in Engl's window, and when I hear a gurgling laugh, I peer through the open shutter. Engl sits on the floor, holding the baby's hands. He works his tongue, straining to pull himself up. At last, he rises to a wobbly stand. He is quick to fall on his backside, but he pulls himself up again, over and over. Engl's soft laugh is like bells.

I join the gathering birds at Clodagh and Zinerva's cottage. The ravens make their harsh cries, and Zinerva's owl swivels its head to look at me. Clodagh has been gone these three days. Though I fear she makes for the altar, I am not yet ready to follow. I step closer, until I am near enough to look in the shutter. Inside, there is nothing remarkable. Zinerva sits in a corner, her eyes fluttering in meditation. The owl screeches, and I slip away in silence.

Next morning, I catch a glimpse of Calder as he passes by the hut. In his hand is a browning bundle of flowers for Shannan.

*I would take this blight if I could. I would drink up a river, an ocean, of bitter water, so that you could bring yellow blossoms to your bride in the mornings.*

He crosses the stiles and makes his way toward the flaming canopy of the ash.

I wrap my bedroll and push it against the wall and go out. It falls to me to make the crowns for the celebration of Bloodmoon. This year I feel no dread. Frost sparkles on the blackthorns' yellow leaves, and I walk the grove with the satchel over my shoulder, ready to gather any sloe that were overlooked in the early harvest. I weave my arms through the branches, cutting the ends of the smallest ones and wrapping them into crowns. After each is finished, I stack it under the tree that was its home. Three times nineteen twisted, thorny trees. I have not even taken the trouble to wrap my hands.

Strange that I should feel her eyes on me, as I did last year at Newmoon. I move into the clearing to see Zinerva seated under a blackthorn with her owl in the branches above. Her orange shawl is changeless. The wind stirs her braids and the strands of hair that are wrapped in thread. The rest rises up from her face like wisps of yellow cloud. She stares at me through narrowed eyes, the lids lying heavy as always. Her face is pale. There is no color in her lips and cheeks.

"Hello, Bard," she says.

How young she is! How frail among the thorns!

Her owl wakes at the sound of her voice. It raises its head from the cover of its wing and spins toward me. It covers its yellow eyes in a slow blink before fixing me with the heat of its glare.

"Ovate," I say, with the slightest incline of my head.

"You prepare for the Bloodmoon," she says.

"Yes. Are you preparing as well?"

"I am."

The sense of calm I feel, the sturdiness of the ground beneath my feet, surprises me. This is not how I met Zinerva last Newmoon.

"Your first rites," I say.

"And my last."

"Your last?" I say. "You do not believe you will survive the Bloodmoon?"

"I am one of the Antae, am I not? We all come to our end, Bard. Only you, you who stand among the blackthorns and weave the crowns, are blind to the truth of it. Why do you resist?"

I am slow to answer. All this time, I had imagined that Zinerva meant to endure, that she thought, somehow, to triumph over us. The Antae believe she has conquered death. But she has not even allied with it. She has surrendered to it. Somehow this is more terrible. Why is there not more horror in her face? More sorrow?

"Zinerva," I begin.

She flinches, opening her eyes wide in a moment of shock. I am supposed to address her as "Ovate."

"At Newmoon, you said Madigan told you he'd found peace in the eternal quiet of the Underworld."

"That was the message he gave," she says.

"Yet I have stood on the threshold of the Underworld, and the sound of screaming, the clamoring of ten thousand times ten thousand tormented voices filled my mind."

Her eyes remain wide, but now I begin to see the fear in them. I have never seen fear in those eyes.

"Did you not hear them?" I ask. "When you went into the Underworld?"

She pauses, gathering herself. Her lids slide down to shade her eyes, and she flicks a glance toward the owl. "Do you challenge the word of the ancients, Idris?" she asks, putting special emphasis on my name.

I ignore the question. "Are you not afraid to leave the sunlit world?"

Zinerva looks toward the dolmen. Under the capstone, the bones of our ancestors rest. Can she hear their voices? Does she listen for them now? For a moment, the space of a single heartbeat, I feel the portal tomb yawn and gape. Within, there is darkness and an unutterable, outthrusting pressure. It seems as if the stones will not hold, as if they will burst their bounds and scatter over the clearing. The vision passes as quickly as it came.

Zinerva rises. The owl flutters to the capstone and waits for her to follow. She leaves the grove without a backward glance.

The answer comes as I weave the last crown. A thorn pricks my palm, and the blood flows. Suddenly, I do not see what is before me. I see Tír Ársa and the Blue Sea, Gormára, and the fields and meadows of Baileléan. I see a plain of battle and the hidden groves of the Tullagh Sé.

*The Tullagh Sé are the center of all our stories.*

I see Perth, seated in the sacred groves, searching the sky, seeking the balance. I see lovers parted on the summit of a strange hill, an iron charm, an iron tree. The sky roils with storm clouds, and lightning flashes.

*The tree is our supreme teacher.*

The banshee peers out from behind the old yew. The puka spreads its black body over the entrance of the cave and calls to me. The creeping bog spreads and poisons, spreads and poisons. The crops wilt, the flowers vanish. The Crone cackles, and the door to the Underworld swings wide. The graves are open, the water passes through. The dark and the cold and the voices rise like a fog from the bottomless heart of Half-Bald Hill. The captive sits on the summit, imprisoned in iron. We stand on the western shore, bound to walk an inescapable path.

*Whatever you ask, I will give, if it is in my power to give.*

*I would take this blight if I could. I would drink up a river, an ocean, of bitter water, so that you could . . .*

*So that you could . . .*

*It's not so much her beauty she pines after. It's the* life *we had. That's what she misses.*

*I would take this blight if I could. I would drink up a river, an ocean of bitter water, so that you could* live.

The sacred Word comes to me, in the moment when I stand to speak it. Etain returns from the brink of death and smiles into my face. The baby sucks life from my thumb like honey from the comb.

I see Corann, cloaked in falling snow, leading us through the storm by the light of druidic fire.

Bard, Ovate, Druid.

*Conquer Death, Idris.*

My eyes clear, and I blink them, looking around at the familiar grove. I set the final crown under the nearest tree and walk to Calder's cottage. I stand under the shade of the ash, under leaves as red as the blood that wells from my hand. I choose a stone from the drystone wall, one with a sharp edge, and wedge it into the trunk of the ash. I wipe my left palm with my right forefinger and press the blood into the gash in the tree. This time, there is not a night's waiting. The bark knits itself back together. I look at my hand. The skin is whole. I wipe the last traces of blood on my tunic. There is nothing beneath but smooth flesh.

I know what I must do.

# 28

THEY HAVE BURNED THE RING-FORT AT RATHROE.

In six days the Bloodmoon comes, and already the Antae journey to Blackthorn from Beltrá and Kilveagh and Eyebright and Seaswell and Moy Catha. They come for the celebration. They come to await their end. They have spread their camps around the grove, and I hear their low murmuring as I wake.

I sit up on my bedroll and look across the low embers of the fire to where Corann sleeps. Yes, he sleeps. Once I believed that he was not a man, that he had no need of food or rest, but here he lies. I remember his gruff welcome when my father first brought me to the hut, his prickly frustration when I could not learn a history after one hearing. I recall the cheering sight of his face when it appeared through an opening in the stones that covered the entrance of the cave where I meditated.

He bowed to me and called me "Ollamh." Now he lies on his side, his head propped on his left arm, his hazel wand resting just beyond the reach of his right hand. One lock of white hair has fallen over his face, caught in the short tangle of his gray and white beard. The folds of his gray robes cover him, all but his thin, weathered feet and his right hand. Even in this pale morning light, when every man looks bloodless, that hand is beautiful. From those fingers leap threads of lightning, and the bright glow of druidic fire. That hand has traveled the sacred groves of Baileléan, brushed the leaves of the hazel tree, and carved the flesh of the salmon of knowledge. It has touched the Upper World, the fingertips grazing the boundaries of the stars, the palm holding sunlight and moonlight like a cup.

Yet he has failed, and I wonder if he can find peace in a world so brilliantly unbalanced. I crouch behind him and lean to kiss his brown cheek. Somehow, the scent of primrose clings to him, mingled with frost and oak and starlight. A tear slips from my eye and falls onto his hair. He does not stir. He must be very weary.

I gather my things—a small sack of oats, some berries, four slabs of freshly salted beef, a water skin, another skin with sour hedgerow wine, a stone blade, and a bedroll. I take Corann's hazel wand and put it in my satchel. That done, I feel a sense of rightness, of completion. I am not leaving Corann behind. I am taking him with me.

So I spend the day, gathering the villagers, tucking them into my satchel so that I need not go alone. Llyr and Murdoch's cottage is empty, but I find a fishbone like the one Llyr wears around his neck, and I claim a fishhook for Murdoch. Some of the other villagers are gathering branches for the bonfire and stacking them in the clearing in the blackthorn grove. Their cottages are left empty. I take a square of peat from the stack by the wall of Etain's cottage. Inside I find a scrap of the bloody bandage that wrapped Sloane's wounded head. Both of these I slip into my satchel.

Calder and Shannan are sitting outside under the ash tree, holding hands. I watch them from the corner of Sloane's cottage, wishing that some of the cattle could have been kept. But who can say how quickly the gorse will rally? It had to be done. I come up behind their cottage and slip my arm through the window. Shannan's mirror sits on a table, a faded gorse blossom on top of it. I take both. The mirror is heavy. It drags the satchel down to my leg, and the strap bites into my shoulder.

I wait out of sight by the Adder, checking to see if Engl is home. Before long, she opens the door and comes out into daylight, balancing the baby on her hip. In her other hand, she carries a basket, no doubt for gathering branches. When she passes the first of the blackthorn trees, I hurry inside. I take the candlepot and tuck it behind the sack of oats so it will not crack against the brass mirror.

I spot a lovely little stone bowl on one of the drystones between Engl's and Barra's cottages. It is empty now, but for a sheen of dew. I have seen the fosterlings play with it often, for it looks as if it was shaped, crafted, not as if it was meant to be a stone at all. It, too, goes into the satchel.

Barra's spear will prove a greater challenge, unless he has propped it against one of the blackthorns while he works. I weave my way through the drystones and over the stiles, trying, in a wide-open, windswept country, to keep from being seen.

A little laugh escapes my lips when I find the spear leaning on the trunk of a blackthorn near the southern edge of the grove. I take my blade and peel a thin strip of wood from the shaft.

When I turn, I am faced with a dilemma. Clodagh and Zinerva's cottage stands a few paces to the west. Will I take them, also? I am not sure if this is a journey they would wish to make. But I remember the fear in Zinerva's eyes when we spoke in the grove. She has been deceived. She has not heard the voices that choke the Underworld. And if she has learned all these years at Clodagh's feet? What, then, does Clodagh know? Does the Crone treat even her thralls with cruelty and deceit?

I step up to the window. The shutter stands half open, and a thick beam of light penetrates the darkness of the cottage. A black robe hangs on a hook nearby. One of Clodagh's ceremonial robes. I reach in the window, cut a scrap of cloth from the robe and place it in my satchel. At that moment, Zinerva moves into the light. She squints toward the window, but my hand is removed. There is nothing for her to see.

The owl's cry startles me, and I press my back to the wall of the cottage and look up. The owl glares down. The blacks of its eyes are thin as needles in the morning light. I smile at this strange adversary. I had begun to wonder how I might bring Zinerva with me, and here is my answer, staring down from the sod roof. I stoop to retrieve a discarded feather. There are several under the owl's perch, some crusted with droppings, others soaked with mud. I choose a clean one of creamy brown.

Now only one cottage remains. But I am not ready to go. I have a few hours before midday.

I walk along the marshy bank of the Adder, down the low slope that rolls to the sea. There are people gathering here. They mill about, listless, watching the horizon or looking toward the grove. I hope they have brought food and drink for their stay, but if they have, they seem to have brought little else. They have come to meet the Bloodmoon. What remains to be said or done? The people of Baileléan are infected with despair. The sun hurries to the roof of the sky. The frost melts and sinks into the earth, and the last of their hope sinks with it.

They do not know me. Without the swan-feather cloak or the gold branch, I am only a young man of slight build who has nothing to offer them. Perhaps they will never know my name.

It matters not. I will remember their faces.

When I can delay no longer, I make my way back along the riverbank to Deirdre and Muriel's cottage. They ought to be in the grove, preparing for the celebration. Nothing should hinder me from taking what I choose and departing. I skirt the hillside, crossing two stiles. I see Deirdre's mallet. It lies on a drystone over a few decaying scraps of gorse. I take a fragment of the beaten gorse and stuff it in my satchel. But I do not know what to bring of Muriel's. How can I bottle her up? How can I reduce her to a tool or a garment? I move to the window and glance inside.

They are there, both of them. Deirdre looks up and sees my

face. She gives a little cry and rushes to the door. She throws it open and runs to me, wrapping her arms around my neck and clinging to me.

"Idris!" she says. Her voice is choked with tears.

I speak into her hair. "I was sure you would be in the grove."

She pulls back and gives me a stern look. "We waited for you," she says.

I study her a moment, wondering how much these two have seen, how much they have kept to themselves. "What do you know?" I ask.

She shakes her head. "Only that you must go, that it is time."

I am surprised at my relief. I had not thought I would look again into this dear face. In her eyes there is pride and hope and grief. I nod. We understand one another.

"Friend of my heart," she says, "I will miss you."

I kiss her freckled cheeks and grip her hands. She glances at the cottage and back at me. She smiles. I kiss her again, on the forehead this time, and round the corner of the cottage.

The sight of the door stirs me. I wish I had knocked here more often, that I had passed through and sat in the firelight with Muriel. What will she do when my task is complete?

For the last time, I step inside. Muriel stands on the near side of the fire pit. She clasps her hands in front of her, drops them, wrings them. I think I understand her now. They have both known, she and Deirdre, that I must go. And they waited here so that they would not miss me, so that they could bid me farewell. I think . . . I think she does not want me to go. I do not want to leave her.

Muriel's hands drop to her sides, and she seems to make up her mind about something. She steps in front of me. She is standing close. I can feel the warmth of her skin. I can smell her hair. She hesitates, studying my face, then raises her hand. She puts the pad of her finger against the skin of my forehead, above my nose and between my brows. Her lids flutter and fall over her eyes. She exhales, and her warm breath touches my face.

I cannot hide from her. All that is in my heart passes before my eyes and hers. She sees what I have seen these four years as I watched her lean against the drystones to talk with the fosterlings, or carry a basket on the smooth curve of her hip, or bathe in the dew of the blackthorn blossoms at the dawn of the Feast of the Fertile Earth. She sees my pleasure as I watch her dance in the light of the sacred fires, sees my longing to brush her hair from her face and kiss the hollow of her temple. She sees the cottage on the edge of Kilveagh and the wind tossing the gold-coin leaves of the birches.

When she opens her eyes, the tears flow in two channels of silver. Her hand falls, and I reach out. I move one strand of spun-gold hair from her face. The edge of my thumb glides over the delicate line of her cheek. She closes her eyes and leans in to my touch, resting her head against my hand. Her lips are trembling—two petals stirred by the wind. I cannot help myself. I bend and kiss them. They taste of hedgerow wine and salt tears. The scent of her hair, like sea wind and moss, envelopes me, and suddenly I know what to take. I lift my blade from the satchel and reach for the hair that hangs down her back. I cut one golden lock and slip it in with the other precious things. And still I cannot pull away from her, from the softness of her mouth. At last, she stumbles back, catching her breath.

I do not think I can bear to linger, to hear what she might say. I inhale the scent of her, drink in the sight of her, then turn and pass through the doorway. Deirdre raises her hand in farewell, and I retrace my steps to the brink of the Adder. From there, I follow the river's edge a ways before scrambling up a grassy ravine. I reach a good height, one that offers a view of the sod roofs of Blackthorn, the fading yellow leaves of the grove, the winking blue sea on the western horizon.

I fill my lungs with air and dash the tears from my eyes. I shoulder my satchel and settle my bedroll in its place and turn to the east.

As I walk the hills of the Tullagh Sé, I feel the press of the Many-Colored Land against my skin. I step from stone to stone, but I seem to hear a wind rushing through a chasm beneath my feet. I come upon a grove of elder, and the small trees seem to stretch higher than oaks. Here and there I catch glimpses of colors too rich and pure for the soil of Baileléan—leaves as red as welling blood, blossoms of rhododendron as purple as sunset, primrose as golden as honey.

Every night I hear the mournful cry of the banshee. I remember the round, pale eyes, the strands of lank hair. And another voice mingles with it, its song cascading over the hills and wrapping me like mourning robes. I wonder, is the coming calamity so great that the banshee must begin already, must sing night after night to lament the swelling numbers of the soon-dead? Or do more of the Antae hurry to meet death, like the girl by the sea or the Druid of Rathroe?

I eat little, just enough to carry me onward. My satchel is a burden. Every day it grows heavier on my shoulder, and sometimes the mirror clanks against the stone blade and the candlepot threatens to crack. But I would not be without this burden. During the nights, I lie against it. In the mornings, it is the thought of those I carry with me that gives me strength to rise.

The six-days' journey seems little more than a moment. I do not pass the Crone's altar, but take the quickest path to the Iron Oak in hopes of freeing the captive. My first sight of Half-Bald Hill strikes me like a thunderclap. A full moon has risen—a ball of soft amber. The colors of the world are changed.

I begin my climb on the southern slope. I place my foot on the soil of the Sixth Hill, and the wind picks up. The trees are on my left hand. They bend, groan. Clouds move in, and lightning splits the dark. I press on, up the hill. My head begins to swim with the sound of voices. My steps are tenuous. I feel as though the ground is a fragile skin stretched over an endless black void. The skin will break and I will fall. I will never stop falling.

A form takes shape before me, rearing up out of the darkness. Its presence fills my mind. It fills the night sky. It fills the Tullagh Sé and all Baileléan. Its age and strength are immeasurable. It devours everything. Its hunger is never satisfied.

I cower, recoiling from that presence, and my fingers graze the strap of my satchel. I remember my weapon, and a sound of bitterness and despair rises in my throat. What good is a stone knife against the Keeper of Death's Door?

The sound never reaches my lips. It is interrupted, caught and silenced by a shaft of light. A memory. The ollamh carries no weapons. He has nothing but the Word.

I stand and square my shoulders. The sacred Word comes to me in the moment when I open my mouth to speak it. But this time the calm, the warmth, the vibrancy, the pressure, the blessing, the healing, have contained themselves inside a single word. The Sacred Word.

I speak it.

It is unutterably, undeniably, unalterably *alive*.

And after the Word, silence.

Far to the west, the Antae have gathered. They wear the blackthorn crowns, and their ritual fires burn. Here there is no more fear, and a red moon sails in a sea of stars.

A banshee's cry breaks the silence and bleeds over the bare half of the hill. I turn and follow the cry to its source, to the woman with white skin who rests against a fine peplos and shawl, to the woman who knows no song of her own. She has never known the taste of venison on her tongue, or the overpowering sweetness of honey. She has never felt the waves lap against her toes or seen the full circle of the sky. She has lived a half-life, and that in the shadow of Death.

When she sees me, she is quiet, subdued. I set my satchel on the ground and carefully remove the food I have saved for her. She takes the sack of oats and the water skin. She cocks her head at the strips of salted beef. But I urge her to take them. I

wrap them in the clothing and hold them out until she takes them in her arms.

I stand and point to her neck. She tucks a finger under the iron band and pulls it to the side. I raise my brows in question. I step closer, bold in my belief that a new power has settled in my fingertips. Another step, and my hands are at her shoulders. She flinches, but she does not step away. That is something.

I remember the fall, the endless fall, of my vision at the summer solstice. The light that arrested my descent was jarring. The fall was easy. The rescue was abrupt. At the very first, it hurt.

This will hurt, too. Will she allow me to do it? To set her free? The band is a second skin. She has worn it from the beginning. She cannot imagine what it means to be without it.

I am close enough now to touch it. The iron is cool against my fingers, but when my other hand takes hold and my fingertips brush her neck, the skin is hot. It burns with pain and pulses with the blood of the Shí. I swallow hard and study her face. In her eyes, I see some of the vastness of the Lands Beyond. The light is brighter there, for it has farther to travel and more to illuminate. It is more akin to the vibrant, throbbing, living light that pulled me from my descent. That light has marked me, invaded me. I think she recognizes it. I catch a gleam of knowing in her face.

Now I undermine the balance again. I have received the Sacred Word; I have healed. One role remains. I do what only a Druid can. I summon druidic fire. My hands grow hot; fire sparks from my fingertips and branches from finger to finger. The captive screams, and there is no mourning in this cry. It is agonized, immediate. I grip the band, pulling one hand from the other, stretching. Veins of red course through the iron, and at last, it shatters. The captive stumbles backward, gaping, the roll of clothes and food still clutched in one arm. I drop the iron fragments to the ground.

She lifts a hand to her neck and runs her fingers over the skin. Already, it is healing. Without the chafing iron, she will soon be well and whole. I smile at her and make a motion for her to move away. She stands where she is. I repeat the motion, beckoning her down the hill, away from the summit, but she does not understand.

She will.

I lift my satchel and place it over my shoulder. I look a moment at the captive, silhouetted against a red moon. Then I step into the hollow in the trunk of the Iron Oak. Here, the darkness is absolute. But I put the palms of my hands to the cool iron and look up. Far above, the Iron Oak stretches its topmost branches to the sky. I look down. There is cool earth under my feet. Beneath that, there are the bones and the door and the spring of water. Beneath them are the black pits of the Underworld, and ten thousand times ten thousand screaming voices.

Can Death die? Corann will smile to know that I have asked the right question, that it carries a world of answers on its back. His face passes before me, then other faces, in quick succession. Father. Mother. Barra. Pixie. Vaughn. Brennan. Sloane. Etain. Llyr. Murdoch. Engl. The baby. Clodagh. Zinerva. Deirdre. Muriel.

The fire of an ancient power burns inside me. It is hotter, fiercer than druidic fire. It is unchanging. It came before Death, and it will outlive it. I have moved beyond the strength of earth and sky, beyond the realm of sorcery. I have left the old ways. Light courses from my fingers, illuminating every ridge of bark, racing out to burn through every vein of every leaf.

It is the light that comes first. The tree blazes with light.

Then the heat. I feel it burning through me. I hear the leaves curling on their stems, hear the branches crack with the growing heat. The fire races along the roots, shooting down into the soil. It burns, it burns, and the heat grows stronger.

I hope the captive is running. I hope she is far from Half-Bald Hill.

The branches above me crash to the ground with a terrifying noise. It is the weight of the Iron Oak descending into the earth. The flames roar. The hollow trunk groans. Now other sounds rise from the belly of the hill, for the destruction goes down to the very roots of the tree, to the tomb, to the pit, to the bottomless dark beneath. On and on and on it goes—the noise of breaking, of crumbling, of falling.

There is tumult and uproar, then silence, an end. I see nothing, hear nothing.

Then, a veil of rain. That is, a veil that shimmers like sunlight through a spring rain. I reach to touch it, and my hand passes through. Another step, and the veil is behind me. My satchel is over my shoulder, and before me is a wide and beautiful country. The air is heavy with the scent of flowers.

# SAOIRSE

THEY BELIEVED THEY HAD COME to the last turning of the wheel. That is how Deirdre tells it. The wheel had rolled off its course, and it spun into darkness. Until its fall was arrested.

Two winters have passed since I came to Blackthorn, since the cry of the banshee was silenced forever. At first, they were slow to understand, for I stumbled naked into the heart of their village, and I did not know their speech. At the time, they still wondered at the strange events of Bloodmoon, when the earth quaked and trembled and a great fire shone in the east.

I saw it. I heard the banshee cry for the Crone, for Death itself. And since I have learned their speech, I have tried to tell how I fled down the eastern slope of the hill while the Iron Oak burned with unearthly fire. I have tried to say how fire shot into the earth, how far, far down in the depths of the Underworld, there was upheaval. I have tried to describe the way in which the hill opened its mouth and swallowed the Iron Oak. I have tried, and failed, to tell of the voices that fell silent, that found peace.

Half-Bald Hill, the place of my birth, the cradle of my bondage, is no more. That ground is a ruin and a monument.

*For that is the place where Life entered Death and burst its bounds forever.*

That is how Deirdre tells it.

*That is the place where the door to the Many-Colored Land was opened wide. Now, at Newmoon, the Antae may pass through, to journey in the glorious lands beyond, where eternal light laps on the shores of golden seas, and even the memory of Death has passed away.*

Not long after the Bloodmoon, I took them there—Corann and Deirdre and Muriel and Barra. They stood over the rubble and wept. I did not know how to comfort them. But a chattering spring gushed from the ruin of the hill, and we drew close. Corann put a hand to the water and cupped a mouthful in his palm. He raised it, looked to each of us, and drank. The water dripped from his beard and mingled with the tears that fell from his eyes. Then he smiled, nodded once, raised his arms to the sky, and laughed. We filled our water skins and brought some of the sweet water home.

It took months for the river to clear completely, longer still for the bog to stop its advance and begin to dry out. Now spring has come again, the second since the Bloodmoon, and everywhere I turn my eye, the fields are bright with flowers. There are the blues of bluebells and spring gentian and eyebright. Pink foxgloves stir in the wind, and I think I can almost hear them tinkling like tiny brass bells. Hare's tail stands up from the grass in snowy white tufts, and meadowsweet blooms in every hedgerow. Calder teaches me the name of each new flower as it appears—the white wood sorrel that grows among the rocks, the elegant spotted orchid with its deep purple markings, the mint and vervain and keck and honeysuckle, and a large flower of pale purple that Calder says he has not seen since boyhood. Sheep's-bit, it is called. I like the feel of the word in my mouth. Sheep's-bit.

But yellow is the prominent color on the hillside. The primroses are everywhere, little clusters of sunshine you can scarcely avoid with your tramping feet. And the gorse is taking over. Even now, Sloane and Etain are cutting it back and bringing the scraps to me. I have taken Deirdre's task of beating the gorse, and every day I help Calder feed the cattle. We have two cows and one bull. Last summer, Llyr and Murdoch traded a boatload of salmon for them, and the cows give sweet milk. I have never tasted the like. It is as if the clouds fell to earth and kept all their substance, all the thick, rolling mystery of their ridges and hollows.

I have taken an empty cottage on the brink of the Adder. Engl lived there with little Farrell before Barra took her to wife. Now the whole rowdy clan lives together in the center of Blackthorn, and Vaughn and Pixie walk the drystones with Farrell on their shoulders. They have yet to drop him, and that is a mercy.

Deirdre has gone to study with Corann. Twice now, we have sat around a fire on the north side of the grove and listened while she told the history of the Antae, while the brass bells tinkled in time with her voice. She has many years' study ahead, but she learns quickly, and Corann is fond of her. The old druid has taken up his metallurgy. Calder tells me he was a great craftsman in his younger days. He says that before water became the one thing of value in Baileléan, there were gold coins and gold torques, and instruments of brass and finely wrought iron. It may be so again.

Clodagh has not been seen since she went into the Tullagh Sé, and Zinerva disappeared after the Bloodmoon. Corann dug a hole near the portal tomb and buried the things they left behind. But their herbs and ceremonial cloaks he burned.

Muriel waited impatiently all that first year, and when the wheel turned at last toward Newmoon, she made her farewells, clasped Deirdre as though she would not let go, and set out for Kilveagh, to bring Idris's father and mother with her into the Many-Colored Land.

We speak of Idris with profound love and deepest esteem. Deirdre insists that when she receives the gold branch, she will not take the title of Ollamh. She will be only the Bard of Blackthorn. "There is no other who can claim that title," she says. "There will never be another like him." Her voice breaks on the words.

Calder whistles while he tends the cattle. Shannan comes to chat with him, to bring him draughts of water or bits of food. There is a warmth to her skin and a brightness to her eyes that tells me she must have been a great beauty in former years. And there is not a day that passes when she does not wear a blossom of gorse on her cloak or a cluster of primrose in her hair.

They mean to go, Calder says, and follow the ollamh through the veil. I understand. There is much I long to see in that place, and when the stars sing out of the night sky, I find my thoughts drifting to the mysteries of the Lands Beyond. But for now, as there is no ovate in Blackthorn, I am learning of teas and syrups and salves. I am learning how the sap of an ash tree can cure an earache, how a poultice of nettles can stop the bleeding in an open wound.

It is a small service to offer these people, for they have given me a life, and a home.

Yet it was the ollamh who gave me my freedom, who brought freedom to all the Antae. It is the name I chose for myself, when the language came more easily. Saoirse. Freedom.

*For the Keeper of the Word passed through clay and water, through fire and iron. He carried us with him when he conquered Death.*

That is how Deirdre tells it.

*He carried us with him when he opened the gate of glory.*

# Acknowledgements

The seed for *The Door on Half-Bald Hill* was planted when I saw a distinctive hill near mile marker 100 on I-24 South between Nashville and Chattanooga. I am forever indebted to the landowner who chose to clear half his hill and leave the other half wooded.

I am grateful to James Stephens, whose extraordinary use of language in his collection *Irish Fairy Tales* (Abaris Books, Inc., © 1978) left such a mark on this story.

Ming-Wai Selig and Hetty White helped with research by hiking in the rain and clambering over drystones on the west coast of Ireland with me. Let's do it again, ladies.

Several early readers offered feedback and words of encouragement. Thanks to Gene Sorensen, Allen Sorensen, Hetty White, Jonny Jimison, Stephen Hesselman, Suzanne Tietjen, Libby Mitchel, Loren Eaton, Jennifer Bast, Christine Peterson, Shigé Clark, Drew Miller, Ron Block, Rebecca Reynolds,

Jonathan Rogers, Jennifer Trafton, Kimberlee Conway Ireton, Glenn McCarty, and James Witmer.

I'm thrilled with Stephen Crotts's artistic vision and grateful for the ways his beautiful work anchors the reader in the world of Tír Ársa.

I will always be grateful to Pete Peterson for seeing in this strange tale something worth fighting for. His contribution as editor has been integral, and arguing with him about the minutiae of syntax and story has been an unexpected delight.

Finally, all my love to Jonathan, Silas, and Lorelei, who destroyed the balance of my little world and rescued me.

Also from
RABBIT ROOM PRESS

FIN'S REVOLUTION SERIES
by A. S. PETERSON
*BOOK 1: THE FIDDLER'S GUN*
*BOOK 2: FIDDLER'S GREEN*

*MIZ LIL AND THE CHRONICLES OF GRACE*
by WALTER WANGERIN JR.

*THE MOLEHILL*
A Literary Miscellany

*THE WORLD ACCORDING TO NARNIA*
by JONATHAN ROGERS

RABBIT ROOM
PRESS
Nashville, Tennessee